ZAIN

SAMANTHA WILDE

Copyright

Zain © 2024 Samantha Wilde
Print Edition

ISBN: 978-1-990385-20-9

Cover design by Covers by Combs
Formatting by BB eBooks

Trigger Warning

This book contains offensive language
and situations.

Situations of kidnapping and violence are depicted,
as well as other events some readers might
find triggering.

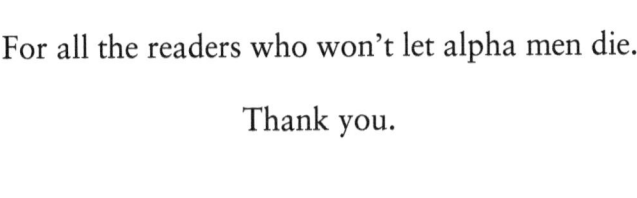

For all the readers who won't let alpha men die.

Thank you.

Table of Contents

CHAPTER 1

Z**AIN SHOULD'VE BEEN** startled by the crack of bullets. But that sound hadn't rattled him in a long, long time.

Nothing did anymore.

Not bombs shaking the ground. Not missiles decimating buildings. Not even the screams—holy fuck, the screams. He liked those the least. But they didn't scare him.

The April night air froze his exposed skin, but he didn't cover his face with the wool shawl draped over his shoulders. He welcomed the cold. The crisp air allowed more oxygen into his lungs and gave him clarity he didn't have with all the noise and Pashto in his ear all day. He spoke the language fluently because he rarely got the opportunity to speak English anymore.

The desert nights were the only thing he enjoyed—though *enjoyed* might be too strong a word. The chilly temperature matched his stone-cold insides.

He'd become desensitized. Didn't know anything but blood, gunshots, and shady motherfuckers he couldn't trust. At one point, he'd just wanted to survive. Now, every throb of his pulse demanded revenge.

He wanted to kill the ones causing the suffering. And he would if he didn't die first. Death wouldn't be such a bad thing, though. What the hell did he live for anyway? Nothing important. Nothing he could remember. And if he stayed in this fucked-up camp with its cave of prisoners and cruelty, he'd turn into one of them.

A howl sounded from the depths of the cave at his back. Zain closed his eyes as the keening turned to guttural cries.

Crack!

The gunshot echoed off the stone walls, so damn loud Zain tipped his head to his shoulder. The hysterical shouts stopped.

Emotion evaded him. Compassion and empathy were gone. In truth, he'd already started to morph into one of them.

Like a vampire's bitten victim, Zain was on the cusp. The poison had already entered his veins. Now he waited with bated breath to become what he despised most. Every day he grew more indifferent. Every minute he lost more of his ability to give a fuck. And every second he forgot more and more about the man he once was.

All he was . . . was this.

Hollow.

Zain ran his hand over his beard. Even the desire to trim the scraggly strands was gone. As fucked up as it was, he accepted this reality. Maybe that's why he hadn't been killed yet. Tilting back his head, he gazed up at the stars.

Christ, the sky was brilliant out here. No light pollution in the mountains of Afghanistan. Looking up at the stars almost convinced him there was more to the world than terrorism.

No, probably not.

Just another illusion.

Picking up his gun, he went back into the moist-smelling cave. He couldn't let himself remember the good.

Not when darkness had become his only ally.

"YOU DON'T HAVE to do this," Dana said softly into the phone. She glanced at the clock on her nightstand. If she wanted to catch her flight to Pakistan, she needed to leave now and not give her travel companion any way out.

Not that she wanted to leave Brick without options, but truth be told, she couldn't make this trip alone. From the moment she'd heard about Rami's missing brother, she'd been riveted.

A Green Beret soldier missing in action wasn't exactly something you forgot about. He'd been gone almost three years, supposedly kidnapped while on a mission in Afghanistan. Dana had been given a photo of Zain taken six months after his supposed capture, and, well, she hadn't been able to stop looking.

That was four months ago. She'd spent countless hours scouring every piece of surveillance data she could get her hands on. Thankfully, she still had contacts from her previous job as an FBI intelligence analyst.

So now, here she was, doomed to traipse into dangerous territory for a man she'd never met—a man who was probably dead or at the very least had been tortured for nearly three years. And she thought she could find him.

If that wasn't a toxic trait, she didn't know what was. It had the whole *I can fix him* vibe. Lord help her.

Brick Slater scoffed through the speaker. "Is that why you called? Look, you and I both know I *do* have to do this. But that doesn't mean I don't want to. Believe it or not, I miss living on the edge. I need an adrenaline rush."

"Rami will be pissed," she said.

Rami would go to the ends of the earth to find his brother, but she couldn't pass on the tip she'd been given. One, she didn't have enough proof Zain was alive. Two, Rami had a whole life now with Ivy Hastings, and not only was he ridiculously in love, but he also had a company to run with his business partner. Jetting off to Afghanistan on a whim could chew up weeks or months, and it could all be for nothing if she didn't get more intel.

Besides the single profile picture that matched Zain's in a facial-recognition search, there was only one other clue she'd found that had prompted her to book a flight to Peshawar, Pakistan, and rope Brick into the shenanigans too.

"I think he'll get over being shorthanded if we come back with his missing brother," Brick said dryly. "Not to mention I was just on a job in Canada for the last five weeks. I'm on vacation for the next two."

Dana grabbed her favorite hoodie and pulled it over her head. Once they got closer to their destination, she'd purchase proper attire for Afghanistan.

"Uber's here," Brick said. "I'll be there in fifteen. You sure you want to go through with this? You know as well as I do Afghanistan is the least safe place for a woman."

For a flicker of an instant, Brick's words threatened to steal the confidence that had rooted itself in her gut the moment she'd made up her mind to find Zain. Yes, this mission was perilous. She was at a great disadvantage as a woman, but with Brick as her companion, she wouldn't draw as much unwanted attention.

Not until she got close to Jaysh, the terrorist group they believed held Zain.

"I'm sure." Her voice wavered, though. "Maybe I'm as twisted as you. This desk job is killing me."

Brick barked out a laugh. "Suit yourself, Mrs. Slater."

She chuckled. Having an alias was one thing, but pretending to be married to Brick was another. In Afghanistan, traveling without a man was largely frowned upon. They needed to have the same last name on their passports to prove their fake marriage, and Brick had borrowed a slim wedding band from his mother and one from his father as well.

"I'll meet you downstairs." She disconnected and stared at her small carry-on bag. She was traipsing across the globe to the most dangerous country in the world with only the necessities. There was no point checking a larger bag as they'd need to get to Zain and get out as quickly as possible.

She dropped back her head and stared at the ceiling. If Brick hadn't seen the same evidence she had, she'd have thought she was losing her mind. But it was unlikely they'd both gone insane.

She barely knew Brick. He'd been away on a lot of jobs since she started at Backcountry Protection Services. But if her brother and the other guys trusted him, that was good enough for her. Rami and Toth had chosen only the strongest ex-military guys they knew to work for their bodyguard security company.

After snagging her bag, she walked through her apartment and made sure the appliances were unplugged and everything was as it should be.

In case she didn't return.

Her stomach churned at the thought of her mom, her dad, and her brother, Taschen, having to go through her belongings and deal with her death. Taschen had been fighting overseas when she was with the FBI. Her parents had aged drastically during those years, and now that both their children were safe and no longer putting their lives at risk, they were happy.

But she couldn't stifle the need to help people. If Zain was alive, she'd find him. And if he was dead, she'd do her damn best to find that out. Because no one deserved to go their whole lives not knowing if their child or sibling was suffering.

She locked her apartment door and moved quickly to the elevator. A familiar sense of urgency washed over her. She'd been a field agent for only three of the six years she'd been with the bureau. The other three, she'd been analyst and loved it. She was good at tracking data. Good at finding inconsistencies and consistencies and seeing outside of the box.

But part of her had missed carrying a gun. Missed the adrenaline and the rush.

Well, she was back at it.

And her mom was gonna kill her.

CHAPTER 2

"KEEP YOUR EYES down," Brick commanded. She stayed close to his side as they walked through the streets of Kabul.

She wanted to point out that she couldn't scan the crowd for Zain's face if her damn gaze was on her feet. Every inch of her face was concealed behind a niqab, and the cloak of material made her feel invisible. Less vulnerable. Still, keeping her eyes in check was hard. She wanted to look for Zain.

They'd rested at a hotel in Peshawar, and then Brick's friend Ali arranged for his men to drive them into Kabul, Afghanistan, where a protest was about to take place. Flying into the neighboring country and then driving across the border made things a little less dangerous, especially for Dana. Now they were in the thick of an angsty crowd, though.

Definitely not an ideal situation. But through recent footage she'd found online, she'd discovered that Zain—or his doppelgänger—had captured prisoners at previous protests and riots.

If they had any shot of finding Zain, this was it.

Men shouted in Pashto or Persian, she couldn't be sure which language. Women circulated, too, all dressed similarly to Dana. They held signs with messages written in Arabic. No one met her eye. But dread crawled up her spine.

Every fiber in her being screamed they were in danger. Not only were they clustered among the group egging on the Taliban, but from what she'd gathered, they were pissing off Jaysh too. Brick had explained that the men and women of Kabul were fed up with the lack of safety—enough to risk their lives in hopes of change.

The rattling of engines stirred the air. The screaming crowd got louder. Brick's hand wrapped around her wrist and protectively tugged her to his side. She stayed close, letting his six-foot-something frame swallow her up.

A fleet of pickup trucks rounded the street corner, dust billowing in their wake. Black flags danced high as the wind whipped them proudly, and the white symbols coupled with the assault rifles in the men's hands were as threatening as a swastika.

"Oh god," Dana mumbled.

Regret wasn't something that struck her often. But right now, it was fermenting deep in her gut. She tried to tug her wrist from Brick's hold, the movement involuntary and desperate. "We need to go," she hissed over the din.

His jaw hardened beneath his unkempt beard. "It's too late."

He was right. The vehicles had boxed in the crowd. Tears stung her eyes as she watched men leap from the back of the pickups waving their guns angrily. Dust particles swarmed like angry bees. Dana's burka protected her skin from the sting, but not her lungs.

Fear anchored her feet to the spot. She couldn't run. Couldn't hide. Couldn't take back the decision they'd made.

There was no other way to find him. It wasn't as if terrorist groups had goddamn employee directories. Dana pictured the last image she'd seen of Zain. The photo depicted a similar situation, though it had been taken months prior. Jaysh had come to break up a protest and silence people with fear. Someone's cell phone camera had caught Zain's profile as he'd pointed his gun at the innocent crowd.

With his description fresh in her mind, she rapidly scanned the dozens of men shouting threats at the civilians. Zain was six foot four—not a small guy—and of Lebanese descent. His dark hair and olive skin would blend in here, but hopefully his size would make him easy to spot.

The people yelled back, and one Jaysh leader standing on the back of a truck aimed his gun at the sky and fired bullets in rapid succession.

Dana clapped her free hand over one of her ears. Each blast increased her heart rate.

Brick's hold bit into her wrist. He bent his face close to her ear. "I don't see him!" he shouted.

She couldn't respond. He'd have a hard time hearing her through her burka and over the rioting. The gunshots hadn't calmed the crowd. They'd only angered them more.

The leader who'd fired the weapon glowered at the people. Rage contorted his face. Menace shimmered in his dark eyes. He leapt off the back of the vehicle and advanced on one of the loud men in the clusters of people in front of them.

He snagged him by the cloak at his throat and hauled him to the front of the crowd. The man's face turned pale as the terrorist leader shouted ferociously. Spit flew from his lips. The protestors' hollers of defiance became cries of indignation. A woman pleaded for the man's life.

Dana curled her free hand around Brick's forearm. They could shoot everyone in the crowd just for disobedience. Tears stung her eyes, and her breath wheezed in and out of her lungs. The man's desperate gaze searched the men and women calling for his release.

The leader shoved the man to his knees, brought the gun to the back of his head, and fired.

Chaos erupted. People rushed up from the back of the crowd, throwing Dana against Brick's side.

His hold on her tightened, but they both got carried forward. Dana let go of Brick's forearm so she could brace herself against the person in front of her.

Weight slammed against her back, and she stumbled to the ground. Dana cried out as her knees connected with the dirt. Pain shot down her shins.

Angry feet and legs bumped and kicked against her as the riot intensified. Dust clouded around her as she tried to get her feet under her before she got trampled. Brick caught her firmly under the arms and hauled her against him. He shoved people away, his brown eyes wide with uncertainty.

Another wave of people made Brick stumble. Dana was forced to move with the crowd or get trampled. Bodies crushed her on all sides. Panic shot through her. A scream caught in her throat. If she didn't find a way out of the mob, she'd be killed.

Using all her strength to push against the backs of the people in front of her, she craned her neck in search of Brick.

Jaysh members screamed and yielded weapons. The leader once again grabbed an innocent man. This time, the crowd settled. Some of the pressure on Dana's back eased, and she pushed her way through the group. Scanning each bobbing head, she looked for Brick. If she could just—

Her gaze landed on a hulking man. One of the

terrorists. His wide shoulders and muscular frame stood out. A gasp hit the back of her throat.

A pakol hat covered his dark hair, and his thick and full beard almost hid the chiseled line of his jaw, but the bone structure was recognizable. Her insides stirred with wonder. The cries of the people fell away from her ears. No sound penetrated Dana's brain.

Could it be him?

Before she could get a good look at his eyes, he swiveled to face one of the Jaysh leaders. She needed to get closer.

Elbowing her way forward, she reached the front row. Blood sprayed the barren ground, and a woman knelt next to the dead man's body. Dana shuddered. She'd come this far. All she had to do was confirm it was him. Then find a way to talk to him. And, of course, get him away from his . . . captors?

She didn't want to think about the brainwashing Jaysh could have done on Rami's brother. Didn't want to acknowledge that the Green Beret soldier could very well be deeply entrenched in a terrorist group and have no desire to leave.

The man she suspected was Zain waved off the leader he'd spoken to and turned to face the crowd again. She stood within arm's reach. Close enough that she could spot the lines of ink jutting out from his collar. She couldn't be sure they were Zain's tattoos, but they were in the right location.

She needed to see his eyes. She'd studied his golden irises for months. All she needed was one good look to be sure . . .

Come on, dude. Look at me.

The leader shouted something, and the note of finality in his voice struck fresh fear into her. Were they leaving? Rounding up everyone to shoot them?

She might not get another chance. If she was wrong, she could be staring down the end of this man's rifle.

She reached forward and caught his wrist. He jerked his face toward her, and his warm skin stayed in her grasp as he stared down at her. His mouth went slack with shock. He blinked, revealing the most gorgeous golden eyes.

"Hey." She spoke loudly, terrified her voice might not carry through the cloth covering her lips.

His yellow eyes widened. "Who—"

Crack, crack, crack!

Dana dropped his hand and covered her head. Her pulse hammered in her ears, and she sank to the ground. Everyone in the crowd dropped to their knees as someone from the back fired at the terrorists. The leader's face filled with fury and more gunshots broke out.

Brick!

Dana stayed low. If she stood, she'd probably get shot just for being an easy target, but where had he gone? Was he injured?

Please, God. Let him be okay.

She turned her attention back to where Zain had stood moments before, but he was gone. Desperation clawed at her. No. She couldn't have lost him. She'd just found him, for god's sake.

Moisture splattered her face, soaking through her burka. She lifted her hand and wiped at the damp material. Crimson coated her shaking fingers. Her chest squeezed her lungs until no air could enter. She had to get up. Had to run. Find Brick. But she couldn't move.

Stark horror froze her in place.

Her brain flickered with the need for oxygen. Pressing her knuckles into the pebbly earth, she sent a prayer skyward and dragged a breath through her nose.

Booted feet came into her vision, and a brutal hold seized her elbow, pulling her to her feet. Dana let out a strangled cry as she stared at the leader who'd shot the man moments before.

Terror stopped her heart.

★ ★ ★

DREAD CLUNG TO Zain's skin like burs. Five protestors had already been shot. When one of the members zeroed in on a kid, Zain nearly lost it.

But that woman . . .

Christ, who was she? *Where* was she?

He'd gotten Rakesh to leave the boy alone, but now Zain couldn't find the woman who'd grabbed his arm. Her electric-blue eyes had held his with a firmness and a confidence that were unusual for a woman in Afghanistan. Not to mention her earnest hold on his wrist.

If she'd done that to any other Jaysh member, she'd have been shot in the face. But she'd grabbed him. Spoken English. A language and greeting from his past. Words he'd almost forgotten.

Whoever the hell she was, he had to find her before she became the next victim. And he needed to get Isaad to pull the troops out. They'd come here to scare off truth-speakers, to rule with their iron fist. He'd figured there'd be bloodshed. There always was.

But hearing her voice . . . it'd done something to him. Pulled him back to a time when he wasn't okay with this level of brutality.

Zain ignored the cries of the people on the ground by their loved ones. If he had the patience, he'd tell them they shouldn't have come. Shouldn't have angered Jaysh. He didn't dare utter the words because he'd be next. Not for one second did he believe they wouldn't kill him without a second thought. He'd played their game this long. Learned to adapt by shutting off his emotions.

His gaze landed on Isaad, the group leader, who sneered down at a woman cloaked in a black burka. His grip on her slight arm was ruthless. Even though she was covered from head to foot and he couldn't see her eyes from here, he knew it was her. Maybe it was the way her head tipped up to stare at Isaad with insolence, maybe it was the balled, defiant fist at her side, but goddammit it was her—and by the look on Isaad's face, he was ready to put a bullet between her eyes just for existing.

Zain stalked across the dirt road, protectiveness washing over him. He had to stomp it out. Couldn't show Isaad he gave a damn about civilians.

"Isaad," Zain hollered.

The man turned his face toward Zain. If he'd heard the growl in Zain's voice, he didn't react. Zain spoke quickly in Pashto, telling Isaad he'd overheard someone say the authorities were on their way.

Since they'd brought only a small fleet of men to disperse the protest, Jaysh wouldn't want to fight law enforcement. Isaad's face tightened, but he didn't let go of the woman. Rakesh approached and Isaad repeated what Zain had said about the authorities.

"Farid," Isaad said, addressing Zain using the false name he'd been living under. "Make sure everyone loads up."

Isaad turned to Rakesh. "Take her as prisoner." He shoved the woman at Rakesh. "She's disobedient." He gestured to the crowd with two fingers. "And grab two more. Let's go."

Rakesh called orders and towed the woman

toward the waiting vehicles. She dug her feet in the ground, fighting. Warning bells went off in Zain's head, and he mentally pleaded with the woman to keep calm. Acting out wouldn't end well for her.

"No! Let her go!" A man broke through the crowd, blood dripping from his lip. He spoke in Pashto, but an American accent clung to his voice.

What the hell were these two doing in the middle of an Afghan protest?

Zain advanced on the man and held out his palm. Several of the troops had already jumped in their vehicles, but a few loomed uttering threats to warn the crowd against future revolt. "Hey." Zain spoke in Pashto even though he'd bet his right arm the guy spoke English.

The guy's eyes locked on Zain's and something flickered in them—recognition? No, it couldn't be. He'd never seen this man in his life. Of that he was almost certain.

Unease made Zain want to back away. To steer clear of whatever this man had brought to his door. Because he couldn't take the fucking risk. Still, curiosity buzzed his cells.

The man took a step forward, his brown eyes flickering with fear as he swept his gaze to the woman being loaded in the truck. "You can't take her," he cried. "She's—"

Smack!

The man crumpled to the ground, unconscious. One of the guards had slammed the butt of his gun into the back of his head. The guard sneered at the fallen guy and mumbled something.

Indecision made Zain hesitate. But he couldn't interfere. Turning, he made his way to the vehicles and hopped in the back of a truck—the vehicle directly behind the one holding the female prisoner.

CHAPTER 3

D ANA'S TEETH CHATTERED beneath her veil.
Not from the cold. Oh, no. This was pure,
undiluted fear stealing her body's ability to pump
blood to her extremities.

She'd been captured by a terrorist group.

This was the absolute worst-case scenario. Being rescued was next to impossible now. She
sniffed back the moisture collecting on her eyelashes. Brick had tried to stop them from taking her.
She'd heard his screams and watched in horror as
he'd been struck in the back of the head.

It's all my fault.

Even if he survived, Brick didn't have the resources to save her. By the time he arranged for
men to get here from Pakistan, where Ali lived, it'd
be too late. She'd either be dead or maimed beyond
recognition.

Stupid, stupid, stupid.

If they'd done things differently. If she'd stayed
closer to Brick. If she hadn't taken on this godfor-

saken suicide mission. She knotted her hands on her knees. Feeling sorry for herself would do absolutely nothing. Keeping her legs drawn tightly to her chest, she stared at the shackles the terrorist—others called him Rakesh—had locked around her wrists. The tarnished metal was heavy. Nothing short of a bullet or key would crack it open.

The truck bumped and rattled beneath her. On the other side of the truck bed sat two young men, who'd also been taken prisoner. From what she could tell, they didn't speak English. Some of the terrorists sat on a crate in the middle and some crouched low, hanging on to the sides of the truck. Each vehicle held at least a dozen people, and she'd counted five vehicles.

Zain. Where was he? From the low corner of the truck, she couldn't make out any faces in the vehicle behind or in front of them. She'd glimpsed the other vehicles only when she'd been ushered onto the truck bed.

It had been him. She was sure of it. His eyes had flashed with warning when she touched him, but she hadn't been afraid. Because something else screamed from his amber eyes. Concern. For her. She was sure of that because he didn't flinch or remove her hand from his arm. He didn't retaliate. Instead, he'd stood frozen, as if electrocuted by her voice.

But he'd heard.

Was he one of them now? The chances of her seeing him again were slim now that she was prisoner. She'd made it all this way and found him only to be captured and have the whole damn thing blow up in her face.

Even if she was lucky enough to speak to him again, he might just tell her to go to hell.

She closed her eyes as a torrent of fright swelled in her belly. They were traveling fast, and the whirr of the tires made bile creep up the back of her throat.

She lifted her gaze to see Rakesh. Heat burned her face. His eyes burrowed holes through her burka and his tongue slid over his bottom lip just above his beard. Revulsion crawled up the back of her neck. His eyes continued to hold hers as he kept the handle of his gun braced on the floor, the nozzle pointed to the sky.

Dana lowered her gaze. Her chest ached and a deep, black hole of self-pity wanted to suck her inside. The only certainty right now was the predatorial fire in Rakesh's eyes. If she ever faced him alone, it'd be when she took her last breath. Because she'd rather fight until he killed her than suffer at his hands.

★ ★ ★

THE DESIRE FOR murder flooded Zain's arteries. He pressed his tongue to the back of his teeth as he stared at Rakesh. The guy was inches shorter than him. If Zain lost his temper, he could snap Rakesh like a twig. And he wouldn't regret it either. Rakesh was one of the cruelest bastards in this godforsaken place, reveling in the suffering he imposed on innocent people.

Lanterns flickered on the cave walls as they walked together, sending insidious shapes over Rakesh's face and the rock surrounding them. Rakesh's dark eyebrows bobbed, waiting for Zain's to acknowledge whatever he'd said. Zain hadn't been listening.

Hatred made him want to pull the machete from his belt and slit the bastard's throat. Common sense won out. Zain just grunted. Rakesh meandered down the long windowless hall, and Zain fell into step beside him.

"You check on cell one," Rakesh ordered. "I'll do the other."

Distaste slithered around Zain's spine. Their job was to check on the prisoners. Rakesh had never volunteered himself for the prisoner's check. Red flags waved in Zain's head.

It'd been eight hours since they returned from dissembling the protest, and the woman's haunting blue eyes had stayed with Zain every goddamn minute. A woman captive wouldn't last long here. It'd be a miracle if she hadn't been violated already. Fury skittered over his flesh, but he didn't give in to the stifling need to find her.

He couldn't.

Over the years, he'd learned how to create distance; he'd allowed himself to become desensitized. It was the only way to push through the urge to shield any female from the dungeon's monsters.

I can't get involved.

The linen afghan around his frame offered a shield against the frigid elements as he moved deeper through the cave alongside Rakesh. After steering around the winding corridor, he reached cell one. There were two cells, each one holding two or three inmates, all men other than the woman who'd been taken today.

Rakesh's pace increased, and he disappeared around the corner, where the other cell waited.

Zain slid his assault rifle off his shoulder and poised it in front of him with one hand. With his other hand, he fished out the set of keys from his pocket. No sounds came from inside as he unlocked the door and entered.

Three captives sat hunched against the cave's walls. One on one side and two on the other. Several feet separated them. The flames on the wall sconces danced, illuminating the men's dirty faces.

She wasn't here. Relief and disappointment clashed inside him like two rams fighting to determine dominance.

The stenches of urine and feces stung his nostrils. Pushing down a gag, he made his way toward the captives.

Immediately, a young man from the protest

earlier that day leapt to his knees. "Please, sir!" he said, in Pashto, his native tongue. "My wife. My daughter. I need to find them." Tears coursed down his cheeks.

The dampness in the air was so thick Zain could almost see water droplets. If the men held here didn't die from torture or brute force, they'd die of infection. The prisoner's words morphed into guttural cries that tried to worm through the blocked-off chambers of Zain's conscience.

There's nothing I can do.

Still, the man's deep-brown eyes cut through him. The other prisoners were quiet. They'd been here a few weeks and by now surely knew begging wouldn't get them anywhere. Zain approached the younger man and knelt down. He pulled his canteen from his side and handed it to him.

The man grabbed the leather bag, tears of appreciation in his gaze. He likely thought he'd found a savior. An ally.

He was wrong.

The man drank, wiped his mouth, and handed the canteen back. "Th-Thank you. Please. Can you help me? I didn't do what they say. I'm innocent."

Zain fought the mounting pressure in his chest. This man could scream his innocence and it wouldn't fucking matter. Not only did no one give a shit, but he'd been accused of arranging a riot. Protesting of any kind was unforgivable. Guilty or not, he'd pay the price.

Zain tethered the man's gaze to his. "Don't try to talk to anyone," he said in Pashto, his voice barely above a whisper. "They'll kill you and do the same to your family for fun."

The man sobbed. His wrenching cries made Zain cringe. Without another word, he stood and went back into the hall. The man's pitiful pleas echoed over the stone walls. Zain locked the door and closed his eyes for half a second.

Up until now, Zain's heart had been hardened. Stone cold. But something about the man's desperation for his family ate away at the moat of distance Zain had constructed around his heart. The guy would be dead tomorrow if the family didn't pay the ransom money. Which they sure as hell wouldn't be able to do.

Zain turned and swung the strap of his rifle over his shoulder. Resting his palm on the handle of the machete—he wouldn't walk a step in this place unguarded—Zain looked toward the other cell, around the corner.

Uncertainty anchored him in place. He shook his head, dissolving the unease clouding him. He moved away from the door.

"No!" A muffled female cry split the air.

Zain's senses fired.

Fuck.

★ ★ ★

DANA'S EYES BURNED from lack of moisture. She

sniffed back the stinging pain in her sinuses as she pillaged the walls of her chamber with her gaze. Like a reel on repeat, she produced the same results: no escape.

The high ceilings came to a peak overhead and water droplets fell from the roof to splatter her head and the puddles at her feet. There was no window. No hole. No tools she could use to dig. Except her shackles. She turned her wrists over, and the chain leashing her to the wall rattled. The thin band of metal was secured with a lock.

She could drag the metal against the wall, but she'd probably tear off her skin and get nowhere. She swallowed and glanced at the man sitting across the cell from her. He didn't move or speak. Just stared into nothingness as if he were comatose. She was envious, wishing she could escape to whatever alternate reality his mind had conjured.

A chill shook her shoulders, and she rested her cheek on her knees. A bucket sat a few feet away, and judging by the pungent fecal smell, it hadn't been emptied after the last person who'd been chained in her very spot had been taken away.

Brick. Taschen. Somebody, please get me out of here.

She'd never been one to wallow in despair, but nothing short of an alien spacecraft zooming in and abducting her would get her out of this place. Even if she could find something to use as a weapon against one of the guards, she'd never make the long trek through the bowels of hell without getting caught.

Please, God. Just let my death be quick.

That was her only hope right now.

The tinkling sound of a key in a metal lock made her snap up her head. The chill in her bones spread to her fingers and toes. Her heart thumped against her eardrums, making her brain work harder to assess the threat. Maybe it was Zain . . .

Creak

The door swung open and Rakesh entered.

Dana's stomach revolted. Thank god he couldn't see her expression through her burka. But her spine molded itself to the stone wall at her back.

Rakesh didn't smile, but his thin lips twitched, making his long beard move. He closed the door behind him and stopped in front of her.

Self-preservation kept her gaze on his shoes. He stood still, his energy radiating toward her like a nuclear bomb. Only the gentle *drip, drip, drip* from the ceiling echoed through the room.

"Take off your burka." His broken English shattered the silence.

Dana closed her eyes.

"Now," he commanded.

She brought her hands to the material on her head and pulled it off. Her long, dark strands got tangled in the black cloth. She shook them free and glanced up at him.

His lip curled, and he brought his hand down.
Smack!
Dana cried out and hit the ground. Her cheekbone screamed, as the tender flesh immediately started to swell. She blinked away the shock stealing her breath.

"Do not look at me, whore," he said viciously.

Dana bit back the retort she wanted to hurl at the woman-beating bastard. A high-pitched wail sounded throughout the space. Dana shot her gaze to her cellmate. His knees were curled to his chest, his hands around his ears. He rocked back and forth, eyes closed, piercing sounds coming from his lips.

Rakesh yelled something and the man stopped blabbering. Dana swallowed and slowly pushed herself back to a seated position.

What the hell do you want from me?

The question burned a hole through her tongue, but she didn't raise her gaze from the ground. Rakesh dropped into a squatted position, forcing her to focus on his body. Instinct made her want to look at his face. To read his expression. Search for his intention.

But she couldn't.

Doing so would cost her another hit—or worse. He wanted to scare her. This was nothing more than an intimidation tactic. She had to hold out.

His hand disappeared beneath the cloth he was swathed in, and then he produced a blade. A shudder rippled over Dana. She pressed her trembling lips into a firm line and swallowed.

He was going to kill her.

Cool metal stroked her cheek. "Too pretty," he growled. "You want me to want you, yes? You want to be used."

Her breath wheezed from her lips, the sound raspy.

"Look at me."

Dana swallowed. Her face throbbed from the last time she'd done just that. He pressed the blade against her cheek and her skin threatened to split. She cut her gaze to his. He hovered inches from her face, so close she could headbutt him.

The urge to fight, to use her training, almost overpowered her.

He pulled the knife from her face, and a little gasp of relief left her body. He brought the metal tip to hover at her abdomen. "If you scream, I will cut you from center to teeth."

Cold waves crashed against her.

His hand locked around her throat, and he pushed her to the ground. The unrelenting slab of rock dug into her back as Rakesh pulled at her clothing. Terror as sharp as nails hammered her spine. "No," she wheezed, shoving at his hands.

There was no one to help her.

Calling out would only bring more men to her cell.

"Do not speak to me!"

Wham!

His backhanded slap hit her lips. The tinny taste of blood touched her mouth. He worked feverishly to pull up her long dress, and his hand sunk beneath the waistband of her trousers.

Panic assaulted her senses. "No!" she cried. Using her bound hands like a club, she swung at his face.

Rakesh staggered to the side, and the knife slipped from his fingers. Dana catapulted to her feet, but the chain securing her to the wall didn't let her go far.

Rakesh's brown eyes glowered at her. He wiped his mouth and stood. Words spat from his snarly lips. She was sure he was calling her hideous names.

"Please." She pressed her back against the wall as he closed in on her personal space. "Just kill me." Oh god. She was begging for death. It didn't take a psychic to know he wouldn't carry out her wishes.

"I will, whore. Once I'm done with you."

Creak

Rakesh stiffened and turned to face the door. "Farid."

All the air left Dana's lungs as Zain entered the room, swinging the door shut behind him. Her brain worked at the speed of light. Farid?

Zain spoke in Pashto, words flying from his mouth like stones, firm and authoritative.

Rakesh seized her throat again, towing her to stand next to him. "She is mine," he said, in English. "Find your own whore."

Dana's chest screamed for air, but she wouldn't risk taking a breath. Wouldn't move.

Zain came closer. "I said, leave."

Rakesh's face hardened. He shoved Dana away and she stumbled backward, catching herself on the wall. He held up the knife again, this time pointing it toward Zain. Before, she'd been too close to see the dagger's ten-inch jagged length. Her blood turned cold.

"Don't be a fool," Rakesh said. "You can have your turn."

Zain moved the cloth of his tunic shirt and revealed a machete.

Oh god. No.

Please don't die because of me.

Rakesh let out a sneering laugh then lunged forward, slicing the knife. Zain dodged backward, his torso careening at a sharp angle as if in a scene from *The Matrix*.

Dana's breath came in sharp pants. Rakesh moved in a wide circle. As he moved farther from Dana, she could see the angry pinch of his brow. Zain mimicked Rakesh's movements.

The other prisoner let out a shrill whine, amplifying the tension in the space. Rakesh snarled and dove for Zain, driving the knife toward his midsection.

"Zain!" Dana cried. The word ripped from her throat just as Zain moved swiftly out of Rakesh's reach. His eyes, full of shock and scorched with warning, snapped to hers.

Oh god. What have I done?

Rakesh had called him Farid because Zain didn't go by his real name. But why?

Rakesh's beady eyes turned vengeful. "Traitor," he whispered. His eyes flashed and his mouth twisted. "Tr—"

In one quick sweep, Zain sliced Rakesh's jugular.

Dana brought her chained hands to her mouth to stifle a cry. Blood splattered across the cave wall, just missing her face. Strangled sounds gurgled from Rakesh's throat. His knees buckled and connected with the dirt, then he folded forward, drowning in his own blood.

The prisoner's cries stopped.

Zain's chest heaved. His huge form, dominating the room. Sweat coated his face. His unforgiving eyes homed in on her. "You have no idea what you've done."

CHAPTER 4

Z AIN TUCKED AWAY the machete, bent to Rakesh's body, and pulled out a set of keys. He stood and moved toward the woman. Her mouth popped open and she quickly snapped it shut. Tremors shook her body.

"I—I don't understand," she moaned. "What do you mean?"

He kept his eyes down because if he looked at her, he'd lose his composure. Maybe he'd been too harsh. But Jesus, she'd screwed him. More than she could imagine. It wasn't her fault Rakesh had assaulted her. But she shouldn't be here. Shouldn't have been at the protest. Shouldn't have risked her life.

In the last couple years, he'd witnessed a lot of gruesome shit that went against everything he believed in. Cruelty beyond measure. But he'd never witnessed a woman being raped, and it turned out that was the one thing he couldn't tolerate.

She'd said his name. His mind ripped through a million possibilities. None of them made sense, but he didn't have time to drill her. Rakesh's absence would be noticed. They had to move.

He picked up her wrists and turned them over until he found the lock. In seconds he had her free. Tears coated her cheeks. Instinct made him want to tell her she'd be okay. But that was a lie. Cold hard truth was the only thing that might save them.

"They'll kill us both, that's what." He finally met her eyes, and remorse flooded through him. Grave sadness that creased her forehead.

"I—" Shock was surely taking hold of her brain.

Zain raked his gaze over her. He picked up her niqab and handed it to her. "Can you walk?"

She nodded.

"Did he hurt you?"

She shook her head.

Gestures seemed to be all she was capable of. Not that he could blame her. Hot air rushed from his nostrils. "We need to move fast." His gaze swung to the man who'd been jabbering on the floor. Zain couldn't remember his name, but the guy wasn't a threat. He'd been there weeks and could barely take a piss.

Zain stalked up to him and, in Pashto, ordered him to undress. When the man didn't respond, he pulled out his gun and spoke more forcefully.

The man staggered to his feet and removed his clothes with shaking hands. Grabbing the piles of material, Zain dropped them at her feet. "Change."

Her eyes bulged. "Um, I can't wear that."

"You're the only woman in this entire compound. We won't make it ten feet if you're spotted."

Rubbing her chafed wrists, she nodded. "Okay. But I'm wearing my clothes underneath."

"That's fine. Just hurry."

She'd already stepped into the trousers and had the long tunic over her head before he could say more. He took in her long dark hair as she wound it at the base of her neck and secured it with an elastic she'd produced from her pocket.

Something flashed in her large blue eyes. He suspected she was balancing on the edge of sanity. Her hands shook as she held up the plain black turban the prisoner had surrendered. "I don't know how to wear this." Her voice was hollow. She looked up at him as if this would be the straw that'd kill them.

Tucking his weapon in its sheath, he took the material from her hands. "Come here."

She stepped closer to him and her warm, feminine essence invaded his brain. Her presence was so soft, a sharp contrast to what he'd lived with for three years. She watched him warily as he wrapped the cloth around her head leaving a long tail to hang over her shoulder.

"Obviously you don't have a beard, so we'll be fucked if someone gets a good look at your face. Tuck this around your mouth." He offered her the tail. "And stay at my side near the wall."

She nodded solemnly.

"There's a back way through the cave for emergency exits, but there are rooms at that end too. If we get stopped, well, I'll have to kill whoever it is."

Her breath hissed through her teeth. She caught his fingers, her hand tiny and alarmingly cold. "Zain . . . I'm sorry. I never meant to put you in danger."

Once again, the use of his real name struck him like lightning. It'd been years since anyone called him that. Years since he identified with his true self. It sent him back in time. Questions sizzled on his tongue, but he swallowed them. If he got them both out of here in one piece, he'd get every detail from her.

He grunted. "I was in danger before you got here." He paused then bent and removed a dagger from a sheath at his ankle. It was similar to the one Rakesh had. "Tuck this in your sleeve or against your side. Don't use it unless you have to." Hesitation filled him. He swallowed.

He had no intention of dying today. No intention of leaving a helpless woman to fend for herself against an army of murderers. But shit happened, and she had to know what she was up against. "And if something happens to me, cut your throat before they take you prisoner again."

Tears immediately coated her eyelashes, and he almost wished he hadn't spoken the words. What kind of animal had he become?

A predator, that's what. Top of the food chain. Survival was all that mattered at this point.

"I mean it." He caught her elbow and shook it. "If you think what Rakesh was going to do to you was bad, know that it'll be far worse when they see he's dead and you escaped. Don't hesitate."

The moisture spilled down her cheeks and he hardened his heart. "Do whatever I say."

She dipped her chin in answer. He moved to the wooden cell door and eased it open. Voices sounded in the hall but weren't close. He ushered her out of the cell then swiftly locked the door behind him.

If he could delay them finding Rakesh's body, it would buy them a little extra time.

Keeping one palm on the handle of his machete, he grasped Dana's elbow. Light from the flaming lanterns sent shapes and shadows to tango on the walls. He'd come this way several times and rarely encountered anyone this deep in the cave.

A few vehicles were parked out back. If they could make it there without being spotted, they might be able to get out of the compound before anyone found Rakesh or noticed the woman had escaped.

He glanced down at her. She kept her head tucked and the scarf around her face as he'd instructed. Her movements were quick, and trepidation emanated from her body.

The exit came into view. Moonlight spilled into the cave, illuminating the corridor as far as its arms could reach. He paused at the threshold and eased the woman behind a large rock right at the entrance. Guards circled the property at all hours. He often left to visit his home outside the compound, but right now he was on duty, so it wasn't permissible for him to leave.

Tension gripped his muscles. Voices sounded from inside the cave and Zain cursed. It didn't sound as if they'd spotted Rakesh, but it was only a matter of time.

"See that vehicle?" He nodded toward a beat-up beige truck, similar to one that'd been used in the convoy earlier that day.

"Yes."

If he wasn't on his last nerve he'd commend her for the strength in her voice. "We're going to move fast. I want you to go ahead of me and get inside. There's usually blankets in the cab. Get in and cover up with whatever you can."

She nodded. He held up his palm and glanced around the corners before waving her in front of him. With his rifle in hand, he followed her across the dirt terrain to the truck. He scanned the landscape from east to west ensuring no one spotted them. The unoiled hinges squealed as she yanked open the driver's side door and dove in the back.

Shit, shit, shit. It was Isaad.

Zain turned and forced his face to relax as Isaad exited the cave. "Isaad. I was just about to circle the perimeter," he said in Pashto. "What can I do for you?"

Isaad's gaze narrowed suspiciously. "Who's with you?" The man kept moving forward.

Goddammit. Zain glanced to his left and to his right. The area was deserted. As Isaad reached him, he clapped the leader on the shoulder. "Come. We need to talk."

If he could distract Isaad, he might not have to kill him.

The man jerked from Zain's hold. "Who do you have?"

"A friend." Yanking out his machete, he drove the blade through Isaad's stomach.

Isaad's eyes widened and his mouth gaped. He gasped, and blood sputtered from his lips. Zain yanked out the blade and caught Isaad with one arm across his chest. With his back to Zain's front, Zain dragged him to the large rock the female prisoner had hidden behind a minute ago.

Isaad's glassy eyes stared at the wall as Zain dumped him on the ground. Sweat coated his brow, but not from exertion.

He'd just made things a helluva lot worse.

After wiping the machete on Isaad's pant leg, he sheathed the weapon and crossed the lot. He climbed in the driver's seat and shut the door softly. His pulse beat in a sporadic rhythm against his eardrums. He turned the key that had been left in the ignition. He glanced at the woman in the back. "Stay down."

"Did you kill him?" she asked breathlessly.

He clenched the steering wheel as he shifted into drive. "Yeah, I killed him. Didn't have a choice."

The vehicle hummed, loud like a fucking siren. He rounded the mountain and the guards and group members came into view. Tents were set up outside the cave for the people on duty, and the leaders' quarters were inside.

Turning onto the main road that all traffic entering and leaving the compound used, Zain slowed. "I need to get clearance before I can drive out," he called back, over the drone of the motor. "Don't move or speak until I say."

"Okay," she called.

Jesus. He was insane. He'd lost his damn mind the minute he interfered with Rakesh's assault. It's not like he could have walked away, though. Nevertheless, he'd just made himself a wanted murderer, and one of the biggest terrorist groups in the Middle East would be after him by morning.

If he had that much time.

Tension coiled around his chest like barbed wire. He rolled down the window as he reached the checkpoint. One of the new guards, Zain couldn't remember his name, approached the window with his rifle pointed at the ground.

"Your shift is done?" he asked in Pashto.

"I'm not feeling well," Zain replied. "I'll be back in the morning."

The guard looked at the back seat and Zain's blood pressure spiked, making his head throb. But then the man stepped back, signaled for the arm bar to be lifted, and waved Zain through.

He nodded in greeting and rolled out of the compound. The constriction on his chest eased and he let out a long exhale. Once the entry gate was far back in his rearview mirror, he pressed his foot harder on the gas.

"You can remove the blanket," he shouted. "Stay down though, just in case."

He cut his gaze over his shoulder just in time to see her face poke through the material. It was too dark to see her expression, but the rapid rising of her chest told him she'd been terrified.

"I need to make a call. Do you have a phone?"

He grunted. "I do, but it's undoubtedly monitored. We'll have to wait for calls to be safe."

"Where are we going?"

"Don't worry about that right now." Part of him wanted her to get up front so he could ask her who the hell she was, but the risk was too great.

All it'd take was for a guard with a sniper scope to spot her and they'd be doomed. He also wanted to see her face and read her expressions when they spoke. She might be in danger, but that didn't mean he could trust her.

Not by a long shot.

DANA FOUGHT THE urge to get out of the uncomfortable position. They weren't out of the woods yet, and until he gave her the go-ahead, she'd keep down as instructed. She even held the blanket just below her chin in case she had to duck underneath again. The knife sat nestled on the seat at her side.

He'd taken two lives because of her. The lives of two men who would've killed her without batting an eye. Two men who could be behind past and future terrorist attacks in the US. But lives nonetheless. Was he upset with her? Had they been his friends?

And the biggest question: was he one of them? Because he sure seemed pretty chummy with everyone but Rakesh.

He'd rescued her and for that she was grateful, but there was no way to know what side he stood on.

"Shit," Zain mumbled. He whipped around to glance behind them then brought his gaze to the road. The vehicle accelerated.

"What's wrong?" She fought the urge to sit and

look out the window. She was alive now and wanted to keep it that way.

"We're being followed."

She inhaled sharply. Oh god. Of course escaping couldn't have been so easy. Not that killing two men was a walk in the park, but there hadn't been any gunshots or bombs, which she'd anticipated.

"There's two vehicles that I can see," he said loudly.

Hopelessness flooded her. All this because of her. She sniffed back the pressure building in her sinuses. Crying would do absolutely nothing right now except make them both uncomfortable. But the fact was, neither of them were getting out of this. She hadn't come here to get Zain killed, and that might be all she'd succeeded in doing. "Just let me out here," she said, her voice sounding far braver than she was. "With any luck they won't come after you and will never know your involvement."

He cast a quick glance at her. "Not happening."

She opened her mouth to argue, but he took a sharp turn down a gravel road squashed by forest. Her body rolled, and she grabbed the front seat for support.

"I know these mountains. I've spent a lot of time learning every road and cave. We've got a shot at losing them, but we've gotta be quick."

He drove wildly on the uneven terrain, whipping the truck around corners and bumping down low-grade hills. Nausea sloshed against her stomach lining, and she swallowed the urge to throw up. She didn't have a gun, but she could at least be the eyes in the back. Creeping onto her knees, she hung tightly to the back seat and poked up her head.

"I said stay down."

"You can't see behind you and drive," she shot back. The flash of headlights came around the bend and cut through the trees. "They're behind us." If losing them on the gravel road had been his only hope, then they were sunk.

She clung to the seat, unable to tear her gaze away from the menacing trucks closing in on their tail. Panic buzzed in her ears like an angry swarm of wasps. Zain growled something at her, but she couldn't focus on a word he said.

A rough hand seized her arm, jerking her away from the back window. "Get down, for fuck's sake!"

Crack! Crack!

Bullets pinged off the truck. Dana screamed and covered her head. Zain's hand ruthlessly held her down between her shoulder blades. She didn't bother telling him that nothing short of freedom would entice her to pop up again.

The smack of another bullet hitting the glass pulled a scream from her lungs. Her pulse beat ferociously against her skull, and fear sat hot and stagnant in her chest.

An engine roared behind them, and Dana fought the whimper escaping her lips. More gunfire spewed. A jarring *pop* sounded, and the truck careened to the side. "The tire!" she cried. Dana grabbed the seat in front of her and lifted her head. Zain's chiseled jaw held tension, and his shoulders and biceps rippled.

"Hang on." He spoke through gritted teeth. The truck started to slow, and ice spread through her limbs. He lifted his gaze to the rearview mirror. "Fuck!"

Crash!

A vehicle slammed into them from behind. Dana's head bounced into the front seat. The impact blotted out her vision. Zain's voice sounded far away; his words barely punched through the thick fog dulling her senses. Keeping her hands glued to the seat for support, she found his concerned expression. Blood trickled from above his brow.

They'd stopped. Dear god, no.

A man appeared at Zain's window. "Look out!" she cried.

Zain turned to shove open the door. The crack of punches reached her ears. *The knife.* She had to find it. Forcing down the violent nausea pressing against her palate, she swept her hands along the floor of the truck.

Her fingers brushed the metal handle. *Yes!*

The back passenger door flew open, and rough fingers grabbed her arm and dragged her from the back seat to land with a thud on the road. Someone ripped the turban from her head and shouted in Pashto. A hand sunk viciously into her hair. Fire lit her scalp as she was hauled to her feet. She let out a howl. The scream opened a bottle of rage, and all her training rushed to the forefront of her mind, chasing away the fear.

She tightened her grip on the knife and swept it at her attacker. The man leapt out of reach and the knife licked his shirt, missing his flesh. He let go of her hair but her scalp pulsed from his abuse. The man's eyes turned dark and his fist smashed against her cheekbone, but she caught herself before she fell.

She dove for him again. This time the knife sliced across his forearm. He roared through gritted teeth. His eyes, fiery coals of death, were pinned on her. She threw her weight to her left leg and landed a roundhouse kick to the side of his head. He staggered and fell to the road.

A grunt sounded from the other side of the vehicle, and Dana's heart rate spiked. Was Zain hurt?

The man on the ground dove for her legs, taking her out at the knees. She landed hard on her back and air whooshed from her lungs. A burning sensation spread across her chest and wrapped around her neck, but she forced the paralyzing wave from her muscles and drove the knife into the man's side.

His face contorted as he looked down at the dagger sticking out of his torso, beneath his ribs. Blood spread across his white shirt. Murder flashed in his eyes, and he caught her throat in his hand, his weight bearing down on her jugular. Harsh words flew from his tongue, and spit sprayed her face.

Warmth spread across her cheeks. Her blood stagnant around her ears, trying to move through her body. Her chest ached. She twisted and squirmed, small sounds of desperation coming from her mouth. Consciousness flickered, and she struggled to hang on, to focus on something— anything that would keep her tethered to aware-ness.

His soulless eyes blocked out the beautiful night sky. He brought his face close to hers and shouted words she couldn't understand, hatred she couldn't deny. He produced a gun and ground the nozzle beneath her chin. She closed her eyes, waiting for the bullet to enter her head. Tears leaked out of her eyes, but she swallowed the plea on the tip of her tongue.

Wham!

The sound was familiar. Fist on bone. The grip on her throat went slack, and the gun beneath her jaw fell away. She sucked in a ragged breath and quickly opened her eyes. Zain stood over them, a fierce, towering mass of masculinity. His body seemed to vibrate with fury, and his eyes shimmered with disgust.

He delivered another punch to the man who'd nearly killed her. The attacker's body folded on the gravel road, and blood dribbled from his nose and the corner of his mouth. Zain picked up the weapon, aimed, and fired a bullet into the guy's head. The sharp noise made her jump.

Tremors took over her body. Her scalp throbbed, and tears coated her cheeks. The poignant taste of near-death clung to her tastebuds. Zain pocketed the gun, then bent close to her.

His gaze searched her face, and his knuckles touched her jaw. "Are you hurt?"

She didn't nod. Couldn't move. Couldn't breathe. Couldn't do a damn thing but stare at the savage savior who'd walked through blood and death yet still looked at her in awe.

Blood stuck to his ebony eyebrow and snaked around his eye. Dirt marred his olive skin, and menace gave his amber eyes an ethereal glow. He was the most dangerous, alluring human being she'd ever faced.

She didn't answer his question. Her gaze darted around the road. "Where are the others?"

"Dead."

She looked back at him. He didn't even blink.

"Can you stand?" Concern swaddled his words, the softness a blaring contradiction to his rough appearance.

"Yes." The syllable came out weak. Strained. Pathetic.

But it didn't matter because right now she was all of those things. His arm came around her waist, supporting her weight as he gently lifted her to her feet.

Cortisol infused her cells, her body still anticipating another attack. Zain kept his hand firmly on her side. Her gaze lowered to the split tire. "We don't have a vehicle," she said. As that revelation settled, the forest seemed to close in around them.

Zain held up a set of keys. "We've got a new ride." He led her to the attackers' truck, almost identical to the one that'd just been wrecked, and opened the passenger door.

He moved his hand to her bicep as she climbed into the front seat.

"I lost your knife."

"You saved yourself. There's a difference." His body hovered close to hers as he grabbed the seatbelt and stretched it across her waist then clicked it in place. He shut the door, rounded the truck, and jumped in the driver's seat.

She wanted to correct him. To tell him she hadn't saved herself at all. He had. Stabbing the man had weakened him but not enough. Had Zain not shown up, she'd be dead by now.

A distant rumble sounded. The blood drained from her face. She clamped her hand on Zain's arm. "Do you hear—"

"There's more of 'em." He started the truck and peeled away from the scene. In seconds, they turned down a narrow dirt road. Zain's focused gaze stayed on the road, and he gripped the top of the steering wheel. "One of the guys made a call on his radio before I could get to him. We need to hide."

Fear pierced her tongue with the sharpness of one thousand needles. This was far from over.

CHAPTER 5

N O ONE FOLLOWED them as Zain made his way down road carved between trees.

But they were coming.

He backed the vehicle into the forest, out of sight. He had to walk only half a mile to reach the road that the rest of Jaysh's men would take to find him.

But they didn't know he was ready and waiting.

"Stay here," he said to the woman. "Don't get out for any reason." He should probably ask again if she was okay, but he didn't have the capacity right now. Christ, he'd become socially inept.

He unbuckled his seatbelt and leapt from the vehicle, softly closing the door. He hated that she'd been hurt again. He was being jumped by two men when he heard another drag her out. He'd killed the first two, breaking one's neck and stabbing the other in the chest. But that bastard who'd had her on the ground—*fuck.*

For an instant, he'd thought she was already dead. The possibility had made him feel as if he'd touched a live wire. And he'd almost been too late. While fighting the second man, the one who'd made the call on the radio, he'd caught a glimpse of her through the truck windows. The woman knew how to handle herself. What she'd done was more than run-of-the-mill self-defense. Her posture, stance, and capabilities screamed law enforcement. He'd know that training anywhere.

Earlier, she'd tried to offer herself up as a sacrifice, suggesting he leave her and go. That shit irked him but also made him wonder if she was some kind of journalist who'd realized she'd crossed the line and had endangered too many people.

Later, he'd get a better handle on who she was—and maybe he would just let her out in the woods to fend for herself. After all, she had just blown apart everything he'd been working toward.

No, he could never do that, even if she was a careless journalist. Even if she was another type of operative. Even if she was a spy. She couldn't be more than thirty years old. He was thirty-two, but he still shouldered more responsibility.

At the end of the day, he'd incited all this chaos to keep a woman from a fate worse than he could imagine. So as pissy as he was, he'd only fantasize about ditching her.

He stomped to the back of the truck. Every vehicle held a crate of weapons. He had to hurry before he missed Jaysh's men. Jumping in the back, he ripped off the lid of the crate and pulled out a few hand grenades and another magazine for his rifle.

He moved swiftly down the dirt trail. The men wouldn't be too far behind, but there were several small clearings and paths—a ton of places they could've gone. Hopefully they kept to the main road.

The roar of approaching engines relaxed his muscles. He could handle battle and death. That shit didn't faze him. Women on the other hand, well fuck. He was out of touch with that area. He stayed hidden in the bushes and watched as the first truck came barreling down the road.

He brought the grenade to his mouth and pulled the pin with his teeth. He'd have to step out of the bushes to make a calculated throw at the moving target.

He held his breath as he counted the clicks of the truck. A little more, a little more . . .

Zain stepped out of hiding, drew back his arm, and threw the grenade. In a split second the headlights swallowed his body and gunshots fired. He dove to the ground as the grenade exploded.

He watched with his arms over his head as the first truck flipped on its top and the second swerved around it, rolling off the road.

Flames licked the first vehicle. Zain got to his feet and seized his rifle. He broke into a jog, crouching low, his finger on the trigger. Every one of them would have to die. Reaching the first vehicle, he located three men. Only one stirred, his movements slow. Blood swallowed his face. Without a second thought, Zain blasted two bullets in him and in the two dead guys for good measure.

Breaking away from the scene, he rushed to the second vehicle, which was on its side. One man crawled out of the passenger door. Zain shot him in the chest, and he went down with only a grunt. Then Zain circled around to the windshield and fired two shots at the driver, who appeared already dead.

That was it. No one else. The pressure on his chest eased but only a fraction.

More would come.

HEAT SCALDED DANA'S cheek. She touched the tender, swollen flesh and winced. Then she brought her fingers to her scalp. If he'd ripped out a handful of hair she couldn't tell based on thickness, but the skin smarted.

Everything hurt. With every swallow, she felt as though daggers were slicing her throat, the tendons in her neck ached, and her head still swam from getting the wind knocked out of her. But what did bumps and bruises matter when she might not live to see the next day?

Dana mopped the tears off her cheeks with the heel of her palm. Stupid. All along she'd assumed Zain was some tortured soldier. A captive held against his will and someone in need of rescue. Whoever he was, Zain was certainly not that.

He'd taken out several men without hesitation. For all she knew, he'd do the same to her. Well, perhaps not. He'd saved her life several times now.

But still. He seemed furious she was here. Angry she'd found him. Who would feel that way unless he'd swapped to the other side? A terrorist happy just to kill. Someone who didn't care who was on the receiving end of his weapon. That's who.

Now she was screwed. She stared out the windshield, but she couldn't see a damn thing but trees swathed in darkness.

Bam!

She gasped at the gruesome sound of an explosion. Oh god. Had the terrorists found them? Had they killed Zain?

Fear pierced her heart. She grabbed the door handle. Her stress response kicked in. Fight, flight, or freeze? Definitely freeze. Because she could barely breathe through the cramping around her lungs.

If Zain died before she got to explain everything, she'd never forgive herself. He might have separated himself from where he'd come from, but there was always the possibility she could reach him. Tell him that Rami desperately wanted him to come home. That his family loved and missed him and prayed for him.

That she'd prayed for him.

Her throat cinched, and she blinked away the fresh wave of tears. Zain could be dead, and she was a sitting duck.

Bullets blasted in the night, and she let out a barely audible shriek. She couldn't tell if the firing was from more than one source. After a handful of shots, the sounds stopped.

Her breath wheezed in and out of her nose in frantic little pants. Seconds clipped by, then minutes.

They'd find her. Zain would have been back by now. She clutched the knife in both hands. She had to run. Maybe she could grab a gun from the back of the truck. She'd seen Zain take some from the crate.

Maybe—

A dark figure stepped into the clearing. He moved without hesitation, his head and weapon down.

Zain.

Before her brain could register that he was alive, the door on the driver's side creaked open, and he slid in. The interior light turned on, and he pinned her with his searing-hot amber gaze. His face wore the weathered look of pain and heartache. Tension held his brow high and his jaw tight.

His eyes were sharp like that of a lion—or a wounded animal. Either way, they lacked trust. They'd been hurt. Beaten down.

She inhaled a shuddering breath. "You're okay." Disbelief rang from her statement.

He blinked a few times. Each swipe of his dark lashes seemed to wipe clear a film of distrust from his face. He looked at her cheeks, probably noticing the tear tracks. "I'm fine. They're dead."

"I'm sorry. I didn't mean—"

"Who the hell are you?" he growled.

A lump formed in her throat, and she swallowed over it. He spoke with such disdain that she wanted to curl inside herself. Words evaded her. Fear wound around her vocal cords. *What if he doesn't remember where he's from?*

"You said my name." His voice was a little gentler. A little less angry. "Back at the cave."

She nodded. "Yes, I—" Hauling in a breath through her nose, she knotted her hands in her lap. "I'm Dana McAvery. I work for Backcountry Protection Services."

His granitelike expression didn't change. "Am I supposed to know what that is?"

"It's a bodyguard agency." Summoning up every ounce of bravery stored inside her, she rested her hand on his, which lay on the console separating them.

Zain's gaze shifted awkwardly, but he didn't move. The muscles in his hand twitched beneath his thick skin.

"Rami Mitry, your brother, co-owns it." She watched his eyes widen. Still, he didn't move. "He's been searching for you all this time. And I— Well . . . We came to rescue you."

Zain's head ticked back as if she'd struck him. "Rescue me?"

She squeezed his hand. "You went missing. Right when the troops were pulled—"

He yanked his hand away from her. "Jesus Christ," he mumbled. He swiped his hand down his face.

"I'm sure this is a lot to take in." She inched closer, questions scalding her tongue. "Do you—"

"Fuck!" He smacked his palm against the dash.

Dana jumped, pressing her back to the window. Unease shuddered through her as Zain's body coiled into an angry spring.

"I can't believe this. *Goddammit.*"

She winced. "I don't understand." Part of her wanted to escape the truck. To run from this man who was so angry and confused—a ticking time bomb that might be her demise if she wasn't careful. "Zain?" she asked softly, desperately needing an explanation.

Or some kind of guarantee he wasn't the heartless killer he appeared to be.

Fury emanated from his body. Yet she sensed his anger wasn't directed at her, even though he'd been cold and abrasive.

"Is Rami here?" he asked, keeping his gaze ahead. His voice sounded hollow. Like the voice of a man who'd lost his best friend. But he also sounded cautiously hopeful and . . . afraid? She couldn't be sure.

"No." She cleared her throat. "He . . . uh. Doesn't exactly know I'm here."

Zain swung his probing stare her way. "What do you mean?"

She toyed with a strand of her hair. "Well, everyone who works for Backcountry knows about your case. Rami has been working tirelessly to find you. But it wasn't until August, one of the employees—and Rami's best friend—handed me your file that I really got absorbed in locating you." She couldn't dim the passion in her voice. The excitement when she discovered the video of Zain still radiated through her.

Maybe because she'd always been a thrill junky. Maybe because she'd been so touched by Zain's story.

"That doesn't answer my question. Why isn't he here?"

"I didn't tell him I found you because I wasn't sure it was you. I knew that unless I got closer, I wouldn't know if you were still . . ."

One dark, thick eyebrow arched. "Alive?"

She nodded. "The footage I found of you was old. I was afraid Rami would get his hopes up only to find out you were dead. So I decided to find you myself."

He pinched the bridge of his nose and sighed. The sound was one of defeat.

Her shoulder sagged. This wasn't exactly the rescue she'd envisioned. He wasn't thrilled to have been found. Wasn't eager to go home. Did he even want to leave? What if she had to return to the US to tell Rami she'd found his brother but he wouldn't return?

Devastation spiraled within her. She had to convince him to come with her.

"Zain, please." She wiggled closer, this time a little more confident he wouldn't hurt her. "You've been through a lot. I'm sure you're traumatized and confused. Imprisonment does terrible things to a person. It can take years to get over the hold your captors had on you. Stockholm syndrome is probably a factor. But—"

A deep, rough laugh rumbled from his throat, and his shoulders jostled. She frowned.

"Stockholm syndrome? Are you kidding me?"

"Not in a romantic way," she added. She kept her tone soft, understanding. Hopefully he'd get the message that he was a victim in all this. "Zain, there are a lot of people who want you to come home."

He lowered his hand from his face and met her stare. "Like I said before, lady. You have no idea what you've done."

Apprehension climbed her spine. "I think you

need to elaborate."

A muscle jumped in his jaw. "When the troops were pulled out, my unit was hit with an IED. Eleven men died. Everyone except me."

Dread filled Dana. She kept her hand on his arm. "I'm so sorry."

He glanced down at her fingers then out the windshield. "I still haven't figured out why I'm the one who survived."

The sad note in his voice struck a chord of sympathy in her heart.

He shrugged. "I was in the hospital healing from minor wounds when the CIA came in and told me I was being placed inside Jaysh. I was given a mission to integrate with the group, work my way up the chain, and locate the leader." He faced her again. "That plan and all my hard work blew up in my face the moment you found me."

Her stomach bottomed out as realization struck her with a ten-foot pole. Oh god. She'd screwed up his mission. Endangered him. Pressure built at the corners of her eyes, and she forced down the deluge of tears that threatened to come. She'd almost gotten herself killed. Didn't know if Brick was alive.

And she'd messed up the CIA's plan to take down the leader of a terrorist group.

She covered her lips with her fingers. "Ohmigod. I—"

"Don't. You didn't know." Despite his words,

his voice was rough. Disgruntled.

The last thing she wanted was to send him back to that hellhole, but at least if she went home without Zain now, she'd have an explanation for Rami. Revealing classified information was beyond wrong, but dammit, Rami had a right to know.

He shook off her arm and turned over the engine. "We need to move. I've got a spot nearby where we can change vehicles. We're nowhere near safe."

"Stop." She pulled on his elbow. She was getting way too comfortable with touching him. But his solid strength gave her something to hold on to, the cords of his muscles offering assurance that he was real and she wasn't alone. "You don't have to do this. Just get me to a phone and I'll find my own way out of here. You can go back and—"

"And what? My cover's blown." He shook his head. "If I stay in Afghanistan, I'll be dead by morning. I killed ten of their men in the last hour. You don't even want to know what they'll do to me if I'm found."

The tears she'd managed to keep down rushed to the surface. She hadn't just royally screwed up his mission—she'd put him in a horrible position. She'd made him the most wanted man in the country. "I'm so sorry," she breathed, swiping at the blasted tears on her cheeks.

"Don't be. Just do what I say so we can both get out of here."

CHAPTER 6

A GENTLEMAN HE was not.

Still, Dana's tears affected him. Hurt his chest a bit for some reason. Being around a woman brought back a lot of feelings and shit he hadn't experienced in years. A softness, maybe. Yet there was more to her than met the eye.

He wasn't stupid. She might have a slight stature and a porcelain face, but he'd seen the way she fought. And he'd question her about it as soon as he didn't need to be on his toes every second. He might be seeing only the tip of the iceberg when it came to her, but she wouldn't hurt him. Of that he was positive.

They bumped over the road Zain knew like the back of his hand. He'd asked her to return to the back seat to be safe. Not just to keep her safe from shooters but to keep himself away from her alluring presence.

In a few minutes they'd reach his cave. More like an alcove compared to the Jaysh compound he'd just left. But next to the cave was a car, hidden in the trees. In it, he'd stashed a satellite phone, clothes, emergency food, cash, and a passport.

He'd swap vehicles. No one would be looking for the small sedan he'd use to take them across the border into Pakistan.

As angry as he was that everything he'd worked for over the last three years had been obliterated by Dana's pretty blue eyes, it wasn't her fault.

But goddammit. The days and months he'd spent among people he wanted to kill hadn't been easy. Watching innocent lives taken. Knowing he could've done something to prevent the killings but having his hands tied because of a bigger cause.

Almost three years of lying to Jaysh's members and leaders. Almost three years of sneaking off to his hideaway, where he could call his CIA contact, Maxine. Every time, he'd risked being caught. Every time, he'd managed to evade suspicion.

But now. Christ.

Maxine would be pissed. She didn't have an understanding bone in her body. She was blood-thirsty for Jabar, and rightfully so. Zain had been the one in the field risking his life, but the CIA had taken risks too. They'd worked toward finding Jabar day in and day out, and he'd gotten closer and closer.

So close that if little miss trouble had shown up less than a week later, he wouldn't have to worry about talking with Maxine. Because he'd have already handed Jabar over on a silver platter.

Isaad had trusted Zain. He'd already started pulling him into the inner workings, confiding in him about Jaysh's plans. He'd been scheduled to go on a four-day trip with Isaad next week, and he was almost certain he would've met Jabar.

Now that plan was fucking pixie dust. The moment Jaysh's men found Rakesh's and Isaad's bodies and Zain and Dana missing, they'd known what he'd done.

The headlights illuminated the huge pothole that indicated his turn was coming up. Not even half a mile later, he steered left and drove through the bushes and branches that led them deeper into the forest. He stopped the truck. "Hop out."

He opened his door and waited for her to crawl into the front seat and jump out next to him.

"I can't see anything." Her fingers gripped the sleeve of his tunic as he walked around the vehicle.

He didn't need a flashlight. He'd been here so many times he was familiar with every divot in the earth and every branch that clawed at his skin. He led her to the face of the mountain and searched around for the wall of vines. Pushing them away, he crouched to get inside the hole.

Dana followed. And damn if he wasn't a little stunned by her bravery—or naivety. He couldn't decide which. Either way, she'd held up after a traumatic day.

Finding the ledge where he kept his pack, he snagged the canvas and then pulled down the bag. It landed at his feet with a *thunk*.

He reached inside and pulled out a flashlight. Its bright-yellow glow lit the shallow cave, highlighting every weary line and uneasy crease on Dana's face. Her eyes were red-rimmed—from more crying? Had he caused that?

Scratches and a bruise marred her smooth skin, and his fingers itched to touch her. Not a good idea. She pulled her hair to the side, and once again, her femininity struck him.

He passed her a change of clothes and took out a pair for himself. Their descriptions would be word on the street, so the best thing they could do was change their appearances.

She took the bundle, and glanced around the cave. "Thanks."

"I'll turn around." He spun to face the wall and pulled off his tunic then shucked off his pants. A moment later he heard her clothes hitting the solid ground. Knowing she was naked and close made a channel of need spread to his cock.

Despite the fact that he'd been deprived of female companionship—in any form—there was no denying Dana was a beauty. Striking.

To be fair, a cave woman would probably turn him on right now, so maybe he wasn't a good judge of attractiveness.

"Okay," she called, sounding a little winded.

He rotated to face her as she wrapped a turban around her hair. But she wasn't doing it properly and wouldn't have a long-enough end. "Here." He stepped forward and took the turban from her.

Keeping his gaze on her hair as he swept the cloth around her head for the second time that day, he tried to ignore the faint scent of cherry blossoms that wafted from her silky strands. The aroma filled his nostrils and went straight to his head like intoxicating fumes.

The memory of the cherry blossom trees on his mom's property filled his mind. In seconds he was thrown back in time, running through her yard and climbing trees. He and Rami always competed to see who could climb the highest.

Usually Rami because he was older. Zain would always stop to pull cherry blossoms off the tree to give to his mom, who'd beam when he came in covered in dirt with the partially crushed flowers in his hand.

"There." He dropped his arms.

Dana picked up the long tail and draped it over the opposite shoulder. "Thank you. I'd try harder to get the hang of that, but I hope it's not something I have to practice for much longer."

He grunted and scooped up his backpack, fishing the set of keys from the inside pocket. "Wish I could promise you safety, but I can't."

She chewed her bottom lip, her eyes downcast. She'd been more hesitant since he told her about the CIA operation. Clearly she blamed herself. And hell, she was at fault in a way. But only because she hadn't known.

She bent and picked up the knife. "Here."

He glanced down but didn't take it. Instead, he reached into his duffel and took out a sheath. "This clips onto your pants."

She accepted the leather and peeled up the shirt she swam in. Her fingers worked to pry apart the clip at the back, but she struggled to do so with the knife still in her hand.

"Let me see." He took the sheath and extended the waistband of her pants. Creamy skin peeked out from the gap in her clothing. His knuckles brushed her soft flesh, and he had to fight the urge to stroke her skin. Biting his tongue so he wouldn't do anything stupid, he slid on the clip. Then he took the knife from her and fit it into its new home. "There."

He moved toward the entrance of the cave. "Look," he said, stopping and turning. He fought for words, for a vocabulary full of decency and understanding he'd lost years ago. "You didn't know about my mission. You were only trying to help Rami."

Her eyes found his. They were so bright and bottomless he could lose himself in them for hours—days.

"Thank you."

He lifted the corner of his mouth. "Don't thank

me. We might not live another hour."

She brought her fingers to his elbow. "I mean it. Thank you. Rakesh would have—" Her throat moved on a swallow. "Even if I die tonight, I'm grateful you spared me that trauma."

Fresh anger bunched his muscles. If he could bring Rakesh back from the dead and slit his throat all over again, he'd do it in a heartbeat. Shoving down those words because they'd probably scare the shit out of her, he gave a brisk nod. "As long as I'm here, no one will hurt you." Normally he didn't make promises. Not to himself and sure as hell not to anyone else.

But this wasn't a promise. It was a guarantee. He barely knew this woman, but he wouldn't let anyone touch a hair on her delicate head, let alone violate her.

The lines of tension on her face softened, and the corners of her lips turned down. "Thank you."

"You said that."

She sniffed.

Ah, hell. Don't cry.

"Yeah. I know. I just—It's been a rough day. You know?" Her voice grew impossibly small. His war-hardened heart melted a bit but Jesus. How could he comfort her when he didn't have an ounce of compassion left in him?

Well, maybe that wasn't true. Because whatever he felt for Dana's pain was something. Without dropping his bag, he brought his free hand to wrap around her shoulders. Her slight frame clicked against his like a magnet to stainless steel.

She rested her cheek against his chest, her hand gripping his shirt. Her shoulders shook and he mumbled comforting sounds that probably didn't make any sense. He might not have the right words, but he could give her a moment to process shit. He rubbed his fingers in small circles between her shoulder blades as her raspy little cries twisted his insides.

She was a lot smaller than him. Tiny even. Which only made him more furious with Rakesh. He hadn't witnessed Rakesh's assaults on women, but he'd heard about them. Knew that she'd have been unrecognizable if he'd had even ten minutes alone with her.

The possibility blurred his vision. He took a slow, deep breath to lower his heart rate before the strained organ beat out of his chest.

"Sorry. I don't know what's come over me."

"You're fine." His tone was gruffer than he wanted it to be.

She chortled and pulled away, wiping her tears with her knuckles. "I got your shirt all wet."

His hand stayed rooted to her back as if it had a mind of its own. "Come on. We've got a long drive ahead."

He led her from the cave with the flashlight illuminating their path. He might have canceled his contract with the CIA, but it wasn't for nothing.

★ ★ ★

DANA SAT IN the front seat of the small sedan, both the bottle of water and the protein bar Zain had given her half gone.

She was grateful the prisoner's scent—of urine and god knew what else—was off her skin. In the cave, she'd removed both the other man's garments and her own.

Now, only Zain's heady scent surrounded her. The aroma of pine and spice was all him, and she didn't mind one bit. It would beat artificial fragrance any day.

They'd ridden in silence for the last fifteen minutes. Zain seemed on edge, and he routinely checked his rearview mirror, but no one followed them.

She didn't want to break his concentration, but the need to locate Brick strummed through her. The last thing she wanted was for him to ambush the compound they'd just left and be attacked. "Can I use your phone now?"

Zain slid his gaze her way. "Yeah, but we'll be in Pakistan in an hour. Can it wait? I'd feel better with more distance between us and Jaysh."

"I got separated from my colleague at the protest. I'm worried he didn't make it."

His jaw clenched, and he seemed to be struggling to make a decision. Slowly he nodded. "Yeah, I guess you should call him. I'm assuming that's the guy who tried to run after you?"

Regret pulled at her heart. "Yes. He was hit in the head."

"I saw." He stretched toward the back seat, rummaged through his duffel bag, then passed her a device. "It's a satellite phone. Works the same as any other, though. Just more reliable without the need for cell towers."

She held the smooth, bulky plastic. "Will the CIA be angry about your mission?" Stupid question. Of course they would. She couldn't stand the thought of him going through any more turmoil, but what was done was done.

"I'll deal with it. Call your friend."

She hit the buttons on the keypad—no flimsy glass screens for this military-grade phone—and pressed the device to her ear. The line rang and she closed her eyes. *Please pick up. Please pick up.*

"Hello?"

The sound of the husky, cautious male voice made Dana choke out a laugh.

"Brick? Is that you?"

"*Dana?* Holy hell. Where are you? What happened?"

"That's a long story. We're almost in Pakistan. About an hour away. Where are you?"

"I'm at Ali's. After they took you from the protest, I came here for cover so I could arrange a team and plan an extraction strategy. But—Wait, who're you with?"

She didn't hold back the smile that pulled at her lips because as wild as this mission was, she'd succeeded. "Zain."

A beat passed. "Dana, I think you're in the wrong line of work. Rami's crazy to keep you behind a desk."

She chuckled. "I think that's my brother's doing."

Brick scoffed. "Yeah, he's pretty pissed right now."

Dana winced. In all the chaos, it hadn't crossed her mind that Brick would alert Taschen to her being in Afghanistan and captured by Jaysh. To say he was pissed was probably a mega understatement. Not something she could handle right now. As soon as they had their footing, she'd call her brother. And not a minute sooner. "Let him know I'm okay. But we need to find you. I want to make sure we all get out together."

"Absolutely. Put Zain on and we can arrange to meet you as soon as you cross into Pakistan."

She hit the speaker button and held the phone between them. Brick introduced himself to Zain, and they spoke briefly about their locations and made a plan. Brick, Ali, and Ali's men would be waiting when they crossed the border.

After ending the call, Zain asked, "How well do you know these people?"

"I work with Brick and so does your brother. I met Ali, but I really don't know much about him."

Zain grunted. "And what does Ali think you're doing in Afghanistan? Does he know you came for me?"

"Brick told him it was a secret rescue mission. He doesn't know anything else and I think Ali is smart enough not to pry. Why do you ask?"

He tucked in the corner of his mouth, and his face clouded with distrust. He was so dark and dangerous, just looking at him made anticipation heat her skin. Mystery surrounded Zain, and she'd always been a sucker for a good case. That had to be the cause of her quickening pulse.

"Because I'm leery of people with money in these parts. By the sounds of it, Ali has a good-sized team. Which is expensive. And in this area of the world, you don't really get into a position of power without Jaysh knowing about it."

Anxiety tugged at the muscles in her neck. She just wanted this to be over. She was exhausted, running on nothing but fumes, and at any minute a missel could strike their car and wipe them both out. It wasn't just a matter of tomorrow not being promised—she didn't even have a survival guarantee minute to minute.

And if what Zain had said was true, they were entering the lion's den. And Brick was caught in the middle.

CHAPTER 7

ZAIN FOUGHT THE urge to place his hand on Dana's jumping knee. Instead, he kept his eyes on the road and his palms on the steering wheel.

By now, Jaysh would've alerted any contacts at the border. He'd changed his clothes and had new identification, so that was a good start. Dana would be caught in a second, though. She'd left her ID at his hideout, but she was easily identifiable as an American.

He'd deliberately chosen the smallest border crossing, which was a little farther out of the way, but that didn't offer much guarantee. Not when there was plenty of air and land patrol on both sides. He slowed the car and pulled to the side of the road.

Dana straightened in her seat. "Why are you stopping?"

He braced his hand on her headrest and zeroed in on her smooth, panicked, pink lips. "You need to hide again. People could be looking for us at the border."

Her face paled.

"Their organization spreads far and wide. We might sail through without a problem, but my bet is there will be moles looking for us."

She compressed her lips.

"You'll need to go in the trunk. I've got blankets back there you can hide under. I promise I won't keep you in there a minute longer than necessary, but they're looking for a male and female. I have a false identity. You'll raise suspicions without a passport. Not to mention your appearance will give you away."

"Okay," she said, her big eyes wide. "Now?"

He nodded. She unbuckled her seatbelt and got out. He did the same and met her at the back of the car. Popping the trunk, he pushed aside an emergency medical bag and then lifted a folded blanket. "Go ahead."

As he watched her climb into the trunk, irritation rattled through him. Goddammit, he hated making her get in there. Hated that she'd be afraid. But there was no help for it. If they got caught, he'd be too outnumbered, and he couldn't let them capture her again.

She curled into a ball, her arms bundled tightly to her chest. Her wary eyes stared up at him. His chest spasmed. He spread the blanket over her. The trunk light illuminated the purple coloring on her cheekbone, a stabbing reminder of why he had to do this.

He reached out and brushed his knuckle over the bruise, wishing he could erase it from her delicate features. She blinked, her gaze curious.

Balling his hand, he pulled away. "Cover your face when I slow down. We'll be at the border crossing then." A beat passed. He couldn't seem to tear himself away. "Won't be long." With that, he shut the lid with a sharp *clank*.

He hoped to hell the last thing he'd said to her hadn't been a lie.

★　★　★

WELL, THIS TOOK *a turn*.

When they'd switched to the less-distinct vehicle and called Brick, she'd thought they were in the homestretch. That escaping Jaysh was as easy as crossing an invisible line into another country.

Boy had she been wrong.

Although the air outside was cold, inside the trunk, it was thick and stale. The heavy wool blanket was scratchy on her neck and chin, but she gripped the edge tightly, ready to dive underneath when they stopped. As if a blanket would hide her. If the trunk opened, they were screwed.

The vehicle bumped along the gravel road, and every pitch and sway made the undigested protein bar hit her stomach lining, as if a toddler were throwing a plate of food at it. If they made it into

Pakistan, she'd surely get sick.

After a few minutes, the car slowed. The brakes squeaked, the high-pitched noise only agitating her nausea further. She pulled the blanket over her head. Her rapid breath made the confining walls shrink around her.

Please, God. Let us get through.

ZAIN KEPT HIS hand loose on the wheel as he inched toward the border crossing. Every muscle in his body clenched, ready to attack. His rifle sat on the passenger seat next to him—too far away for his comfort.

Thankfully, carrying a weapon was normal in these parts. Pointing one at the guards, however, would be a problem, so he'd avoid that unless necessary.

He'd promised Dana he wouldn't let anyone hurt her. And while he'd meant every word, he didn't like promises. The fact that he'd made one at all, let alone to a woman he didn't even know, was stupid.

A guard approached his car, and Zain rolled down the window. Lights from lampposts lit the checkpoint like a concert stage. The desert around them was nothing but black sand and black sky. With a machine gun held loosely, as though it were simply another appendage, the man motioned for Zain to hand over his ID.

He dipped his fingers inside his shirt pocket and pulled out his passport. The guard read the identification stating he was Yusuf Syed, native of Pakistan. Zain had no doubts about the ID. It would pass any security system with flying colors because it had come from the best—the CIA.

No, the heartburn heating his chest wasn't a result of the damn passport. It was the result of the stowaway in the trunk.

The guard lifted his steely brown gaze. Something flashed in his eyes. Zain lowered his hand to his lap, ready to snatch his weapon and shoot. Tension vibrated the air between them. He focused on making his breath even, not taking his eyes off the guard. If he flinched, he'd look guilty as hell. If he reached for the gun a second too late, he and pretty miss blue eyes were dead.

"Out of the vehicle," the guard shouted in Pashto.

Sweat dampened the back of Zain's collar. His muscles bunched. If he got out of the car without his weapon, he might as well just hand himself over. "Something wrong?"

Distaste twisted the man's features. "I said, out!" He shouted something else over his shoulder, and another guard approached.

Fuck, fuck, fuck.

For a moment, indecision paralyzed him, but then he pushed open the door and stood next to the car with his hands up. There was no easy way out of this. All he could do was hope the bastard wasn't trigger happy and that he could talk his way out.

"What's the holdup?" Zain asked. "I've got somewhere to be."

The guards mumbled to each other, and his brain worked to process the fast-speaking Pashto. The only word he could pull from their conversation was a name: Isaad.

Fuck. These men were eyes and ears for Jaysh. And his gun was several feet away.

"Open the trunk," the first guard said, gesturing.

Hell no.

Zain clenched his teeth. He shouldn't be surprised that Jaysh's men had gotten word to the border-crossing guards. Maybe he should've tried crossing through the mountain, but they'd likely have expected that as well. And Pakistan didn't take kindly to illegal crossings.

He had to act. A cloak of calm spread over Zain's shoulders. He didn't normally lead with emotion. The only reason he was bent out of shape right now was because of the helpless woman he'd somehow become responsible for.

He never went down without a fight, and this time would be no exception. With that conviction in mind, the calmness became satisfaction. He'd already killed ten men today—what were a few more? He did a quick, subtle survey of the area. At this hour, there weren't many people around.

In the next lane was only one car; the man in it spoke to a guard. Including the two guards Zain was dealing with and the one operating the arm barrier, there were four he'd have to take out.

He'd need to act fast. He'd hit the two men in front of him first, then the guard at the next lane; the one behind the bulletproof glass would be trickier. Not the best odds, but not the worst either.

He stretched his lips into a grimace. Let them think he was begrudgingly compliant. "Sure. One sec."

The guards bent their heads together and spoke rapidly while Zain leaned inside. Rather than hit the trunk button, he grabbed his rifle. The smooth, heavy metal like home in his hands as he dragged it into the driver's seat.

"What's going on?" Another guard approached, his tone authoritative. Zain straightened, leaving his rifle inches from his grasp and out of view.

"This man's suspicious and noncompliant." *Bullshit.* "We need to search his vehicle."

The new, heavyset guard reached for Zain's passport and held it close to his face to study the shiny paper. Lowering it, he took a step forward, his gaze watchful.

"What are you doing, Abdullah?" asked one of the other guards. "We need to search."

Abdullah cocked his head. "Are you a friend of Ali?" he asked quietly.

The tension gripping Zain's chest eased a fraction. "I am," he said with a slight nod, remembering the name Brick had mentioned.

His dark eyes sparked with warning. "Get in your vehicle."

Zain took back his passport and slid into his seat, pushing his weapon out of the way. Had Abdullah not shown up, every man at the checkpoint would be dead right now. He shifted into drive and sped away from the men arguing behind him. The first guard shouted at Zain, but he kept going.

★ ★ ★

DANA'S BREATH CAME in and out in sharp gasps. She hated this. Terror screeched in her ears. And with all her panting, the air only grew thicker. Sweat clung to her skin.

The warm, musty smell made the nausea in her gut heavier. Carpet fibers irritated her nose, threatening to make her sneeze. She covered her nose with her hand and pressed her tongue to the roof of her mouth.

Great. With her luck they'd want to search the vehicle.

The men's voices grew agitated. Zain spoke, but she couldn't make out what he was saying. She took tiny breaths through her nose, but it wasn't enough to settle the anxiety pressing against her chest. Her eyes watered with the need to break free from the confines of the vehicle. But she couldn't do a damn thing but lie there and fight the rising hysteria.

The car door shut with an abrupt slam, and the engine started. Anxiety ripped through her muscles as she anticipated a blast of bullets. She covered her head with her arms, but no shots were fired. Only men yelling. Was Zain fleeing?

There was no way to tell. Not a fragment of light reached inside of the trunk. She might as well be at the bottom of the ocean for how dark it was.

She kicked the blanket away and greedily dragged in one breath after another. The inside of the trunk began to spin.

The tires whirred beneath her. Every bump over the uneven earth made breathing more difficult. She had to get out of here. Using all of her strength, she banged on the trunk lid. Her arms burned with the effort it took to use the last of her energy.

The car turned and slowed.

Her breath ran shallow, and the need to get outside into the cool, fresh air was almost too much to bear.

Click

Light flooded the dark space. Oxygen rushed in, and she choked on the fullness that hit her lungs. Hands seized her beneath her arms and hauled her out of the trunk.

"Dana." Zain's sharp, distinct voice calmed her slightly.

He held her perched on the edge of the trunk, one arm wrapped around her back, the other bracing the base of her neck. "Look at me, dammit."

She struggled to bring in more air. One deep, shuddering breath after another. The cool night breeze caressed her sweaty skin, quickly dropping her body temperature. Bringing her gaze to Zain's took a painful amount of effort.

His dark beard shadowed his jaw. Angst locked his mouth in a firm line and his brow in deep channels of worry. The gold flecks in his eyes anchored her, pushing away the possessive arms of terror.

"You're okay." His expression said otherwise. His thumb swept over the flesh where her jaw met her ear. "Sorry I kept you in there so long."

She swallowed and shook her head. "It's fine. I just . . . panicked, I guess."

"It's not fine."

Her chest rose and fell, her system still trying to adjust to the abundance of space around her.

"Need some water?"

She swept her tongue over the dry tissue in her mouth. She nodded but caught his wrist so he wouldn't walk away. If he let her go, she'd surely fold to the ground.

He must have understood because he brought his arm beneath her knees to lift her off the edge of the open trunk. Then he shut the lid. Setting her on top, he kept a steady arm around her. She let her body lean forward so her chest rested against his abdomen, her head just beneath his shoulder.

The solid wall of his abs tensed beneath his clothing. He seemed to hesitate before resting his palm on the middle of her back.

"Are we out of the woods yet?" She hated the way her voice wobbled. Hated that she needed confirmation from someone else. This wasn't field-agent Dana. This was beaten-down Dana. After everything that'd happened today, she was fine with returning to a desk job.

Zain grunted. "Let's hope. Your friends will be here any minute."

"You don't sound happy about that."

Two large SUVs turned onto the road, their headlights bright. Zain's body went rigid, his hand on her no longer hesitant but firm and protective. She lifted her head and found he had his rifle pointed at the newcomers.

The vehicles stopped side by side, and the passenger door of one opened. A man stepped out, hands raised.

Dana gasped with relief then slid off the car and out of Zain's arms. "Brick!" she called. He ran toward her.

His large, muscular arms wrapped her in a hug

and he rocked her. "Jesus, I'm so glad you're okay." He pulled away and looked down at her face. His features clenched. "Those bastards."

She forced a smile. "I'm okay. Promise." She looked over her shoulder to see Zain walking awkwardly toward them, his expression cautious, brooding, and guarded.

Dana backed away from Brick and caught Zain's hand. "Zain, this is Brick." She beamed at him. "We're going to take you home now."

CHAPTER 8

Zain studied Dana's friend. What kind of name was Brick anyway? He could only imagine the fun people had cracking jokes, but Zain had long since lost his sense of humor.

Brick gave a friendly smile and shook his hand. "We're happy you're okay, man."

The guy seemed nice. Sincere. Zain flicked his attention from Brick to Dana, and a seed of jealousy rooted itself in his gut. Was she with him? Their embrace seemed platonic. But the fact that there could be more going on between them made hostility heat his skin.

Christ, why did it matter? He'd known Dana less than a day. Had no reason to care if she was with someone or not.

Yet he did. And when the timing was right, he'd find out if she was off-limits. Because for some reason he needed to know. Normal curiosity about an intriguing woman—nothing more. "Thanks." His tone was flat, emotionless. He didn't have it in him to tell Brick what he and Dana had screwed up. She could fill him in on that later.

Warmth reached Brick's eyes. "Rami's going to flip when he hears we found you."

At the mention of his brother, emotion churned in Zain's chest. He'd put his family out of his mind for so long. He hadn't forgotten them but had forbidden himself to think about them. Doing so, knowing his brother and mom would be bereft, would've only made Zain's mission that much harder.

"Can I talk to him?" Urgency rushed forward. The opportunity to connect with his brother was almost too good to be true.

Brick clapped him on the shoulder. "'Course. Let's get to Ali's first. I think we could all use a rest."

Zain nodded. "I'll follow you."

Brick looked at Dana. "You can ride with me if you want. Tell me what the hell happened."

Zain's hackles rose. He balled his hand into a fist to stop himself from overstepping. She had every right to be close to her friend right now, so why the fuck did Brick's suggestion bother him so much?

Dana smiled wearily. "Thanks, but I'll stick with Zain. We'll chat more at the house."

He relaxed his hand. Her words were like aloe vera gel on a fresh sunburn: calming and . . .

welcome.

Interest sparked Brick's eyes, but he didn't appear affronted by Dana's refusal. "Sounds good. It's about a twenty-minute drive." With that, Brick strode back to the SUV and got in.

Zain waited for Dana to get into the passenger seat, then passed her a bottle of water before shifting into drive and following Brick onto the main road. "You okay?" he asked, after several minutes of silence.

Maybe his people skills were improving.

He flicked his attention her way and saw her drop her head back against the seat.

"I feel oddly alert. Exhausted, but I don't think I could sleep."

He brought his focus back to the taillights ahead of him. "That makes sense. You're still running on adrenaline. Probably in shock."

"Do you think Jaysh will continue to pursue us now that we've crossed the border?"

The same question was nestled in the back of his mind. He wanted to reassure her, but there was no knowing to what depths Jaysh would go to find them. Not only had he killed off a chunk of their team in one night, but he'd been working undercover. He'd bet his head was their top priority. And Dana's—collateral damage. "I think it's wise to assume they will. The sooner we get back to the US, the better off we'll be."

Dana sighed, and her hand covered his. "You

mean that? You're coming home?"

He scrunched the corner of his mouth and had to fight to keep his eyes off the hope dancing on her face. "What else would I do?"

She shrugged. Her hand stayed on his knuckles, and the cool softness of her skin made him want to turn over his palm and fit her hand in his. "I dunno." Her tone suggested she had a theory in mind.

He raised his eyebrows. "Go on. What'd you think I was going to do?"

She wrapped her long, dark locks behind her ear and tucked her chin. Once again, he tore his gaze back to the road before he rear-ended Brick's SUV.

"I didn't know if you'd want to leave."

"Well, if I had the choice, I'd finish my mission. But that's not the hand I was dealt. So I'd be stupid to stay here when everyone on the street—and probably some crooked law enforcement too—wants my head on the chopping block."

She scoffed, and it sounded like a hiss. "Don't talk like that."

"It's true. But it's not going to happen."

"I won't let it," she stated solemnly.

He turned his head away a fraction so she wouldn't see the smile her vow had invoked. Hell, it was the first time he'd smiled genuinely in a long time, and it felt good. Human. Imagining this cutie going toe-to-toe with Jaysh was unsettling at the least. But her desire to protect him—that was endearing as hell. "That reminds me." He let his gaze drift toward her earnest eyes. "You've got quite the fighting skills. Where'd you learn that?"

This time, she was the one who steered her face away. "Um, well. That's a long story. Prior to working for Backcountry, I was an FBI analyst." She inhaled. "And before that, a field agent. So I've had training. Honestly, after that fight I think I need a refresher course."

"You did fine." FBI. Interesting. With the skills he'd witnessed he'd assumed she had some type of law enforcement background. But picturing her as an FBI agent both agitated his nerves and made his dick hard.

She scoffed. "I was on my ass with a gun to my throat before you showed up."

He grunted. "You did better than most. But if you want, when we get stateside, we can spar a little." The suggestion made desire swim inside him.

The thought of seeing Dana in less clothing, sweaty and swinging at him, made his dick twitch. It was too dark to read her face, but her lowered eyes told him her thoughts might have gone in the same direction.

Or he'd made her uncomfortable. Fuck.

"Sure. But I hope never to fight for my life again."

Zain clenched the steering wheel. Dana must

have a guardian angel watching over her. She'd fought for her life more times in the last twelve hours than any woman should have to.

And if he stuck around, she'd never have to again.

★ ★ ★

"It's just for one night."

Brick's placating tone was wearing down her patience.

She was grateful to be alive. Grateful he'd met them and had a safe place for Zain and her to regroup. But she wouldn't feel safe until Jaysh was across the ocean.

"There's just no way I can sleep. It seems careless to just . . . *hang out* when we could be putting distance between us and the men who want Zain dead."

Well, Zain and her, but she didn't say that. She'd already told Brick everything but the nitty-gritty details about Rakesh attempting to rape her. He was a smart man and had probably deduced enough from what she'd said.

"If you rest your eyes, you'll feel better."

She puffed out an exasperated breath. She wasn't getting anywhere. Brick was insistent that they all spend the night and arrange for a private flight out of Pakistan the next day. From his perspective, it was a logical request.

"Fine." She crossed her arms over the clean

tunic Ali had provided, a beautiful afghan he apparently kept on hand for guests—although it was after 2:00 a.m. and she really didn't care what she was wearing. They were in a high-tech mansion in the mountains, and her brain was still struggling with the contrast. From damp, haunting caves to a stunning property and massive, impersonal house in a matter of hours. It was almost too much for her system.

"You're beat. Go to sleep." He squeezed her shoulder. "The guards lock female guests' bedrooms. It's for your own safety. And, uh—" He glanced over his shoulder. "Every bedroom has a camera. So if you want privacy, be sure to use your bathroom."

Unease scampered over her skin like the legs of a centipede. She fought off a shudder.

"I'm right across the hall and Zain's next door. Safe as a baby."

She grimaced at the reference and lifted her gaze to the glassy eye watching her from the ceiling. The soles of her feet itched to hightail it out of here. Zain's words about a wealthy man in this part of the world careened through her mind.

Ali had been more than accommodating and polite, but his men, who all resided on the property, made her uneasy.

She'd met two—exhaustion prevented her from remembering their names—and they'd treated her like some of the men in Afghanistan had: as if she were invisible and her presence was unwanted.

News flash, dudes. I don't want to be here either.

"Go to bed." Brick drifted to the hallway as Zain appeared at her door.

"You can come in," she said.

In the bright fluorescent lights of the home, Zain's tall stature and sharp jaw line stood out more. The dirt on his skin seemed like a permanent coating, and blood splatters that she hadn't noticed in the dark decorated his forehead. "I just wanted to check on you before I call Rami."

She gave him a tight smile. "I'm all right. But I'll be better when we're home."

He dragged the tip of his thumb along the hairline of his beard. "Same." He stepped farther into the room, drawing short of touching her toes with his. His gaze raked over her face. She'd showered before putting on the clean clothes and had seen the bruises on her face. The sight of her reflection had brought tears to her eyes. Not because she looked like shit, but because the markings were a constant reminder that she'd come close to dying.

"Those must hurt."

Touching the spot beneath her eye that still throbbed, she stifled a wince. He stuffed his hands in his pockets, his expression now stoney. "I just wanted to tell you . . . the promise I made you earlier. It still stands."

She drew her eyebrows together. Fatigue made

her thoughts muddy and slow. "I don't know what you mean."

He stepped closer to her, blocking the camera with his back. Leaning in, he withdrew his hand from his pocket. His fingers brushed over the material of her pants, and he slipped something inside her pocket. His lips dipped close to her ear, his breath warm and teasing on her skin. Her body temperature rose and her loins clenched at his closeness. Despite her response to him, his actions lacked sexuality. "As long as I'm here, no one will hurt you."

Her eyes flickered, and she leaned into him. His words caressed her battered soul, and she swallowed the emotion clogging her throat. She gripped his shirt for the simple reason that she needed to touch him. Needed more of whatever promises he'd give, empty or not.

He stilled at her touch, his body going rigid. He pulled back an inch, just enough so that his face hovered near hers. The amber coals of his eyes glistened with uncontrolled attraction.

She gripped tighter. "You don't think we're safe here." Her words were barely a whisper.

"I don't think we're safe anywhere." He brushed his fingers across her forehead, and heat radiated through her core. God he was tempting. Dangerous. Hot. "But I want anyone watching to know that you're protected."

Oh.

She wet her lips, not breaking eye contact. He wasn't coming on to her. Who was she kidding? Of course he wasn't. They'd been through hell and back the last few hours, and he wanted to follow through with his promise. That's all this was.

His closeness; his tantalizing scent; his warm, gentle touch; the watchful flare in his eyes—all nothing more than him wanting to stand between violation and her.

Her reaction to him? Well, that was an entirely different story, and one she wasn't going to unpack while running on fumes and sleep deprivation.

"Time's up." A guard appeared in the doorway. His authoritative voice made Dana jump, but she didn't back away from Zain.

Zain sent the guard an annoyed glare. Once again, he brought his mouth close to her ear. "If you need me, scream," he whispered. "Don't hesitate. And use what's in your pocket if you're in danger. I'll take care of the rest." He pinched her chin and backed away.

Her body ached at the lack of his contact. It was all she could do to keep her feet rooted and not follow him. "Sleep. You're safe." He reached the hallway, and the guard shut the door.

But not before Zain's penetrating gaze locked on hers and sent her heart into palpitations.

The lock clicked.

CHAPTER 9

Z AIN SAT ON the edge of his bed, satellite phone between his hands. It was almost 3:00 a.m. but there was no way he could sleep. Not yet.

He'd showered in the ostentatious bathroom— the only place without a camera. He was more of a prisoner here, wrapped in the stone walls, than he ever had been inside the Jaysh compound. The forced separation from Dana agitated his nerves. And Ali had insisted they relinquish their weapons, which also didn't sit well with him. He'd managed to slip Dana one of his knives.

Nevertheless, the half-hour-long piping-hot shower—Jesus he'd missed running water—was a luxury he was happy to indulge in. His clean skin was new to him. He'd shave in the morning.

He stared at the screen but couldn't think of the right words to say to his brother. There weren't any. It had been three years since he'd spoken to his brother, and he'd changed. He dialed the digits he'd committed to memory and held the device to his ear. With the twelve-hour time difference, it was afternoon for Rami.

"Hello?"

The sound of his brother's voice took Zain back in time again.

"Hey, man. It's me."

Rami's sharp inhale made Zain get to his feet and start pacing. He wished he could be there to see his older brother's face.

"Jesus Christ. Zain," Rami blurted, his voice strained. "I thought you were dead. All this time . . . *What happened?*"

Zain palmed the back of his neck and closed his eyes. What *hadn't* happened? "It's a long story."

"Brick told me he thought they'd found you but—hell, I didn't believe him. None of it feels real." Rami's tone was pained.

Remorse swallowed Zain's heart. His decision to harden himself for the mission came back to bite him. He'd hurt his family, and there was no way to ask for forgiveness. Rami might understand, but it'd take time.

"Why didn't you contact me?" Rami's question stabbed through his chest. "We were worried, bro. Mom—I didn't think she'd keep going. The only reason she hasn't had a heart attack is because she's been waiting for news about you. Closure."

Pressure weighed on Zain's lungs and hit the corners of his eyes. He was too exhausted to do this. To explain something his family would struggle to understand. But he owed Rami an explanation. "I know." The admission came out weak, contrite. Pain and guilt burned his throat. They'd suffered because of him. "I—" He rubbed his thumb against his fingers, wishing he was better at this shit. "I'm sorry. I hope you know that."

Silence. "You're alive. That's all I care about. Just come home."

"On it."

"Are you all right?"

That was a loaded fucking question. "Probably not," he said with a scoff. "But I'm coming back in one piece. Dana almost didn't."

Rami muttered a curse. "I had no idea she went on a self-appointed mission. Had I known—hell. I would've gone myself. I'll have words when she and Brick get back, that's for damn sure."

"She's fine now." He wouldn't say she'd been assaulted. Wasn't his place. But his hand clenched into a fist at the memory of interrupting Rakesh.

They spoke for a few more minutes then hung up. Zain lowered himself to the bed and kicked his legs up on the mattress, then clicked off the lamp on the bedside table. That was one tough phone call off his plate. Tomorrow he'd make the other— to Maxine.

His muscles ached as his cortisol finally reached a normal level.

Sleep came fast and hard.

But his mind never drifted far from those pretty blue eyes.

"YOU'RE NOT LISTENING." Dana didn't hide her exasperation. Talking to Taschen when he was riled up was like trying to tell a hurricane to change direction.

He had every right to be worried and pissed, which was why she hadn't chewed him out yet.

She plucked a grape from the extravagant fruit spread on the kitchen table and popped it in her mouth. A guard had unlocked her door at 9:00 a.m. and told her breakfast was served, as if she were some kind of criminal being summoned to the prison cafeteria.

However, after the gourmet breakfast of a three-egg omelet, toast, bacon, hashbrowns, and fruit galore, she couldn't exactly be mad.

"I'm listening to you try to justify a really careless decision that almost got you killed."

She grimaced. She hadn't *just* been almost killed. She'd have endured far more than that if Rakesh had gotten his way with her, but she wouldn't share that with her brother. By the sound of his voice, he was on the verge of a mental breakdown.

Brick sat across from her with a large plate of food and double the bacon she'd had. As Taschen yammered at her, she shifted her gaze to the hallway for the twenty-zillionth time since sitting down. Zain hadn't emerged from his room, and she was about to go knock on his door.

Though she'd fallen asleep immediately after Zain left her room, intense nightmares about the man she'd fought on the road pulling the trigger on the gun had woken her several times. Each time, she'd hear the gunshot and would writhe in bed until she realized she was alive, and it was all a horrible dream.

Nonetheless, she'd made it to morning without any more attacks, and for that she was grateful. Now if they could just get on a plane to the US today, she'd be slap-freaking-happy.

She talked to Taschen for a few more minutes and promised to call him again as soon as she could. After hanging up the satellite phone Brick had lent her, she slid it across the table.

"He's still pretty pissy," Brick said, as he ripped off a large bite of toast.

She snorted and took a sip of her orange juice. "I hope he calms down before we get home."

Brick brushed off his fingers over his napkin. "Has Zain said anything to you about why he was here all this time? I haven't wanted to ask. But he clearly wasn't a prisoner, like we thought."

Dana fought the urge to squirm in her seat. Zain's story wasn't hers to tell, especially given the nature of his mission. She didn't want to lie to

Brick, but saying anything about the CIA could create a huge problem for all of them. "No," she lied. There were too many eyes and ears everywhere. Later she'd tell Brick more—or at least explain that she couldn't divulge any details regarding Zain's time in Afghanistan.

Her gaze pinged toward the doorway as Zain entered. Her insides swirled with appreciation and desire as his eyes landed on her and a small, genuine smile softened his face.

He'd shaved. Not the whole length of his beard, but several inches; the bristles darkened his jaw just the right amount. His skin was deeply tanned, and his yellow irises seemed to glow in contrast.

Good lord he was gorgeous.

He wore American-style attire: a long-sleeved charcoal henley and jeans. He must have had the items in his go bag. Tattoos peeked out from the collar of his shirt, making his appeal that much stronger. Sexier. She pressed her knees together to stifle the urges coursing along the insides of her thighs. Even her nipples jumped to attention. Thankfully the loose-fitted black shirt she wore concealed her breasts. After the night she'd had, just slipping into the clean top and linen pants, even if they weren't her typical style, seemed like a luxury.

Brick swiveled his head over his shoulder to see what had stolen her attention. He swung his face back to her, and a smirk lifted his lips.

Ass.

"Morning." The sound of Zain's husky baritone made her cheeks flush.

"Good morning." She kept her tone light, even though the emotions inside her were anything but. "Sleep well?"

He grunted. "Slept like shit. But I always do." He sat in the chair next to her and shuffled it closer to the table. "This looks amazing."

A chef appeared with a tall glass of orange juice and asked Zain how he wanted his eggs cooked. He ordered three over easy with all the fixings.

Zain picked up his glass and chugged half the contents, then placed his elbows on the table and studied her face. She'd never get over the searing intensity of his gaze. Scrutinizing, yet in a pensive, thoughtful way that seemed to dial into her every emotion. "How about you, Dana? You sleep okay?"

She scrunched her face. "I'll sleep better when we're out of here." She shot a look at Brick. "Any luck on a flight?"

He shoved another bite of eggs and hash-browns into his mouth as if now choosing to ignore the heat between her and Zain. He wiped his mouth then took a sip of his coffee. "Yup. I've got us a private plane."

Dana sucked in a breath. "We sat here for half an hour and you didn't think to tell me that?"

He shrugged. "Tellin' you now."

She rolled her eyes with annoyance. "Men." She'd let Brick tell Taschen about their flight because she really didn't want to get on the phone with him again.

"When do we leave?" Zain asked.

"We'll head out at eleven. It's a two-hour drive to the airport."

Dana glanced at the clock. It was ten o'clock. She could wait one more hour.

Zain nodded. His gaze held a weight she couldn't put her finger on. Worry?

"Did you speak to Rami?" Brick asked, taking another sip of his coffee.

"Yeah. We talked last night." He looked at Dana as if he wished he could boot Brick from the room so it was just the two of them.

Or maybe that's just the impression Zain gave. He had the unique quality of holding her attention and also making her feel as though she were the only person in the world. He never broke eye contact when she spoke, never interrupted, and seemed to analyze her every reaction.

The effect was addicting.

He made her want to talk more, made her want to bare her heart. Things she rarely did—and certainly not with someone she'd known for about eighteen hours.

The chef entered the dining room and slid Zain's plate beneath his nose. Zain thanked him and reached for his fork. "What about you, Dana? Did you speak to your brother?"

Her stomach knotted. "Yes, just before you got here."

He cut off a chunk of runny egg, placed it on his toast, and bit into it. He wiped his mouth and spoke again. "And was he as angry as you'd expected?"

A warm fuzziness washed over her. She was surprised he remembered her brief mention of Taschen. "To say the least."

He frowned as if the idea of her brother being short with her irritated him.

"He'll be fine once I'm home." Not necessarily true. She'd probably be put through the third degree when she saw Taschen in person, but that was something she could handle.

As a matter of fact, in a day or so, when she did have to face him, she'd have a little more energy and her trauma would be a little further behind her—so she could blast him for underestimating her capabilities.

She loved how protective Taschen was. It was his nature, not a quality he reserved just for her. He'd always been protective of women, including their mom and a couple of Dana's close friends growing up. He carried groceries for his elderly neighbor, Zelda, and shoveled her driveway in the winter. Taschen cared. He just didn't know how to tone that shit down.

She'd made it pretty damn far in her adult life without his protection. She wasn't a piece of fine China. She could defend herself.

As the three of them continued talking, Dana tried to hide her fascination as Zain gobbled up his enormous plate of food then asked for seconds. Brick's serving appeared small by comparison.

When was the last time he'd eaten a good home-cooked meal? Her heart grew heavy. He probably hadn't cooked for himself often, and whatever Jaysh provided surely wasn't much when they had so many men to feed. Though if Zain had been lacking food, his size didn't show it.

Ali entered the room and rubbed his hands together. "Good morning, everyone." He made eye contact with all of them, including Dana. They all greeted him.

He looked fresh and dapper in a navy-blue suit and silver tie, his brown hair combed back neatly and his green eyes bright. "I guess Brick's given you the news?"

"Just," Dana said, shooting her friend playful daggers.

Brick sighed. "You're not gonna let me live that down, are ya?"

"Nope."

"Your brother said you're a hard ass."

Ali blinked, seemingly uninterested in their exchange, but Zain's mouth lifted at the corner.

"Well then," Ali cut in. "I'll arrange for your

transportation to the airport."

"You don't have to do that," Brick insisted.

Ali beamed. "Of course I do. You'll have a hell of a time finding reliable transit without my help. But that's what friends are for."

"I hope you'll send Backcountry Protection a bill for your services these last couple of days," Brick added.

"Don't mention it."

Zain took a bite of bacon and eggs then set his fork down. "Tell me," he said to Ali. "What do you do for a living?"

The chef brought in Ali's plate, and he thanked him in Pashto before shaking out a linen napkin and laying it across his lap. "Many things," he finally replied. "My work is primarily in mining, but I dabble in technology."

The vague response made Dana shift her attention to Brick then Zain, who bobbed his head slowly. "Must be hard running such a successful company under Jaysh's nose. I'm sure they're particular about who they allow to profit around here."

Ali held his fork and knife with the tips of his fingers, almost awkward in his properness. Yet Zain's question didn't seem to ruffle his feathers. He didn't even blink at the insinuation.

Brick cleared his throat before Ali could respond. "Ali's a powerful opponent. He's done many things to fight radical ideals."

"One learns to make the deals that are necessary to stay afloat. Sometimes your enemies are your closest friends." Ali finally drew his focus from his plate and smiled around the table. "Please let me know if there's anything you need for your trip home. I'm happy to accommodate."

If that was his way of shutting down the conversation, he'd done it well. Zain's brow stayed in a fixed, even line, and Dana wished she could stretch her leg far enough to kick him under the table.

It was one thing to have suspicions, but another to make accusations. If Ali suspected they distrusted him, they could very well get on his bad side. And she really, really wanted to board that plane today.

"If you'll excuse me, I'm going to pack." She looked in Zain's direction as she stood.

He also got to his feet and smiled at Ali. "Thank you for breakfast and your hospitality. I have a phone call to make before we leave. Dana, I'll see you to your room." He waited for her to round the table and precede him down the hallway.

She reached her bedroom and slipped inside, waiting for Zain to follow her. He came in and closed the door, his face hard and his stance rigid. "Cameras," he whispered.

Shit. She'd completely forgotten. To talk, she'd have to get close. She took a step forward, bringing her body against his.

His hand snaked easily around her waist, and he turned her so his back shielded them from the camera.

Let Ali think there was something between them. She didn't care. What she needed was to find out what the hell Zain was worried about.

He brought his lips to her ear. "You do inconspicuous really well." His warm breath tickled her skin and her loins clenched.

He was so big. His body encased hers with its broad build and staggering height. Delicious need danced along her nerve endings.

"Just following your lead from last night," she said, feigning innocence. Yes, she wanted to talk to Zain without suspicion, but she also wanted to test the waters. To see if her body responded to him the same way after some food and sleep—and yup, sure did.

The tingling sensation deep in her abdomen had had nothing to do with exhaustion or confusion and everything to do with the large alpha male warming her core with his steely abs pressed close to her chest.

Good lord, she was playing with fire.

He nuzzled her neck, and ripples of gooseflesh raced down her back.

"Act like you like this." His hand tensed on the small of her back, pulling her closer to him.

She tipped back her head and closed her eyes.

To an onlooker, she'd appear to be lost in her lover's arms . . .

But that's not what this was.

His lips touched her earlobe, so soft she thought her overstimulated brain had imagined it. She gripped his shirt, needing to feel his mouth on her again. Would he kiss her?

Her heart sped up.

"Ali's a threat," he murmured.

She tensed but didn't open her eyes. "Mm-hmm."

"I want you to stay away from him. Stick by me until we get to the US."

"Okay," she breathed.

"I mean it. Brick's blinded by his friend's generosity. I see through it. We're walking into a trap, and I don't want you on the wrong side of this."

The racing of her heart reached a dangerous level, her senses jumbled with fear and arousal. She couldn't land on rational thought.

He tipped his head back an inch, and his face hovered above hers. His stare bore into her eyes, watchful, concerned . . . protective. Heat emanated from his chest. Even more powerful was the desire in his eyes. Scalding. His dark eyelashes rimmed the golden embers imprinting on her soul.

Some of the fear left her body—the one thing Zain had proven over and over was that he'd protect her. He'd get them out if it cost him his life, and it was both exhilarating and terrifying being surrounded with such a force of masculinity.

"Understood" was all she could manage.

His gaze drifted to her lips. "One more thing for good measure." He touched his mouth to hers and electricity shot to her toes. Pressure pulsed through her body, so forceful it rattled her knees.

His tongue glided between her teeth but only for a fraction of a second. He pulled away and his arms fell.

She swayed forward, wanting his warmth and desperate to read his expression, but he'd already locked it down as he moved toward the door.

"I'll be back in half an hour. I've got a call to make." He disappeared into the hall.

She brought her fingertips to her lips, and an ache channeled through her. Getting involved with Zain was all kinds of wrong. Dangerous even.

But she was already in over her head.

CHAPTER 10

ZAIN PACED THE room. Speaking with Maxine had only intensified his stress. She wanted intel and fast—not that he could blame her. The quicker they could get a team to immobilize Jabar, the better, but there was only so much shit he'd collected. Plus, it was almost impossible to put his mind in work mode when his brain had one fucking function: Dana.

He'd kissed her. Christ. *Stupid* was too weak a word to describe his actions. But goddammit, he hadn't been able to stop himself. For the last three years he'd lived on adrenaline, in survival mode and lonely. Having that familiar ground ripped out from under his feet was as foreign to him as hearing his real name.

The moment he'd laid eyes on her, Dana had shaken him. And she continued to knock him on his ass with every doe-eyed look and every touch of her small, fine-boned hands.

He couldn't get enough.

Pulling her into his arms last night had been the right thing to do. He'd needed everyone to know she was off-limits and that if anyone hurt her, they'd have to face him.

But he shouldn't have kissed her. Doing so had only invoked more desire, more need to explore her mouth and body. More, more, more.

And he couldn't have more. He was too unhinged to be with someone like her. Dana was smart, beautiful, and probably as dependable as a lucky penny. He'd just spent part of his life killing and living under an alias in the most dangerous part of the world. Not only were his senses blunted—he also didn't trust himself.

He hadn't had sex since he left the United States. Celibacy wasn't for the faint of heart. Many of Jaysh's men frequented brothels, but Zain never partook. Not when so many women were in the brothels because of trafficking. He'd have no part in that.

And he hadn't been able to meet anyone legitimately. His position was much too dangerous. But Dana . . .

Hell, she brought out a primitive, basic need he'd kept buried for so long. Looking at her made him want to touch her. Touching her made him want to see more of her. Kissing her made him want to undress her.

Just breathing the same air as Dana put him on a slippery slope. He had three years' worth of pent-up sexual energy. Not to mention he'd closed himself off from humanity. He could hurt her without realizing it. Unlikely, but he'd probably need to jack off ten times before he dared to lose himself in her. Because once he got started, he wouldn't want to stop.

Dana needed to leave his head. Besides, she probably thought he was some kind of blood-hungry barbarian, given all the men he'd killed yesterday.

But the way her soft lips had parted and she'd leaned into his embrace said otherwise. Hunger rumbled through his nerve endings. Fuck, he needed to keep Dana at a distance for her own damn good, at least until he could wrap his head around the drastic change in his atmosphere. He was too eager, too hotheaded, and way too fucking horny to get involved with her.

But keeping away from her wasn't an option. Matter of fact, separating himself from her right now would only endanger her further. So he'd have to learn some self-control really fucking quickly.

Tucking his phone into his bag, he fought a rush of irritation. Maxine had responded to his call exactly how he'd expected. Even so, her cold, callous attitude made bitterness chew through him.

He'd sacrificed three years of his life for the mission.

And it had gone to hell.

But what was he supposed to do? If Maxine had any say in how he'd handled the situation, she'd have told him to leave Dana with Rakesh. Or kill her. Maybe not in so many words, but her shock regarding the fact that he'd sacrificed everything to keep a woman alive screamed volumes.

With his bag packed, he had nothing left to do except wait for Brick to tell them it was time to leave. He opened his bedroom door, crossed the hall to Dana's room, and rapped his knuckles softly on the wood.

She opened the door, her brow rippled with trepidation and her face pinched. Her gaze quickly took him in and she relaxed. Standing back, she let him enter then closed the door. "How was your phone call?"

He sat on her bed and laced his fingers together. "About as good as I anticipated."

She wrinkled her nose. The action made him want to stroke the cute slope that turned up a bit at the end. Too damn cute.

"I'm sorry." She wore long bone-colored linen pants and a navy tunic that reached her knees. In the time that he'd been gone, she'd braided her long ebony locks over one shoulder. She looked so soft and pretty it took every ounce of effort not to draw her back into his arms like he had last night.

Like he'd dreamed about. But in his dream, she'd been naked.

"S'not your fault." He shifted his attention to the polished marble floor at their feet.

Dana sighed and sat next to him. "It is and you know it. But that doesn't matter right now. What did she say?"

He flicked his gaze to the camera before swiveling to face her. "We'll talk more later," he said on a breath.

Sharing details with Dana was one thing. Sharing them in this house was another. There were probably audio bugs and cameras everywhere. Brick might be confident Ali wasn't a threat, but the information was highly confidential, and if Ali knew Zain was CIA, well, that could pose a big problem. A thought struck him. "Did you mention anything to Brick about me?"

Worry flickered in her eyes. "No, of course not."

"Good."

Dana pressed her lips together then reached forward and covered his hand. "We'll all feel so much better when we get home."

Home. Right. What was that?

Knock, *knock*

Zain was on his feet before the knuckles stopped hitting the door. He crossed the room and cranked open the wood. Brick stood there with a bag slung over his shoulder. "Ready?"

Dana was already at the door with her small backpack in hand. "Let's get this show on the road," she announced.

He couldn't agree more. "I'll need my weapons back."

Brick smiled. "Of course. I'll see to it they're ready."

★   ★   ★

DANA STOOD OUTSIDE next to Brick and Zain. Two extended SUVs had pulled up in the circular driveway. The drivers stood near the passenger doors with their hands crossed in front of them, waiting for their cue to assist their travelers. The whole situation seemed unreal.

They were almost out of here. It was hard to believe.

In a couple of hours they'd be on a plane, putting Afghanistan even farther behind them. She wouldn't fully be at ease until she set foot on her own soil, but she'd breathe a hell of a lot easier thirty-thousand feet above the terrorist group that wanted them dead.

Ali came out of the house, his footsteps quick on the stone stairs. Reaching Brick, he extended his arms out to his sides and then embraced him. "It's been a pleasure having you all."

"Thanks for your hospitality." Brick pulled away and gave Ali a handshake.

Ali smiled at the three of them. "I have business in Peshawar, so I'm going to accompany you to the airport if you don't mind."

"Not at all," Brick said quickly.

Dana shifted her weight to one side and lifted her gaze to Zain. His eyes darkened a fraction, and a bell of warning rang inside her.

"Great. Brick and Dana, you'll ride with me. Zain, feel free to rest your eyes in peace while Darrian drives your vehicle."

Dana jerked her gaze to Zain then Brick, and her heart beat in double time. Zain had made it clear that she was to stick by him at all costs—what the hell was Ali doing?

Brick tilted his head and looked puzzled. Zain stepped forward, dominating their circle. He stared down at Ali, and his body vibrated.

Zain clamped his hand around Dana's wrist and hauled her to his side. "She stays with me."

Dana rested her hand on Zain's ripped abdomen. His muscles were prominent beneath his shirt, and his skin radiated heat.

Ali laughed lightly. "No threat, my friend. You're free to ride with whoever you want."

Zain's glare shifted to Brick then back to Ali. "Like I said, she stays with me."

Brick cleared his throat awkwardly. Dana searched her friend's face. Even Brick seemed put off by Ali's suggestion. They locked eyes, and everything in Brick's demeanor told her to stand down.

She swallowed as the tension in their circle amplified.

Brick elbowed Zain. "It's all good, man. You and Dana chill together, and Ali and I will chat." His response far too lighthearted for the moment, considering the blaze of fury coming off Zain.

His hand moved to her waist, locking her in place against him.

Not that she'd planned on moving. Something was going on, and she was no longer eager to get in the SUVs. She wet her lips, watching the silent exchange between the two men facing off.

Then Ali took a page from Brick's book and laughed. "Everyone must be exhausted. It'll be nice to get home, I'm sure. Why don't we get on the road?"

Brick followed Ali into the back of an SUV. Then Darrian, their driver, opened the passenger door and motioned for Zain and her to get inside.

She hesitated. Something wasn't right. Ali was acting as cool as a cucumber, but there wasn't a logical reason for Zain to ride by himself, as he'd suggested.

"Did you sweep the vehicle?" Zain asked the guard.

Darrian frowned. "Yes, sir." He spoke English with a bit of an accent.

"Then you won't mind if I have a second go?"

The man shifted then straightened his tie. "Suit yourself."

Sweat dampened her palms, and the hair at the back of her neck tingled. Zain broke away from her and began to move around the vehicle.

He checked every nook and cranny of the exterior, even getting on his stomach to search the underbelly of the vehicle, before searching the interior, the trunk, and beneath the hood.

Ali's driver got out and jerked his head at Darrian. "What's going on?"

"He's doing a sweep."

The other driver shook his head with annoyance and got back in his car. Zain slammed down the hood and walked up to where Dana waited. He caught her elbow and gestured to the still-open passenger door. "All good."

That at least made her a little more comfortable. Her mind hadn't gone to explosive devices, but it was sure there now. Agitation still jumped along her pulse.

She searched Zain's face. Tension hardened his brow and his eyes sparked with wariness. He squeezed her hand and gave a slight nod. "It's fine," he confirmed once more.

She'd just have to take his word for it. He held her hand while she climbed into the SUV, and then she scooted across the leather bench seat. Zain got in beside her. The freshly treated interior held a lemon scent. Two bottles of water sat in cupholders on either side of the vehicle. Darrian closed the door and got into the driver's seat. He asked a few questions about their comfort then started the engine.

When the vehicle didn't burst into flames, Dana relaxed. Zain's hand went to her knee and kneaded her skin briefly before pulling away.

A minute later they were on the road. Zain pressed a button and a divider went up between the front and the rear of the vehicle. Zain finally sat back and sighed.

"What the hell was all that about?" she whispered.

"Fuck if I know, but I don't like it."

She buckled her seatbelt, and Zain did the same. She hated being in the dark. There was more going on, she was sure of it now, but there wasn't a single thing either of them could do about it. Like it or not, they were walking through a minefield of enemies and distrust.

"Do you think we're even going to the airport?" she whispered.

His gaze slid toward her. "I think we need to be really careful," he said, and his tone indicated he was referring to both the mounting danger and the need to watch what she said.

She closed her eyes, wishing she could wipe away the doubt expanding in her chest. Reaching into her bag, she grabbed her phone and then powered it up. She'd left the device and passport in her backpack with Ali's driver before attending the protest two nights ago. Luckily, otherwise she wouldn't have one right now. But with all that'd happened, she'd forgotten to charge it last night.

The battery was at 17 percent.

She opened the Backcountry Protection group chat, which included Rami, August, Brick, Taschen, and her. Toth, Rami's best friend and part owner of the company, was also in the group, as was Ghost, an enigmatic contract employee she'd met only once.

The chat group was typically quiet. Only the odd meeting reminder or event was posted. Right now, it was her best shot at getting out a distress signal.

Zain and I are in danger. We're en route to an airport, but lots of red flags. Not sure if we'll make it to the flight. If anything happens to us, you need to look at Ali.

The message wasn't much. Hell, she might as well be sending a cry for help from a deserted island because the capable men on the receiving end were thousands of miles away. Dana, Zain, and possibly Brick would be dead long before Backcountry could do anything about it.

But if they happened to escape, at least help would be on the way. Or her brother would know where to find her murderer.

She placed her phone back in her bag after making sure the location was on. Cool air pumped from the vents in the vehicle, circulating the trapped tension. Agitation fermented in her gut. She had no way of knowing if they were headed in the right direction, as she didn't know what airport they were going to.

She almost wished Zain would lower the divider so she could see out the front windshield. Having no view of where they were going only worsened her anxiety. He sat rigid next to her. His thick, jean-clad thigh touched hers.

He'd opted to sit in the middle, and his closeness made some of her fear abate. He was so large he seemed to eat up more of the oxygen in the vehicle.

Not that she minded. She'd breathe in his carbon dioxide all day. God, she had it bad.

At least he'd gotten his weapons back. Ali's guards had handed them over before they left the house. She'd watched Zain stuff a pistol in the waistband of his pants and swing a rifle over his shoulder. Also not something she minded.

Turns out there were a lot of things about this mammoth of a man that she didn't mind.

The vehicle started to slow. Not a lot, but enough that Dana anticipated a stop. Only the stop didn't come.

Apparently Zain sensed it too. He hit the button for the divider and the window powered down. Ali's SUV was well ahead of them. "Why are we so far behind?" he demanded.

"Just giving room, sir."

Zain's gaze shifted from the windshield to his window then Dana's.

"What's wrong?" she breathed. The question was moot. The energy in the vehicle was as charged as a battery pack. A wave of foreboding chilled her skin. She reached for Zain's wrist, but his arm was already belted across her.

"Something's up."

Her heart hammered in her chest and perspiration dotted her top lip. She circled her arms around Zain's protective one, expecting a bullet to enter her head any minute.

A vise squeezed her lungs, making every breath an effort.

Zain jolted next to her. "Look out!"

Her heart lurched into her throat, and she shot her gaze to the windshield. Some kind of weapon was hurtling toward their SUV. A trail of smoke spiraled in its wake. Zain's body crushed against hers, his heavy weight shielding her.

Bang!

The explosion burst against her eardrums. She opened her mouth to scream, but the sound didn't reach her ears. Her body was weightless as the vehicle lifted into the air. The screeching in her head intensified.

A thundering crash shook her body. The sound of glass and metal crunching was the last thing she heard before everything went black.

CHAPTER 11

BLACK-AND-WHITE IMAGES FLICKERED through Zain's brain like a broken video tape from the 1940s. Images of his mom and brother. His parents' property near the water in Seattle. The warm, salty air on the breeze and the smell of . . .

God, that smell. So familiar. So comforting.

Home. No. Cherry blossoms.

His mind zapped as if he'd been tased, and he lifted his head.

Dana. Her fragrant cherry-blossom scent held the pieces of his shattered heart.

More information rushed back.

Ali. Brick. The IED he'd seen pointed at the car and—

Dana again.

She lay beneath him. The sharp angle of the SUV told him it was on its side. Smoke and debris filled the air, thick and pungent.

Urgency flashed through him, and he brought his palm to Dana's cheek. "Dana, wake up." He cradled her face, pressing his thumb against her chin. He didn't dare shake her in case she had brain trauma.

Blood trickled from her temple, but that was the only sign of injury he could spot.

"Dana!"

She dragged in a shuddering breath, and her eyes wobbled open. "Zain." She coughed and choked on the acrid air. She looked past his shoulder, taking in their dire fucking situation. "What happened?"

"We were hit with a bomb. Are you hurt?" He spoke loudly, and the deafening sounds of fire and cracking metal made him reach for her seatbelt before she answered.

"I—No. I'm okay." She lifted her head, and he watched as her gaze turned distant.

"Hang on, honey. Don't pass out on me." He needed to get her to safety, but first, he needed to make sure there weren't any more threats out there. He glanced at the driver. His eyes were wide, staring straight ahead. A piece of metal had impaled his chest.

Zain unclipped Dana's buckle and caught her waist. Men shouted, and the scampering of feet on gravel sent fury pulsing through his pores. Adrenaline lit his flesh. He snagged both their bags and tossed them over his shoulder. They couldn't risk losing their passports and IDs.

He wrapped his arm around her. He had to

stand parallel to the bench seat since Dana's door was against the ground. "We're gonna have to climb through my window. Can you stand?"

She nodded again.

He let her get to her feet and shimmied up the length of the bench seat, bracing his foot on the front passenger seat for leverage. Thankfully, his window had smashed; he wouldn't have to break it. The temperature in the SUV was rising rapidly. Sweat dripped down his face, and the sharp, nauseating scent of gasoline hit him. Christ, it was going to blow up any second.

"Climb to me!" he shouted, extending his hand down to Dana.

She lifted her arm, and he clamped his hand over it. Then she placed her foot next to his on the side of the passenger seat and climbed her way up until she was sandwiched between the back of the driver's seat and him.

"Hold tight. I might need to shoot. But I'll get you out, I promise."

Crack, crack!

Bullets tinged off the vehicle. Zain ducked his head and kept Dana away from the opening. Her small hands gripped his shirt. He steadied his rifle, lifted his head a few inches through the window, and spotted the shooters.

The two men who'd bombed them.

Zain aimed and fired. Down they went. He quickly scanned the road. Ali's SUV was heading in their direction. It was likely bulletproof. But he'd shoot everyone in the vehicle if he could—Brick included if need be.

Slinging his rifle over his shoulder, he caught Dana beneath her arms and hauled her through the window, lifting her to sit on the edge. "Hang on. Let me get down first."

He quickly heaved himself through the opening, then slid to the ground. With every second that passed he anticipated the explosion. Ali must have had it built damn well. "Jump!" he held out his arms, and Dana leapt from the overturned vehicle.

She landed in his hands, and he lowered her feet to the ground. She hesitated, as if the jump had rattled her, but they didn't have another moment to waste. He scooped her over his shoulder and ran down the gravel road.

His chest ached from smoke inhalation, and every pounding footstep made his head throb.

"Zain, I can walk!" Dana shouted.

He didn't respond. He ran another twenty feet until he was sure the blast wouldn't hit them. Ali's vehicle roared up behind them. Zain brought Dana to stand next to him. Her hair was askew, her clothes covered in debris. Even her long braid had pebbles of glass stuck in it.

Her chest rose and fell erratically as she stared at the fast-approaching vehicle. She mopped the sheen of sweat from her cheek. "I don't understand. Was Ali responsible?" Her question came out on a gasp, and he couldn't help but worry about further injuries.

But he didn't have the opportunity to check her over. The SUV screeched to a stop, and Brick leapt out. "Shit! Are you guys all right?"

Boom!

Glass and metal exploded like a firework from hell. Zain covered Dana with his arms as smoke billowed from the vehicle they'd just escaped. Thankfully they'd made it far enough to avoid any remnants of the blast. But the fact that they'd just about been blown up made fresh rage singe his brain.

Zain shoved Dana behind him and took aim with his rifle. "Stay there!" The roar shook his chest. If Brick was in on this, he was about to eat Zain's entire clip.

Brick lifted his palms. "Dude. I'm with you guys. You're hurt. Let me help."

Zain wiped a trickle of blood from his eyebrow on his shoulder. "Pretty fucking convenient your SUV didn't blow up."

Brick's eyes widened, and he shook his head. "That's not what this is. I swear to god. I had nothing to do with this."

Ali exited the vehicle, hands extended. "Please. Let me call for help. You both need medical attention."

"Fuck you," Zain spat.

Dana's hand twitched on his side.

Brick's palms shook. "I had nothing to do with this."

Ali's driver approached, gun drawn. "Drop your weapon."

The muscles at the back of Zain's neck pinched. No way in hell he'd comply. He aimed the rifle at the driver's head. "You first."

"Everyone take a breather." Ali took a step forward. "I don't want anyone to get hurt."

"Bullshit," Zain snapped, not taking his eye or his rifle off the driver. "You wanted me in that SUV alone, and when that didn't happen you were happy to sacrifice Dana." Zain itched to assess Brick's expression but didn't dare shift his focus.

Ali placed his hand on his driver's elbow. "Stand down."

"Boss—"

"I said stand down."

The driver scrunched up his face and lowered his weapon to the dirt. Zain's trained eyes spotted his finger still on the trigger.

"We're almost out of here, guys. We've got a little over an hour to get to the airport. Come ride with us." Brick held out his hand, pleading.

Using his instinct, Zain scrutinized him—his earnest eyes, his worried brow. He'd bet the rifle in his hand Brick was innocent in all this, but he couldn't endanger Dana on that hunch.

"C'mon. I'm good friends with Taschen. I'd

never hurt my friend's sister. Or any woman. This is a complete misunderstanding."

Dana inched forward from behind his back. "I trust you, Brick. But you have to admit something's not right. Someone knew what car Zain and I would be in. Knew where we'd be traveling. This wasn't a random attack, and you know it."

Brick dropped his hand, and his expression hardened. "You're right." He turned to Ali. "You have some explaining to do. And until we find out what happened today, you and I are no longer friends."

Anger flashed in Ali's eyes. "Suit yourself. Don't miss your flight." He turned on his heel and headed toward his SUV. The guard refocused the weapon on Zain and retreated backward in his boss's path.

Zain's finger tingled on the trigger. They'd miss their flight if they didn't have a ride. Which meant Jaysh would find them.

They'd get to Dana.

He pulled the trigger. The bullet landed in the guard's head with a sharp *thwack*.

Dana shrieked.

Brick covered his head. "Fuck!" He wheeled on Zain. "Do you have any idea what you've done?"

"Yeah. I'm getting us the fuck out of here."

DANA COVERED HER mouth with her hand. Dear

god, he'd just shot Ali's guard. The implications of his actions hit her like another IED. Before she could even wrap her head around the situation, Zain caught her arm and towed her alongside him.

Brick cursed a blue streak. Dana's eyes landed on the guard's large, unmoving body. Crimson blood tainted the light-colored dirt.

Ali ran toward his fallen man, his primness abandoned. "No!" He jabbed a finger at Zain. "You bastard!" Spit flew from his mouth. He bent to grab the guard's weapon, but Zain was on him in a fraction of a second.

"Back up," he warned Ali, his tone without the hysteria of their rival's. Instead, Zain's voice carried a calm authority that seemed entirely foreign in the situation. He should be rattled. After being thrown around a vehicle that was now blown up, he should be on the brink of break-down—like her and everyone else still standing.

Ali froze as Zain approached. Then he raised his hands by his ears. With the gun, Zain motioned for him to back away from the guard's weapon. Ali complied.

"Throw down your phone."

Ali's lip curled.

"Do it now." Zain's voice boomed with authority.

Ali dipped his hand into the pocket of his suit jacket, removed his device, and tossed it into the dirt.

Zain jerked his head to Brick. "Grab his phone. Take the guard's as well, and the car keys."

Brick muttered something but did what Zain asked. Dana could see the pent-up anger in his expression.

Dana's temple thudded. She lifted her fingers to the delicate area, and moisture touched her skin. Blood coated her fingertips, and she winced as pain seared her skull. She'd probably been in shock; she hadn't really felt any injuries until now.

"This guy's a loose fucking cannon," Brick huffed.

She compressed her lips. "Is he?" Dana said, while Zain spoke to Ali. "Because he might have just saved our lives and made it possible for us to catch that plane."

Brick said nothing, but a vein at the side of his head jumped. "I get that. But we're in dangerous territory."

"And you just severed your friendship with Ali. Either way, we were screwed."

He pinched his brow. "Maybe, Dana. But I didn't fucking shoot one of his men."

"He would've killed us all," she snapped. "Tried to. It'll serve you well to remember that."

"Hands behind your head and walk one hundred paces east," Zain shouted to Ali. The man practically glowered with disgust, but he turned his back to Zain and obeyed. When he was a good thirty paces away, Zain circled his hand around her elbow. "Let's go."

Brick followed them to the SUV. Zain opened the front passenger door for her, and Brick got in the rear. A second later, Zain climbed in the driver's seat, tossing their bags in the back with Brick. Ali continued making his trek down the long gravel road in the opposite direction.

Zain fired up the engine, and the GPS screen came up. After asking Brick the name of the airport, Zain plugged it in. The address hadn't been entered by the driver previously—either he'd had no intention of reaching their destination or he hadn't needed directions.

Air conditioning blasted through the vents. Dana rested her head on the seat and the pain in her skull and body intensified. Everything hurt, from her hair to her toes. Her left hip, neck, and right shoulder had it the worst, but if it weren't for Zain's body anchoring her in the blast, she probably wouldn't be able to walk right now.

The IED had hit right in front of the vehicle, sending them flying. Had the shooter successfully hit square on the vehicle, they'd be dead right now—or worse. She shuddered at the thought of what could have happened. Of what had almost happened.

Tears stung her eyes and her throat tightened. She pulled her knees close to her chest, tucking herself into a ball and closing her eyes. The movement outside the vehicle was making her sick.

One more tree racing past her window and she'd puke.

"Are you okay?" Zain's question nudged her from the dark corners of her mind.

She fought back a sniffle. "Yeah."

"You're not okay. But I need to get us to the plane before I can assess you. Can you hold on?"

She wanted to laugh. Hold on for what? Did he have some kind of miracle pill in his pocket to erase the bombing from her mind? A drug that'd take away every ache? Okay, so maybe the latter existed. But that's not what she needed.

She didn't care about the blinding pain behind her eyes. Or her swollen face that had been struck numerous times. Or the ringing in her ears or the gash on her head. None of it mattered because the stark reality was that with every step they took, they created more enemies.

They'd never truly be safe.

Brick's hand on her shoulder made her jump. "Hey. It's going to be okay."

"It doesn't feel that way."

"No, it doesn't. But we'll be home soon." His fingers squeezed. "That message you sent earlier was smart. I got it right before the bombing."

Zain dragged his eyes from the road, and his heated gaze warmed her skin. Comforted her, even. "What message?"

"She sent a group text to Backcountry letting them know something wasn't right and that we were with Ali on the way to the airport."

"Good thinking," Zain said.

This time she did let out a snort. "You're both full of it. How's that message going to help us now?"

"For starters, it let our team know we're in danger. Any reinforcements, even if we don't get them until we land, are better than none."

"Well, I sent it knowing we're going to die. I wanted to cut out the legwork for Taschen when it came to bringing our killer to justice."

"We're not going to die," Zain and Brick said in unison. It was all she could do not to roll her eyes.

Maybe trauma had blown away her optimism. Hell, she could even have a brain injury. Either way, the possibility of them reaching the plane grew smaller and smaller by the second. "Ali is a resourceful man. He'll have reinforcements soon. All he has to do is make one phone call. And then what?"

Neither man answered.

They probably would have been better off dying in the explosion, because once Ali and Jaysh got to them, their fate would be far worse.

CHAPTER 12

EVERY BUMP ON the gravel road made Zain clench his jaw tighter. He didn't like their odds. Didn't like that they were still ten miles from the airport. Nor did he like the way Dana sat limp and quiet next to him.

He fought the urge to pull over and inspect her injuries. He didn't dare. Neither he nor Brick had spoken since Dana had asked her devastating question. Because goddammit she was right. There was no sign that they were being followed. He'd thrown Ali's and the guard's phones out the window about three hundred yards from where they'd left him.

Ali certainly hadn't found the devices, but hell, anyone on the road could've stopped and given him access to a phone.

Zain could only hope to god they reached the airport before Ali got the upper hand. If not, like Dana had said, they wouldn't make it out of here. But he didn't speak his doubts aloud.

They were too fucking close to lose now.

He pulled out his phone.

"Hey man, kinda risky to make a call now, don't you think?"

"It's important." He hit a number on his screen and brought the phone to his ear.

"Who are you calling?" Dana asked, her brow pinched.

"A friend." He gave her a knowing look.

Maxine answered on the third ring. He'd called her private line. "I'm glad to see you're still alive," she said.

"Barely," he ground out. "We're in a predicament and I need your help." He quickly gave her a diluted version of what'd happened and explained that they might need some grease to get through security.

"I'll see what I can do. How long until you get there?"

"Fifteen, twenty minutes."

She made a sound. "I can't promise anything, but I'll try."

"Thanks." He just hoped she cared enough to make the fucking call a priority. They couldn't miss their plane.

Fifteen minutes later, they pulled up to the airport. Cars and trucks lined the parking lot, and Zain found a spot not too far from the doors.

Dana got out and wobbled on her feet. Zain gripped her bicep and held her in place before she could walk off. "I need to know if you're hurt. Tell me what's going on."

She closed her eyes. It seemed any head movement was unbearable. "I hurt. Everywhere. But I think it's just the shock wearing off. I don't suspect anything serious."

He slid his hand under her jaw and examined her eyes. "Nausea?"

"Yes."

"Headache?"

"Mmm."

"Ringing in your ears?"

She bobbed her head half an inch then winced.

He pulled a handkerchief from his pocket, doused it in water from one of Ali's bottles, and wiped the blood from her temple. "You should clean up too," he said to Brick, who was standing mindlessly next to them. Although the guy wasn't bleeding, he was sweating profusely and appeared rougher than he should.

"Good call." He took out a shirt, poured water on the material, and washed his face.

When Zain had the blood cleaned from Dana and she no longer looked suspicious, he worked on himself. After changing his shirt, bandaging the cut on his eyebrow, and washing his face, they could pass for people who'd been traveling too long and were in desperate need of showers.

"If you feel faint, let me know," he told Dana, as he offered his arm for support.

She greedily leaned her elbow against his fore-arm, and they made their way to the entrance.

Ten minutes later they stood in line at security. The airport wasn't busy despite it being midday. They'd probably missed the morning rush. Zain handed his passport to the guard, who examined it under a flashlight. The man flicked his gaze from the passport to Zain, his face stoney. He handed back the small booklet and motioned for him to continue through.

But then Zain saw the guard speak into a mic on his shoulder.

Fuck.

He placed his carry-on onto the conveyor belt, then walked through the metal detectors. No alarms went off, but that didn't stop anxiety from puckering his shoulder blades together.

Two guards approached from the terminal, and warnings screeched in his head. It took every effort for him not to pull one of the guns from the guard's waist. He had to keep cool.

The reality was that a prison for Americans, especially ones in their current position, wouldn't be a safe place for either of them.

Dana came through next. She'd stopped at a store in the airport to purchase a hijab. The fabric framing her face covered the cut on her head and made her appear a little less disheveled. But her sallow skin and wide, wary eyes hit him like a punch to the gut. She clearly noticed the same shifting energy. They were still in danger.

As she lifted her chin and walked through the metal detector, he wanted to hug her for her bravery. Brick came through next.

One of the new guards approached. "Sir, we have orders to escort you to your plane. Follow me, please."

Zain caught Dana's hand and nodded. "Thank you."

Brick handed Zain his bag and carried Dana's and his. Zain's gaze scanned the terminal as they followed the guards. For all he knew, they were being led to police cars. Or a firing squad. But if his instinct was correct, their escort meant Maxine had come through for him.

They reached an exit, and one of their guards scanned his badge over the keypad. The door opened and warm air hit Zain's skin. Dana moved in close to him as they walked outside.

No police cars. No cops. A private plane sat waiting on the tarmac. The pilot waiting by the steps grinned at Brick.

Relief started to settle in around him. Jesus Christ. They just might make it out of here.

"Your chariot awaits," the pilot said jokingly.

Brick pulled him into a hug. "Jake! It's been too long."

"Have a safe flight." The guards turned and made their way back to the airport.

Some of the pressure left Zain's chest. "Can we

get out of here?" he interrupted, before Brick and his buddy decided to get caught up.

"Yeah, we're, uh . . . in a hurry," Brick said.

Jake grimaced as he led the way up the steps. "Is that it? Your message—and bribe—made it seem like you were in some kind of trouble. Lucky for you I was in Dubai."

Brick snorted. "Shit ended up getting even worse. How soon can we get in the air?"

"Soon as you folks are buckled."

Dana's hand was cool and damp in Zain's. He massaged her fingers for reassurance, but until they were well above the ground he wouldn't be at ease.

The air in the plane was cool and the six seats a little tight, but the Cessna gleamed. It had white leather seats and wooden trim accents. At the back was a small counter with a bar fridge and a microwave.

Dana slid into one of the seats at the back, and Zain took the chair across the narrow aisle from her. Brick sat up front, one row separating them.

Jake closed the door, muffling the sounds of the jets around them. Another man popped out from the cockpit. He was several inches shorter than Jake and looked to be in his late forties. "This is Thomas," Jake said. "My copilot. We'll be taking you guys home today. We've got a long flight with a couple of stops to refuel. Help yourself to food from the kitchenette, and otherwise just relax."

Dana buckled her seatbelt and gripped the armrests. Zain did up his own buckle while Jake ensured bags were secured. The pilots disappeared inside the cockpit, and a minute later, the engine fired up and they taxied down the runway.

With the hum of the motor in his ears and the blue sky filling the window, Zain's anxiety lessened. If someone would've told him two days ago that he'd be on a plane back to the US, he'd have laughed his ass off.

He moved his gaze from the puffy white clouds to Dana's pale complexion. A bell dinged, notifying them they could move about the cabin. Zain got to his feet and went to the kitchen. He found chicken wraps, chips, and water bottles as well as a first aid kit.

Making his way back to his seat, he placed some food on Dana's tray.

For a moment she looked surprised, and she stared at him with glassy eyes. His gut tensed. She was either exhausted or injured more than they'd thought.

"Thank you."

He caught her cheek in his hand and slowly peeled back her hijab. "Do you have any pain?"

Her eyes flickered. "Everywhere."

Fuck. "I should have properly assessed you after the crash."

She closed her eyes. "It's my head more than anything."

He dug into the first aid kit and found some

ibuprofen. He shook a couple into her hand and unscrewed her water bottle. She tossed back the pills, wincing as she swallowed. Her hand trembled as she lowered the bottle.

"I'm going to start at your head. If anything hurts, tell me."

He felt her scalp. As his fingers brushed over a goose egg, she winced. He grunted then moved on to her neck. She didn't wince until he turned her head to the side. "Hurt there, too?"

"My neck, yeah."

Using four fingers, he probed down her spine, then went to her shoulders, elbows, and wrists. She winced again when he lifted her left hand. "There too?"

"I don't think it's serious."

He turned over her hand to look for swelling, but there wasn't any. He made a note to check it later. "I need you to lift up your shirt."

She blinked.

"I want to check for signs of internal bleeding or anything that might need bandaging." He hadn't spotted any blood on her, but with the dark clothing it'd be hard to tell.

She shifted forward in her seat, turned her back and inched up the material. Her hand shook, so he took the shirt and rolled it up himself. Her back looked clear, but he hadn't expected to find much there since her back was against the leather when they crashed.

Next, he probed around her hips. She winced again, but not as much. He gestured for her to turn and she did. His male hormones made his focus linger a little too long on her narrow waist. The slim, tanned skin begged for his attention, but he brought his fingers to the neckline of her shirt and tugged it to the side to see her shoulder instead. "Looks like a bruise from the seatbelt. You've got one here too," he said, pointing to the opposite side of her waist. The exact spots she'd assumed had been hit the worst.

Other than that, no alarming bruises called to him. He rolled down her shirt and went on to check her knees and ankles. Once again, she didn't complain.

"Satisfied?" she asked, her voice groggy.

He took a flashlight from the first aid kit. "I'd be more satisfied if you told me more about how you're feeling."

She gave a little sigh as he checked her pupils. "My head feels like it's going to explode, my neck pulses with every movement, and I have a ringing sound in my ears."

"Nauseated still?"

"Yes."

"You could have a mild concussion, but it's hard to tell. I think some food and sleep would help."

"I'm really not hungry."

He popped open the bag of chips. "Then just

have a couple of these and some water and I'll leave you alone until we land in Seattle."

Her lips twitched. "Promise?"

"Cross my heart." He made an X over his chest but quickly held up his crossed fingers, showing he was full of shit.

A smile softened her lips. She wriggled her fingers into the snack-sized bag and removed some plain salted chips. "There," she said, crunching on them.

"Water, too."

She huffed through her nose. He suspected she would've rolled her eyes if she weren't experiencing so much discomfort, but he was happy to see a bit of personality back. She sipped half the bottle of water and then reclined in her seat.

Zain reached for the blanket on the seat in front of him and draped it over her legs.

"Thank you," she said, sincerity in her tone.

He brushed his fingers over her cheek, wishing he could erase all that'd happened to her. But all he could do was mitigate some of the damage. "Sleep."

Dana pulled the blanket closer to her chin and closed her eyes. Part of him wanted to sit and watch her to make sure she didn't suffer any more side effects of the crash. But if seeing his violence hadn't freaked her out, surely having him stare at her while she slept would.

He also fought the urge to talk to Brick. He

wanted to drill him for information on Ali—and anything else he could tell him regarding the crash—but he didn't have the energy. A deep ache twisted his bones, and the pressure from the altitude had brought forth a driving headache.

Plus, his back hurt like a bitch, probably from the awkward position he'd held himself in to shield Dana from the impact.

An explosion. Christ.

He could've lost her. If he hadn't seen the IED coming, if he hadn't been leery of Ali . . . He'd witnessed firsthand the brutality of war weapons. Anger bunched his thighs at the thought of what could've happened.

Unable to sit still, he ate some food, then stared out the window. But no matter how hard he tried, he couldn't keep his eyes away from the sleeping beauty beside him for more than a minute.

CHAPTER 13

"I CAN GO to Rami's," Zain said. "He won't mind."

Dana slid off her shoes, and her feet touched the black welcome mat inside her apartment. The warm scent of cinnamon from her diffuser still hung in the air even though she'd been gone days.

Home.

Fifteen hours ago, she'd thought she'd never make it. She'd half expected their plane to get shot down or for them to be arrested at their fuel stops, but nothing out of the ordinary had happened. She'd slept off and on, only waking once to eat.

It was 4:12 a.m. and Brick had just dropped them off at her place. Zain's face had frozen when Brick had asked if he had somewhere to go. He'd cleared his throat and mumbled something about having an apartment at one time but not knowing if his family had kept it.

Twenty minutes ago, she hadn't thought through her offer. Since it was the middle of the night, it wasn't ideal for him to wake his brother or mom, or go to a hotel. Now, they were alone. In her apartment. In the middle of the night. She toyed with her hands in front of her waist like an awkward teenager.

In her space was a hot Green Beret soldier turned CIA operative. He was too intimidating. Too invasive. And she was too tired to think of a single bad reason to get involved with him.

Yeeeah. She really shouldn't make rash decisions after being in an explosion and traveling for fifteen hours. "Don't be silly. Are you okay to take the couch?"

His eyes glowed in the dim light of the kitchen. His body was so large and formidable, yet she was already accustomed to how gentle his touch could be—how gentle he was with her.

His hands might've killed a thousand men, but that wasn't this man. Not the one who'd kissed her last night, not the one who'd stopped a brutal terrorist from raping her, not the one who'd protected her in an explosion.

No, this man was very different.

She moved away from the gravitational pull that wanted to bind her body to his. Placing her bag on the counter, she went to the cupboard and took out two glasses then filled them with water. "I'm going to shower and go straight to bed if you don't mind."

He removed his shoes and walked into the

kitchen, his steps slow, each one pulling a breath from her lungs. His earnest, scrutinizing gaze lingered on her face. "How's your head?"

She'd popped more ibuprofen before getting off the plane. "Okay."

"Any more nausea?"

"Zain," she said, low and chastising. "I'm fine. Well, I mean, everything hurts. But I'm not going to die." She sighed and dragged her fingers through her hair. "If it weren't for you, I would've already."

His thick lips twitched at the corners. Her fingers ached to drag themselves through the short bristles of his beard, to feel his slightly weathered skin on her palm. He was so big and demanding, yet in other ways subdued.

What was it about him? How could he be so calm and collected yet stir such a response in her?

He brought his thumb to her cheek, touching the bruise Rakesh had given her. "You were hurt more than I ever should've allowed."

She pressed her fingers to his knuckles, holding his hand in place. She never wanted him to let go.

This was dangerous. He was dangerous. No, *she* was . . .

"I put myself there. That's not on you." She gently withdrew his hand from her cheek. "I'm going to take that shower now. Help yourself to whatever you need. There's pillows and blankets in the linen closet. I'll be fast—please feel free to shower when I'm done." Before he could respond, she stepped around him and made her way to the bathroom.

Shutting the door, she let out a ragged breath. She was in way over her head. But the shower and sleep would clear her mind, and tomorrow she could put this all behind her. Zain would reunite with his brother and mom, and he'd probably fade from her life as quickly as he'd appeared in it.

She twisted on the shower and undressed, then stepped under the scalding spray. In fifteen minutes, her teeth were brushed and she was clean, a towel tucked around her. In her haste to escape Zain, she'd forgotten to take clean clothes into the bathroom with her.

She looked toward the hamper and grimaced. Getting back into dirty clothes wasn't an option. She quickly opened the bathroom door and scooted across the hall. Zain looked up from where he stood in the living room shaking out a blanket. He froze, his hot eyes on her.

"Night!" she squeaked. She made it to her bedroom and shut the door, her chest hammering with excitement. Heat swarmed between her legs and her nipples tightened.

God, she wanted him.

No, girl. You need sleep, not sex.

Yes, it was that simple. Sleep not sex. She got into her pajamas, turned off the light, and crawled under her cool sheets. A minute later the bathroom door closed, and the sound of water splashing in the basin reached her ears.

If she ever wanted to sleep, she had to put Zain out of her mind for good.

BUZZ, BUZZ, BUZZ

Zain woke with a start, his eyelids opening so rapidly they ripped moisture from his eye sockets. He reached for his phone with a groan. The clock on the screen read 9:48 a.m., but the sight of the caller's name startled him more than the time: Maxine.

Swinging his legs off the couch, he stood and then went out to the balcony. The cool spring breeze met his bare chest, and he welcomed the refreshing scent of salty air. He'd slept in longer than he ever had, but it'd been a shitty sleep on a too-small couch with a sexy woman in the next room.

Just thinking about Dana made his morning wood ache.

He swiped to answer. "Hello?"

"You made it home I take it?"

"We did. Was that you who sent the escort at the airport?"

"Yes. Glad that worked. How're you feeling?" Her question sounded forced, and the tingling sensation at the back of his neck warned him that Maxine wanted something—probably something big if she had to summon empathy from the depths of her bleak soul.

"Fine. Tired and beat up, but fine."

"Good. And your lady friend?"

He glanced over his shoulder toward the open patio door. Her apartment was even prettier now with the sunlight basking the cream-colored walls, bright accent pillows, and wall decorations. The woman had taste. And even her spare blankets smelled like cherry blossoms. "Alive."

"Mmm," she said absently. "Well, that's nice to hear."

Zain leaned his forearm on the railing and stared out at the beautiful skyline. Beyond it stood Mount Rainier. "Go on and cut to the chase," he said, a little dryly.

She made a sound of annoyance. "Yes, well. You know how it is. There's always something. We need you in Langley."

He propped his elbow on the rail and massaged his temple. He was too tired for this shit. "Why's that?" He'd never been to the CIA headquarters, in Virginia. Of course, he'd never had a reason to since they'd recruited him while he was still in Afghanistan. After his whole unit was bombed.

"We need to debrief you on your mission. We haven't spoken since"—she tsked, probably looking at her calendar—"eight days ago. I'm sure things have transpired since then that will give us information."

Of course they were still after Jabar. Zain's world might've stopped since he left the Jaysh group, but the CIA needed to get the leader. Given that he'd failed, part of him wanted to say fuck the whole mission, but if there was information that could help them further their investigation, it was his duty to provide. "When do you want me there?"

"I can get you on a plane in two hours."

Zain's blood pressure spiked. He'd just gotten home. Hadn't even seen his family. And they wanted him to fly across the country on two hours' notice? "No."

"N-No?" she sputtered.

"No. Hell, no. I just got in, Maxine. I haven't seen my mom or brother in three damn years. I'm not going anywhere until I spend some time with them."

"All right," she drawled. "This evening, then."

He just about threw his phone off the balcony. Burning irritation made his neck itch. If he didn't cool his ass down, he'd be out of a phone and on the wrong column of the government's list. "How about we do the debrief over the phone?"

Maxine let out a long sigh. "I'd prefer that too. But Roger would really like to see you. It makes it easier to ensure we're getting all the information required."

He shook his head. "I can't. If it has to be in person, then this can wait until next week. Otherwise I'm yours for a phone call any time of day. Hell, we spoke on the phone with sensitive information for three years. I don't see why that's not a viable option now."

More silence. "Fine. I'll speak with Roger, and we'll arrange a video call for tomorrow morning."

"Thank you." He hung up before she could say another word that'd pitch him over the edge.

A cool, small hand touched his bare shoulder. He turned as Dana slid in close beside him, resting her arm on the railing next to his. "Everything okay?" Her magnetic blue eyes searched his face. Tiny wrinkles creased her forehead, and her hair danced in tangled waves down to her waist.

His fingers throbbed to sink into her locks, and he ached to kiss her like he'd done two nights ago. God, he could surround himself with her for weeks and he'd never get tired of seeing her pretty face. He forced a half smile. "It's better now."

A pink color touched her cheeks. The swelling on her face had gone down, but the purplish bruise had turned green. He couldn't wait for the markings to fade, but he hoped that her memories would fade even faster. "I hope you slept."

"Like a baby," he lied. "How about you?"

SHE DROPPED HER hand from his skin and steered her gaze to the view, letting out a long sigh. "It was a little restless to be honest." She smiled, pinning her gaze on him. "I heard you mention your mom and brother. I'm sure it will be nice to see them. When are you doing that?"

His mom. She'd either knock him senseless for not telling her he was alive or crumble in tears. If he had a choice, he'd go with the first. "Today. I think if I wait any longer both of them will kill me."

She nodded slowly. "Well, other than getting some groceries, I don't have much on my to-do list. You can borrow my car if you want."

The suggestion warmed his insides. Now that she was home, he didn't have a need to stick around. No one would hurt her here. She no longer needed his protection, yet . . .

He didn't want to leave. The thought of not having her beside him rocked his nerves in a bad way. "Why don't you come with me?"

Her eyes sparked with delight. She tamped down her smile and bit her bottom lip.

Huh. Interesting.

She nervously stroked her hair behind her ear. "Um, sure. I'd love to. I mean, that is, as long as you don't want alone time with your family. I understand if you'd like some space."

He reached for the lock of hair she tormented and gave it a couple tugs. "Actually, I need you there. You'll give my mom someone else to fawn over."

She grinned. "Okay, then. I'll go get ready.

Maybe we can grab a bite to eat on the way."

"Good idea. I'm famished." The words came out on a low growl. He was hungry as fuck, but it wasn't for bacon and eggs.

She rolled in her lips, desire flashing across her face. "Give me ten." She disappeared into the apartment.

A niggling sensation pulled at his gut. She could get back to her life now. In the days she'd been gone, not much, if anything, had changed. But his life was as scattered as missing puzzle pieces. It'd take forever to pick them up, especially when part of him was left behind in another country.

The soldier in him.

He didn't deserve to be here when the lives of his unit had been taken. But looking at Dana, how soft and small she was, he finally understood his purpose. The reason he hadn't been killed that day was her.

If another man had been in his position working undercover for Jaysh, they might not have done the same for her. They might have ignored her screams, might've let Rakesh rape and mutilate her. But he hadn't.

If he'd done anything good in his life, it was taking her home. And he'd do it all again.

CHAPTER 14

DANA'S HEART EXPANDED as she took in the beautiful home at the end of the pine- and birch-tree-lined driveway. A large lawn spread out all the way to the wraparound front porch of the two-story house with white siding. Zain parked her sedan behind two large trucks.

While speaking to Rami earlier that morning, Zain had learned that they'd stored his truck at his mom's house. Which meant he'd now have his own vehicle and they'd part ways. An uncomfortable feeling washed over her. She didn't want to leave Zain, didn't want to just resume life as it had been without him. Her experience with Zain had changed her in a deep way—a way she couldn't understand but sure as hell wanted to figure out.

She also needed to revisit her reaction to him on the balcony. Seeing his bare torso and chest, his tattoos circling his biceps and moving up his neck—dear lord. She wanted to trace every well-sketched line on his olive flesh. The artwork on his body was as elusive and enticing as the man.

"Rami and Ivy are here already," Zain said.

The bundle of nerves sitting in her gut loosened a bit. She'd become friends with Ivy and her twin sister Gigi over the last couple of months. The women visited the office quite often to see their fiancés. Dana had been invited to a couple of gatherings at Gigi and August's house. Last month Rami proposed to Ivy, and they'd all celebrated.

Gigi always cooked wildly delicious meals, so Dana made sure to snatch up any dinner invites. Dana wasn't a pro around the kitchen, so watching a professional food blogger was fascinating. "Oh, good."

He grinned. "Don't worry. I already told my mom we're just friends. She shouldn't give you the third degree."

Dana's heart deflated.

Just friends.

Did friends kiss like he'd kissed her a few nights ago? Would a friend make her belly tighten or give her that heated look?

It didn't matter. She couldn't argue with herself. If he just wanted to be friends, well then that's all they'd be. "Okay."

His fingers caught her wrist, and a gentleness filled his golden eyes. "We might be friends, but I'll never see you as just that."

Her cheeks flamed, and her mouth popped open, but before a question could fly out, he slid from the car.

Great. Now she was even more confused than she'd been a few seconds ago—and she had to meet *his mom* for freak's sake. She climbed out and walked toward the front steps.

"Zain!" A woman with dark hair pulled into a low bun came running out of the house wiping her hands on an apron. Fine lines and wrinkles creased her forehead and the skin around her eyes, but probably more from the emotion twisting her delicate features than age.

She flew down the steps with the litheness of a ballet dancer and gathered Zain in her arms. He pulled her into a hug. He towered over the woman; her head barely reached his chest. "Hi, Mom."

The woman sobbed and pulled away, swatting his arm. "*Hi, Mom?* You've been gone three years."

A dark cloud passed over Zain's face, and guilt flashed in his eyes. Dana wished she could erase that pain. As much as she understood the woman's torment, her son had suffered too. Part of her wanted to scream the truth of what he'd been doing, but it wasn't her place.

"I know. I'm sorry." He squeezed her shoulder. "I'm home now, and I'm not going anywhere."

She wrapped her arms around him again. "I'm proud of you. Dad would be so happy you made it back."

Her eyes shifted around Zain's arm, and her

watchful amber irises, so much like Zain's, took Dana in. She moved away from her son and pulled Dana into a hug. "Rami told me what you did, sweetheart. Thank you for finding my boy."

Dana hugged her back, warmed by her words. "He saved my life. You've got a great son, Mrs. Mitry. Two, I should say."

She beamed. "Call me Greta."

The screen door squeaked shut just as Zain's mom pulled away. Dana glanced toward the porch to find Ivy and Rami standing at the top of the stairs. Micha, Rami's dog, came bounding down the steps. She skidded to Dana's feet then sniffed and licked her hands as she ran circles around her.

"Hiya, girl!" Dana scratched Micha behind her ears.

Sometimes it was hard to believe Micha's story. Gigi was kidnapped several months ago, and Micha had been the captor's dog. The pit-bull mix had immediately taken a liking to Gigi and protected her, earning her a permanent place with Rami. August hadn't been able to keep her, and Rami had always wanted a dog. Now Micha spent her days going everywhere with Rami and Ivy and getting more walks and attention than she knew what to do with at the office.

Ivy had her arms wrapped around Rami's waist, and his arm rested on her shoulders. They laughed as Micha gave Zain a quick sniff then darted off to chase a squirrel.

"Welcome home, man." Rami stepped out of Ivy's hold and moved quickly down the steps.

Rami closed his eyes as he hugged Zain, who stood maybe an inch taller than his brother, if that. Both men were enormous. Both equally as threatening.

Rami had a perpetual scowl, although he smiled a lot more when Ivy was around. The vertical tattoo over his eye gave him an edgy look.

But Zain—everything about him screamed silent authority. The way he walked, the way he stood, even the way he breathed seemed to draw attention. Rami greeted Dana and then introduced Zain to Ivy.

Ivy came down the steps tentatively, as if not wanting to interrupt the reunion. She quickly hugged Zain. "I've heard so much about you. I'm glad you're finally home."

Zain thanked her and drilled his brother with a glare. "Looks like I missed a lot." He touched the skin below his own eye. "What's with the face tat?"

"That's for you," Ivy said, her voice bold.

Zain narrowed his eyes to read the Arabic writing. His face softened, and he cupped Rami's shoulder. "I'm sorry I was gone for so long."

Rami's face was somber. "I'm just glad you're alive. That's all that matters."

Greta clapped her hands together. "Well. Let's go inside for lunch."

★ ★ ★

ZAIN SAT ON the wooden rocking chair on his mom's front porch. The sun had set, and storm clouds were rolling in across the light-gray sky. It'd been a few years since he was home, but hell, it was more like a lifetime.

Maybe because the last few times he'd been here he hadn't been present. Hadn't slowed down. He'd probably come for dinner then dashed away, taking his dessert for the road. Now, life was different.

Because he'd missed a lot of time. He couldn't get over the streaks of white in his mom's dark hair. The added wrinkles around her eyes. His absence had aged her. But more than that, his distance had.

He'd grown up and grown away and now . . .

Well, now he wanted to be back.

As he stared at the sweeping stretch of lawn, he could see himself growing old on this property. Hopefully older than his dad had.

He glanced at the chair beside him. His father's rocking chair was identical to the one in which he sat. If his dad were here right now, they'd have a lot to talk about. But the heart attacked that'd taken him eight years ago robbed them of the moment. The fact that he'd been overseas when his mother had gone through that hell would eat at him forever.

His dad would've liked Dana. He'd always been after Zain and Rami to get married. He smiled at the memory just as the breeze picked up, carrying with it the scent of cherry blossoms and rain.

Damn, those cherry blossoms.

He wanted Dana to come back. Should've gone with her.

She'd left a couple of hours ago, wanting to visit her own parents. Which he understood. Surely they'd been a wreck with her gone. He suspected she'd wanted to give him time to be alone with his family too.

Yeah, he wanted to be with them. But he also wanted her. Without her, he was unsettled. A gnawing sensation of something not being right clung to him.

He should've asked her to stay. But he couldn't just invite himself to her place—and her sleeping at his mom's, well, that'd be awkward as fuck.

Tomorrow he'd swing by her office, and if she was at work, he'd offer to take her out to eat. Lunch was casual, less forward than a dinner invitation, but it'd give him some time with her.

He also needed to get his life together. Rami had rented out Zain's apartment and stashed his belongings in storage. They hadn't sold his things in the hope that he'd return, and for that Zain was grateful. In the flickering moments in Afghanistan when he thought about his old life, he assumed all his shit had been sold and his apartment rented.

Rami had given notice to the current tenant, so Zain would get his place back in thirty days. Until then, he'd have to stay with Rami or his mom.

The screen door squeaked. "Hey," Rami said, as he sat in their dad's chair. "How you doing?"

They'd already talked for hours, and he'd told them he'd been working undercover. Both his brother and his mom had been shocked that his absence was the result of being recruited by the CIA. Of course he left out any further details that could implicate the CIA's mission, but dammit he had to give them an explanation, and only the truth would suffice.

Zain rested his chin on his knuckles. "All right. Guess I'm staying here tonight."

Rami smirked. "Mom will love it."

He didn't hide his smile. Sleeping in his old room would be weird, though. Especially since the bed hadn't been upgraded in the sixteen years since he left home. "You guys leaving soon?"

"Yeah, I've got a meeting at Backcountry tomorrow morning. We've got another big client, so we're gonna need the whole team on this one. You should come by the office and meet everyone."

That'd give him the opportunity to see Dana. "Sure. I've got a call in the morning, but I can swing by around 10:00 a.m. Business is good?"

Rami nodded. "We're growing faster than we can handle. Going to start taking on elite cases now, not so much the smaller gigs. It'll allow us to charge more without having to increase manpower. It's so hard to find good employees nowadays, especially with our background." He elbowed Zain. "Have you given any thought to what you'll do now that you're home?"

Zain grunted. He hadn't. His mind was still stuck in Afghanistan and focused on the job he hadn't completed. He couldn't tell Rami the details about the search for Jabar, but he'd let his brother know things hadn't ended well. "I have enough money in savings to carry me for a bit. I'll figure out my plans while I wait for my apartment. Maybe I'll take a trip."

Mischief sparked in Rami's eyes. "Are you going to take my analyst with you? I mean, I'd hate to be shorthanded, but I'm pretty sure Dana has some vacation days to use."

Zain scoffed and steered his gaze toward the storm clouds so Rami couldn't read his face. "Dana's a sweetheart. She can do better than an unhinged failed soldier." Lightning clapped in the distance.

Was Dana home now? He hated the idea of her driving in the storm. The urge to call her made him reach for his phone. They'd exchanged numbers earlier, but he'd look like a desperate douchebag calling her so soon after she'd left.

Rami nudged him harder. "Hey. Don't be dumb, man. You've accomplished more than most men your age. You got in over your head. So what?"

Zain balled his hands into fists. Rami was only trying to ease his frustration, but the more Zain thought about the mission he'd screwed up, the more it pissed him off.

"And Dana, well, she searched for you for a reason."

"She wanted the adrenaline rush," Zain said dryly.

"Maybe. But I saw the way she looks at you. She thinks you walk on water."

Zain rolled his eyes. "Doesn't matter. My shit's a mess right now. I'm not in any shape to be in a relationship. If she's still single in a few months, maybe we'll connect."

Rami shook his head. "You used to be the go-get-'em guy."

He screwed his lips to the side. "That's when they didn't run when they saw the death toll in my eyes."

His brother's face grew somber. "I'm sorry, man. I wish—"

The door creaked again. Tomorrow he'd oil the damn thing. Ivy stepped out and froze as if she'd walked in on something she shouldn't have.

Rami stood and caught her hand before she could dart back inside. "Ready to go, babe?"

Her worry lines softened. "As long as I'm not interrupting."

Zain stood. "Nah. I'm heading to bed. Thanks for coming, and it was nice meeting you." He hugged them both and went inside.

Rami had found love. Just like his dad had wanted for him.

Zain still hadn't found himself.

A CHILL RACED over Dana's arms as she sat at a red light. She flicked the vents away from her and returned her hand to the steering wheel. Her windshield wipers slapped across the glass, trying to give her a clear view through the sheets of water pelting down on the road.

Several cars had already pulled over to wait out the storm, but it was nearly 9:00 p.m., and after an exhausting afternoon, she just wanted to get in bed. Plus, she was only a block from home.

The light turned green, and she checked the intersection before moving carefully through. Fatigue made her eyes bleary and her body ache. Seeing her mom and dad had been nice despite the chastising she'd received. They'd been horrified by her bruises, but Taschen must've watered down the situation, because thankfully, her parents knew only that she'd been to Afghanistan—not that she'd been captured and barely made it out alive. She had no intention of telling them that.

Though she'd enjoyed her visit, her mind had stayed with Zain the whole time. She'd wondered what he was doing, when she'd see him again. And now she wondered if he'd already gone to bed. She turned into the parking garage below her building. At least she wouldn't get drenched.

A few minutes later she walked tiredly down the hall leading to her apartment and stifled a yawn. Reaching her door, she stuck the key in the lock and paused. Had the lock clicked open? It must have. She just hadn't been paying attention.

She pushed open the door and flicked on the light. After dumping her purse and keys on the small entryway table, she shut the door and removed her shoes. She padded through the kitchen to the living room. Her gaze automatically fell to the couch, where Zain had slept just last night. He'd left the spare blanket neatly folded; the pillow sat on top.

Stop. Don't even think about snuggling his pillow all night, for god's sake.

But why not? He'd never know. She practically rolled her eyes at herself as she reached her bedroom and clicked on the light.

The soft scuffle of footsteps on the laminate flooring sounded behind her. She wheeled around. A man lunged for her from the bathroom. She gasped and staggered backward, and her stomach dropped to her feet.

A black mask shielded his face, and a black long-sleeved shirt and black pants covered his body. Blue latex gloves coated his hands like a second skin.

Terror drugged her like morphine, numbing her from the inside out.

The bedroom light caught the sheen of a metal blade. A scream swelled in her throat, but fear clamped down on her vocal cords like a bear trap. The man plunged the knife toward her chest. Dana jumped backward, her training kicking in. Fight instantly overcame freeze.

She jabbed the man in jaw, and his head snapped back. Before he could recuperate, she kicked him in the stomach. He grunted. Blue eyes glared at her through the holes in his ski mask, and a silvery scar sliced through his left eyebrow.

He dove for her, tackling her to the ground. Dana let out a scream as her back slammed hard against the nightstand. The solid wood tipped, dumping the lamp and clock to the floor with a *crash*.

She kicked and squirmed but he got on top of her, pressing her back into the floor. He held her arms down with one hand and lifted the knife to her throat. She let out a guttural cry and twisted, throwing him off balance.

He staggered to the side, and she bucked hard, forcing him to let go of her arms to catch himself on the bed. She jammed her knee into his groin.

"Fucking cunt!" he bellowed. He sliced the knife at her stomach, but she blocked it with her arm. Searing heat spread through her forearm.

She scrambled backward, and her hand bumped into the fallen lamp. She closed her hands around its heavy porcelain base and brought it down on his head.

The man's neck buckled. His eyes went vacant and his mouth slack as he sank to the floor.

A ragged cry tore from her throat. She dropped the lamp and ran. Her bare feet slapped against the cool floor, sweat making her skin slick.

No noise came from behind her. She threw a gaze over her shoulder—nothing. She'd knocked him out.

She skidded to the front door, picked up her shoes, purse, and keys, then fled the apartment.

CHAPTER 15

*R*ING, *RING*, *RING*

Zain blinked and rubbed his eyes. He'd just lain down in bed and had forgotten to turn off his ringer. Sitting up, he picked up his phone.

Dana's name on the screen had him surging to his feet. "Hello?"

"Z-Zain. It's me."

The fear in her voice shook his senses.

Without a second thought, he turned on the lamp, reached for his jeans, and pulled them on. "What's wrong? Where are you?"

A shuddering inhale. "Someone attacked me in my apartment."

His blood turned to lead. "Are you hurt?"

"N-No. I knocked him out."

Pride welled in his chest, but he didn't waste another second. "Where are you exactly?"

"In my car. I just left my building. I should call the police. I don't know what I'm doing. I—"

"It's okay. Just keep driving. Stay on the line

with me, and I'll get to you. Can you head toward Evergreen Point bridge?"

"Yes," she said, steel entering her voice. "I can do that."

Goddammit, he just wanted to hold her. To let her come unglued. He should've been there. Fuck. He should have stayed with her. If he hadn't been such a pussy and asked to stay with her, he could have protected her. He swiped his keys from the dresser and ran from his room.

In seconds he was out the front door and shielding his head from the rain. He was a good fifteen minutes from the bridge. Which was fifteen minutes too fucking long. He peeled out of the driveway, probably waking his mom from a dead sleep. Bluetooth kicked in, and he heard Dana's soft breath over the speakers in his truck. "Did you get a good look at him?"

"Um, no." Her voice was hoarse, making the ache in him run deeper. "It happened so fast. I knew something wasn't right when I went to unlock the door. But nothing seemed out of the ordinary, and—"

"It's not your fault. Can you remember anything that might identify him?"

"He wore a ski mask. All black. And—" She made a choking sound. "Gloves. Latex gloves. He was going to kill me."

Zain muttered a curse. Obviously killing Dana was the asshole's motivation, but hearing her come to that realization undid him. He'd murder the bastard with his bare hands. "What about a tattoo? Piercing?"

"Not that I saw." She exhaled. "Wait. He had a scar through his eyebrow."

"Okay, good. That's something." He kept her talking as he drove through the city on autopilot, grateful as hell he'd grown up in Seattle and didn't need to plan his route. Dana had already parked near the bridge and was waiting.

A few minutes later he pulled into the concrete boardwalk lot that hosted food trucks in the summer. A few cars were in the lot, but Dana's sedan stood out like a beacon. He pulled up next to her vehicle and hopped out.

He was at her door before she even had it open. Catching her around the waist, he lifted her into his arms and held her to his chest. Her fragrant scent tickled his nostrils. He smoothed his hand down her back, and she shook in his arms.

Pulling away, he lowered her to her feet and cradled her cheek with his palm. Tipping her chin up with his thumb, he examined her face. A streetlamp illuminated her smooth, pale skin, accentuating her bruise. He couldn't wait for it to vanish.

Tears filled her blue eyes, and his heart twisted. "I'm sorry I wasn't with you."

She sniffed. "It's not your fault. There was no reason for you to be with me."

He clenched his jaw. "There is now. Someone's after you. Probably because of me. And until I find out who, you're staying with me."

She lowered her gaze to his mouth then slowly dragged her eyes up to meet his again. And damn if that look didn't stir his desire.

"Is that okay?" He should've asked, not told her, but he also wasn't letting her out of his sight whether she liked it or not. He could at least be polite about it, though.

She swiped a tear from her cheek. "Where will we go?"

He dragged his thumb along the slant of her jaw. So fucking pretty. He wanted nothing more than to kiss her again. To tell her he hadn't stopped thinking about that kiss at Ali's, and that he needed to know if she felt the same.

He swallowed the words before he said shit he couldn't take back. Right now, she needed to feel safe, not poached by a sexually depraved dick.

"Let me figure that out, okay? We're gonna leave your car here for the night, though. Come on." He caught her arm, and something warm and sticky touched his palm. She winced and let out a sharp whoosh of air.

Lifting her arm, he froze. Blood dripped from her forearm down to her wrist. A thick gash, probably two inches in length, split her skin. "Shit. You're hurt."

She twisted her arm to look at it. "He tried to

stab me. I blocked it."

He locked down his expression, fighting the urge to put a hole through her window. Rage rattled his muscles, but he forced a composure he didn't feel. "I have a first aid kit in my truck."

He led her to his vehicle and lifted her into the front passenger seat. She probably could've gotten up there herself, but he couldn't stop touching her. He'd carry her around all damn night if it meant no one would hurt her again.

But that was stupid. She was in danger because of him, not despite him. It might be his fault she'd been attacked, but he wouldn't let it happen again.

The fierceness of this realization made his hands shake. He'd never trembled over a woman. Never worried so much about anyone else's life. When his unit died, he'd been shaken. Distraught. Furious.

But this was different. Maybe because the blame fell on him. Maybe because she was a woman. Or maybe because his heart was getting in the way and Dana was a lot more dangerous than her dazzling blue eyes let on.

IN THE TRUCK, Dana watched as Zain methodically cleaned up the blood coating her arm. Strange, but she'd forgotten about the gash until Zain pointed it out.

Now it hurt like a bitch.

"This is gonna sting."

She cringed and turned away as he squirted liquid fire—alcohol—on the wound. She let out a sharp hiss as the astringent disinfected her as effectively as bleach.

"Sorry."

At least he sounded apologetic. A second later, a cool breeze lessened the sting eating at her flesh. She opened her eyes. Zain held his lips close to her cut, blowing gently over the injury. "Okay?"

She nodded because she couldn't do anything else but wish those lips would linger in other places.

Before she could haul her mind from the gutter, he had a laceration bandage on her skin and gauze wrapped around that. "How'd you get away?"

She swallowed, and the dry walls of her throat nearly stuck together. "I hit him with a heavy lamp. Knocked him out."

Zain blew out a breath. "Must've been a heavy-ass lamp."

"Porcelain."

"You're tough as nails. I'm sorry you've been through all this." He smiled, and if she didn't know any better, she wouldn't suspect there was fury burning behind those glittering eyes. Not at her. The anger had flashed in his tightened face the moment he asked about her escape.

He quickly collected her phone, purse, and shoes from her car and returned. They were on the road a minute later. Part of her needed to know where they were going, but she was mostly too tired to care. The adrenaline crash was making her brain mush.

"Should we call the police?" she asked.

He grunted. "I don't think they're going to help. Besides, I'm sure he's long gone. I'll call Maxine when we get settled. She'll know the best way to handle it." He covered her knee with his large, warm palm. "We're gonna get a hotel for the night. I'll have Rami bring me some clothes, and we'll stop at your place tomorrow."

"Okay." She rested her head back against the seat. Nothing mattered right now except getting to a bed as fast as possible.

Half an hour later, they had checked into a ritzy hotel downtown with a view of the harbor, and Dana sat in the one-bedroom suite while Zain spoke low on the phone in the living room, on the other side of the door.

Hearing him relay the details of her attack told her he was speaking to either Rami or Maxine. Her body hummed with the need to lie down, but now her brain fired with activity. Her mind kept replaying the memory of the man lunging at her, knife inches from slicing her throat.

She pressed her fingers to her closed eyes and tried to focus on her breath.

You're okay. He's gone. He didn't kill you.

This time.

She shuddered and got to her feet. She desperately wanted to get out of her clothes, the feel of the attacker still fresh on her skin. Breezing to the closet, she pulled out a housecoat and then went to the bathroom. She stripped and pulled on the robe. A shower would make her feel better, but she was too damn tired and probably shouldn't get her cut wet.

After tightening the tie, she scrubbed her face clean, rinsed her mouth with the complimentary mouthwash since she didn't have a toothbrush, and finger-combed her hair.

When she exited the bathroom, Zain was just entering the bedroom. "Hey," he said, his voice smooth as he scanned her from her toes to her hair.

A little thrill swarmed in her tummy as she sank onto the bed. "Did you talk to Maxine?"

He folded his arms across his chest, his expression murderous. "Yeah. She sent agents to your apartment. She'll give me an update when we speak in the morning."

She nodded slowly, lowering her gaze to her bare feet. "Thanks for coming. I'm sorry."

He sat on the bed beside her, cupping her neck. His hands were so thick and comforting, she could melt into them for hours. Lifting her lashes, she met his stare.

Determination blazed from his irises. "Don't be sorry. I shouldn't have let you leave by yourself earlier. It's my fault this happened."

She frowned and gave a light laugh. "How? You had no reason to stay with me. It's not like we expected this to happen."

Something blipped across his face, and the hard, chiseled planes softened. "No, I didn't expect you'd get attacked. If I'd thought for one minute you were in danger, I would've gone with you." He shifted his gaze toward the window, his hand twitching on the base of her neck.

Then he pinned her with his unwavering stare again. Some of the rage that always seemed to burn at the edges of his demeanor had diminished. The anger was still there, but she sensed it more than witnessed it. He was unraveling from his mission. And maybe, just maybe he'd reveal the true Zain to her.

"I should've stayed with you because it felt wrong when you left." The words rasped out on a hungry whisper. "I don't know how else to say it. You left and part of me stayed with you. It was a fucked-up feeling."

His words engulfed her heart. She bit down on her bottom lip as warmth spread through her. But she reminded herself that he was being protective. He'd guarded her from the moment he rescued her from the prison cell—that's why he had those feelings. He felt responsible for her.

Nothing more.

Still, she leaned into him. "I wanted to stay

with you too." Her voice cracked as she spoke.

If Zain had been with her, nothing bad would've happened. He'd have caught the man, and they'd have answers. But that was only part of it.

The other part was that she wanted him. She wanted him to hold her. To kiss her like he'd done. To not be afraid to touch her because god, she needed him.

Soft breaths came in and out through his nose. His fingers toyed with the sensitive strands at the back of her head, and she rested her hand on his shoulder. "You make me feel safe, Zain. It's not your job to protect me, but . . ." Words failed her.

She sniffed as a rush of emotion flooded her, stealing the resolve that'd kept her trauma at bay.

Zain pulled her to his chest, tucking her face into the crook of his neck. "Shhh. You don't need to say anything else. I'm not going anywhere."

With her snuggled in his arms, he stretched out on his back. She let her body mold to his side, let his arms envelop her like a cocoon. His broad length was the only solidity in her life right now. And so help her, she'd cling to him until she reached stable ground.

She wanted out of the robe. His body against hers. His flesh touching her. She propped herself up onto her arm and stared down at him.

His black T-shirt stretched over his stacked chest. He bent one arm behind his head and lifted a thick, quizzical eyebrow.

She kept her hand on his pec. She shouldn't do this. Shouldn't touch him. But for some inexplicable reason she couldn't stop. "I owe you a thank-you."

The corners of his mouth dipped. "You don't owe me shit."

Dammit. She was screwing this up. She wanted more than to thank him. Zain did something to her. His touch brought her to life, and his kiss had detonated her. She wanted more of that. Even if just for one night. Casual sex wasn't her thing. She'd never been about that. But she needed to feel connected to someone, needed to feel Zain's hands on her again. She'd die if he thought she was only doing it to say thank you, though. And he surely wouldn't want an appreciation fuck.

She slid her hand over his stubble. The short, coarse hair tickled her skin and sent a rush through her core. "Yes, I do. You saved my life, Zain. You were there when I needed you and—"

He caught her wrist and rolled into a sitting position. His fast movement brought her up to sit before him. His grip on her arm was firm and urgent. "I mean it. I don't want to hear that. You came looking for me. At the time, I thought you showing up was trouble." His jaw rocked. "I didn't save you, Dana. You saved me."

Tears burned her eyes. His words surrounded her heart. From the moment she'd learned he was missing, she wanted to help. Wanted to bring the wounded, tortured soldier home. But he hadn't been what she'd thought. That miscalculation had hurt her pride more than she wanted to admit, but his risking his life for her time and again had been her biggest failure.

She shook her head. "If you hadn't killed Rakesh and those other men, I'd be dead. If you don't think that's worthy of my gratitude, then you need your head examined."

His frown morphed into a grin. He chuckled and rubbed his beard with the back of his fingers. There was a spark in his golden eyes that hadn't been there before. She loved watching him come to life. Every emotion he expressed was like another layer peeled off an onion, and if she'd done anything this whole mission, she'd helped with that.

"Honey, if it's your gratitude you want to give me, I'll take it. But nothing more."

Her stomach hardened. She curled her fingers away from his face and tucked her hair behind her ear. "Of course. I didn't mean it like that."

Heat blasted her cheeks, and shame kept her from looking at him. Zain's hand caught her chin firmly. "Don't think for a fucking minute I don't want you. It's not that." Fire blazed from his brooding face. "I don't want you to feel obligated to . . . be with me."

He expelled a breath through his nose, his nostrils flaring. "I don't want to hurt you, Dana. It's been a long time for me." The confession came out softly but as loud as bullets hitting metal.

"You'd never hurt me."

His eyelids flickered. "I haven't been with a woman in over three years. And I don't want to screw up our first time."

She wrapped her fingers around his wrist, and his thumb twitched near the corner of her mouth. She brought his palm to her lips and placed a kiss on the meaty, calloused part of his hand. "I'd rather you try it out with me than anyone else."

The fire in his eyes turned to an inferno of desire, burning its way to her loins.

CHAPTER 16

Z AIN SHOULDN'T BE on a bed with her. Shouldn't even be in the same goddamn hotel room, because nothing short of another IED would make him keep his hands off her.

Which was dangerous.

She was dangerous.

Her rounded, glassy eyes stared at him. Scared and hesitant. Fuck, she should be scared. He didn't have the capacity to handle sex right now. But the last thing he wanted was for her to think that he didn't want her.

The thickness pressing against his jogging pants confirmed his desire. If he was smart, he'd kiss her full, pink lips, get up, and walk away before he got in over his head.

"I'm sorry. Look, let's just go to bed." She hiked up one shoulder and gave a light laugh, as though they hadn't just been talking about sex.

The front of the hotel robe gaped around her frame, making the smooth line of her shoulder visible beneath the terry cloth. He lifted his fingers and dragged them over the indent above her collarbone. "You do something to me, Dana." He spoke carefully, evenly. Because if he let out every jumbled word that weighed down his tongue, she'd bolt.

She tilted her head slightly, listening raptly.

"I'll do whatever you need to feel better right now. If that's leave, I'll leave. If it's staying here, in this bed, I'll stay here in this bed." He let his hand move slowly to the belt around her waist. "But if we start this, you need to be damn sure."

Her lips parted ever so slightly. She jutted out her small tongue, and something broke inside him. He leaned forward, but she surged to meet him, her mouth slanting over his.

He caught her around the waist, and she came down on top of him. Her mouth was so fucking soft and sweet. She moved to straddle him and placed her hands on either side of his face. Her warm, torturous scent invaded his nostrils, and he gripped her hips.

Fire channeled through his body, singeing his nerve endings with passion. Her tongue swept inside his mouth, making his cock throb ferociously.

The material surrounding her needed to be gone. He had to touch her. But if he didn't operate with self-control, this whole thing would be over before it started and he'd embarrass himself.

Breaking contact, he stood, forcing Dana's hands to fall away. He stalked away from the bed and threaded his hand through his hair. What the hell was he doing?

He couldn't get involved with her. He was too unstable. Pretty fucking crazy that he couldn't even trust himself.

"Zain, what's wrong?" Dana's soft question pulled at his heart.

He turned slowly, giving the window his back and facing her. She stood, combing her long, dark hair over her shoulder. Her face was pinched with concern, and self-consciousness rippled in her blue eyes. His chest tightened.

She kept a couple feet of distance between them, as if she worried getting too close would make him jump through the window.

"It's not you, babe. I want to be with you, believe me."

She tilted her head to the side. "Then why are you upset?" The housecoat swallowed her slight structure, and he had no doubt that if he peeled away the thick material, he'd find her naked beneath. The thought of her bare and so close was almost enough for him to say to hell with whatever anxiety was plaguing him and just do what they both wanted.

"I'm a mess, Dana." Despite his words, his voice didn't quake. He wouldn't allow it. Admitting he was broken was one thing. Her watching him crumble was another.

She took a step forward.

He crossed his arms over his chest so he couldn't touch her. If he did, it'd be game over.

"You've had a hard three years, Zain. Nerves are expected." She shrugged as if she were speaking about someone who'd lost their job. A smile tipped up the corner of her lips. "You make me feel safe. No one's ever done that."

He swallowed. Her words wound around his heart, and hell if he didn't cling to them like a drowning man to a life raft. "I want to protect you. Sleeping with you is the opposite of that."

This time her smile turned into a guffaw. "How?"

He shook his head and looked away. She wouldn't understand. He couldn't even put his thoughts into words, let alone bear his fucking heart.

"Zain." She was in front of him, her head tilted back to stare up at his face and her fingertips gripping his crossed arms. "I'm not asking you for anything. I just—" She wet her lips. "I don't want you to be alone in this. You've spent a long time being disconnected. You're the most dangerous man I've ever met. You've protected me, but I hope you know . . . you're safe with me too."

Violent images fermented deep in his mind. "I've killed a lot of fucking people, Dana. More than you can imagine. Some—" The thickness in his throat grew tenfold. Her fingers squeezed harder, urging him on. He locked his gaze on her, willing to expose the monster he was because if he didn't, she'd continue with the lie in her head. "Some not guilty of anything but being human."

Tears clouded her eyes. and the tip of her nose turned pink. She pressed her body closer to his, her abdomen against his groin. He wanted to hate himself for the arousal building inside him. Wanted to deny what was real and natural, but he was losing the battle . . . and fast.

"You're human too."

He scoffed. "Am I? I just told you I'm a murderer."

She lowered her gaze, then brought her eyes back to meet his—and what was reflected in them stopped and restarted his heart. Raw emotion laced with compassion. "You're a hero who had to do impossible things to survive, and I don't blame you for that."

"I blame myself."

She drifted one hand from his bicep to cup the back of his neck. "There's a lot of people who've prayed for your return. Me included. Don't live in the past, where you can't change anything. Live here," she breathed, rising onto her tiptoes. "With me."

He stared into her fervent, teary eyes, and relief spilled over in his heart. A cataclysm of trapped emotions were released.

He needed her.

He belted an arm behind her waist and lifted her. She swooped her legs around his hips, and he caught the neckline of her housecoat and shoved it off her shoulders.

The material parted to dangle at her waist, stuck beneath the arm that held her. He brought his free hand to her breast and closed it over the full, hard-nubbed globe. She dropped her head back, and he lowered his lips to her neck, kissing and sucking her soft skin.

Dana's back arched in his hold, and she squirmed. "Take me to the bed," she rasped.

He followed without hesitation. But instead of spilling her onto the mattress, he sat down before reclining with her on top.

She sat up, her legs straddling his waist, and the damned housecoat pooled around them. He drifted his hands over her narrow waist to her full hips. Her skin was like therapy for his hands, with their ruthless history.

"Is this okay?" She wiggled exceedingly close over his groin, and blood rushed to his demanding appendage.

His mouth wouldn't form the words. He should be the one asking for consent and comfort, but that was the blasted thing about Dana. She seemed to know what he needed before he did. She never hesitated to put herself on the line, never broke away from being true to herself. He both admired and envied her for those qualities.

Catching her around her ribcage, he tilted her forward until her mouth touched his. No matter his inner turmoil, Dana's mouth calmed him. "It's more than okay," he finally said.

As if his words were a shotgun at a race, she traced his bottom lip with her tongue. He closed his palms over her thighs, needing to anchor himself as desire pushed through him.

Her hands slipped between them, wiggling beneath his shirt. He sat up, and she dropped onto his lap while he tugged his T-shirt over his head.

She splayed her fingers over his abdomen and moaned. He yanked the housecoat from around her hips and tossed it to the ground. She sat on his thighs, glorious and naked.

Jesus Christ.

He ran his fingers everywhere he could reach, exploring each contour from her thighs to her spine. It was as if she'd been exquisitely sculpted for him by God himself. "I could touch you all day," he murmured, meaning every word.

She smiled against his mouth, and her hands stroked his pecs. "Sounds good to me." She rocked her hips over his junk, and he almost came in his fucking briefs.

As if understanding how close he was, she moved her hand to the waistband of his pants and tugged. He helped kick them off and managed to snag his wallet from his pocket before settling her back on top of him.

Eagerness thundered through him as he opened the leather flap and removed the condom he'd taken from his car earlier. After ripping the wrapper with his teeth, he rolled the rubber over his throbbing member. Dana braced her hands on his shoulders and nestled her slick heat over him.

She placed her hand on his cheek and her eyes blazed blue fire. "I need to hear you're okay with this."

His heart beat at a Herculean rate. He dragged his hands up the length of her legs to cup her ass. "Baby, I'm in heaven." He swept his fingers between her cheeks, reaching around to slide two digits over her slit.

A moan soared through her lips as he gently swirled his fingers over her opening, getting her good and soaked. Then he rubbed her fluid on his knob, using it as lube.

Dana guided her opening to his head and sank down.

"Christ," he choked. Her walls closed around him, squeezing him from every angle. Pleasure swarmed his senses as his nerve endings crackled.

He caught Dana's waist and pulled her on top of him, burying his face in her neck. Every muscle in his body bunched, craving release. But there was no way he could surrender yet. Not when he savored every curve of Dana's delicious body. Not when—

She raised her hips and then dropped low. He filled her to the hilt. She cried out against his jaw, and her hot breath only stirred the deprived animal inside him.

How was it possible that he could have every inch of her gorgeous body at his fingertips, his cock swallowed inside her, yet it still wasn't enough? Catching her neck, he brought her mouth to land on his.

Yes, this was what he was lacking. As much as he needed to be inside her, he needed to be closer. To taste her. He swept his tongue around the cavern of her mouth, loving the feel of her smooth teeth and the slipperiness of her mouth.

She moaned again. Her tongue darted out of reach, then she nipped his bottom lip. Pinpricks of pleasure shot to his dick. His body convulsed. He needed to get on top, to drive into her, to take what he desperately wanted . . .

But he refrained. He gripped her hip bones to keep her on top. With her controlling the speed and pressure, there was less risk he'd lose his mind and accidentally hurt her.

She rode him deep and hard. Her breathing reaching a frantic level as she pumped her hips. He grabbed her ass, relishing how her smooth cheeks bounced in his hold. Then he brought his thumb between their bodies and touched her clit.

She jolted as if the sensation was too much. He circled the little nub, and she fucked him harder, grinding against his shaft. Her cry broke against his lips, and he let her mouth go to watch her face tense with ecstasy.

"Let me see your eyes, honey."

Her lashes flickered open, and he watched her hazy blues focus on him. He lifted his hips with every thrust of hers, taking himself deeper and watching her come apart right on top of him. Her body shook and trembled.

"Zain, yes! Harder."

He moved his attention from her clit to clamp his hand around her lower back, driving into her. Sweat coated his skin as he filled her. A maelstrom of pleasure shot through him, blotting out his vision and leaving only Dana. Her sweet cherry-blossom scent the only smell. Her damp, satiny skin all he could feel. Her body and his was a perfect combination.

His dick nearly exploded with pressure as he came. Dana rolled her hips in long strokes, bringing him over the cusp. He savored the foothills of his climax until his heart rate slowed.

Her moans became hoarse little sighs as she melted on his chest. He nuzzled her soft neck and the dark waves over his shoulder. All this time, he'd wanted to lose himself inside Dana . . . but Jesus, he'd done so much more.

He'd found himself.

ZAIN BLINKED OPEN his eyes. Bright, unfiltered sunlight swathed the room in a warm, yellowy glow. He hadn't even remembered to shut the blinds last night before passing out.

Because he'd been consumed by Dana.

Scrubbing his face with his palm, he brought his other hand to the sleek arch of her spine. She lay snuggled against his side, her head pillowed on his shoulder, one knee bent over his thigh and her petite hand curling around his neck.

His heart strings twanged. Her brow had a cute little frown line, as if even in sleep she resisted being woken. Her pink lips were soft and full, making him want to kiss them. Her dark eyelashes rested on her creamy cheeks ... Hell, she was incredible.

A few days ago, he wouldn't have thought himself worthy of such beauty. But they were magic together. He couldn't deny that now. After a short snooze, they'd made love a second time. This time while he spooned her. Her ass bouncing against his groin was something he intended to relive.

He dragged his fingers over her shoulder ever so gently. Maybe if he woke her up with his mouth between her legs, she'd be ready for round three—

Ring, ring, ring

He lifted his head. His cell phone was blaring in the other room. Carefully, he slid out from under Dana and stepped into his jogging pants. He glanced at the clock: 6:49 a.m. Who the hell was calling him so early? His call with Maxine and Roger wasn't until 9:00 a.m.

Padding out of the room, he closed the bedroom door and then picked up his phone from the coffee table. He swiped the screen. "Hello?" he answered, groggy as shit.

"Zain. It's Maxine. Roger and I need to speak with you right now. It's urgent."

"Okay." His brain was nowhere near ready for this conversation. He hadn't even had a cup of coffee yet, for Christ's sake. But the uncompromising tone of Maxine's voice made him swallow any argument.

"I sent you a secure link. Log in and we'll chat on a video call."

He disconnected and slipped into the bedroom to grab his shirt. Once he'd closed the bedroom door and the material was over his head, he followed Maxine's directions.

The screen split into two windows. Maxine took up the left side of his screen and Roger the right. Maxine's red hair was pulled back into a severe bun. Her face was rigid, and the pale skin around her eyes was like wrinkled tissue paper. Maxine wore the years of a hellish career even though she couldn't be older than mid-forties.

Compared to Maxine's strict stature, Roger looked almost relaxed, his shoulders slouched. His military-cut gray hair made his clear-blue eyes stand out. "Zain," he said. "Nice to finally to meet you. Thank you for your service."

Zain returned the sentiment and then Maxine interjected to grill him with a series of questions about the deaths of Jaysh's men. Maxine and Roger both listened, expressions stoic, as he described what he'd had to do. Roger's face twisted with annoyance when Maxine clarified that he'd killed ten men.

"I assumed you didn't get out clean and easy," Maxine said, her tone chilly. "But the number of men you killed has thrown our plan completely off target. Jabar's gone into deep hiding now. Our mission will have to start—"

"That's enough," Roger said. "Zain doesn't have the clearance to hear details regarding CIA operations. All you need to know," he said, focusing his stern expression on Zain, "is your actions spooked Jabar."

Zain gave a solemn nod. If they had a better suggestion as to how Dana and him could have gotten out of there alive, he was all fucking ears. Pushing his tongue to the backs of his teeth, he kept the words inside.

"When we spoke yesterday, you told me about the woman, Dana," Maxine said. "Is she with you now?"

Zain forced his jaw not to lock. He didn't want to talk about Dana. Hated that he'd had to give them any information at all about her, but there was no help for it. She was a liability. "She is, yes.

But she knows nothing about the details of our mission." He'd already told Maxine that, but he'd make sure Roger knew it too.

"We might like to speak with her to ensure she understands the gravity of the situation."

"I think she does," he retorted.

"Maxine, let's move on," Roger urged, probably wanting to get to the bones of the mission before Zain got too pissed off and left the meeting.

"Of course." Maxine straightened. If she got any fucking straighter her head would pop from all the pressure. "You told me that Isaad planned to introduce you to Jabar."

"Correct." He relayed the date, time, and what little travel plans he'd been given. Maxine and Roger listened, but their tension was so thick Zain thought his screen might crack.

They talked some more about Isaad and things he'd said prior to his demise. Zain also gave them information he'd obtained from Rakesh's frequent rambling regarding other Jaysh compounds he'd visited. Maxine hadn't been aware of one, so at least she'd learned something from him. He talked more about the business dealings Isaad had mentioned.

With Isaad dead, it was unlikely the CIA could infiltrate another undercover agent. Zain was the perfect candidate because of his military background and his coloring, which allowed him to blend more easily with locals.

The intel they'd received in recent months indicated Jabar had a major attack planned—something Zain could've prevented.

"Thank you for meeting with us today. We'll talk soon." Roger clicked off, but not without striking annoyance in Zain.

Maxine's stern face dominated the screen. "Well, that had to be done. But I wish we had more information."

Zain was over talking about Afghanistan. He had a more pressing matter now. "Did you find out anything about the intruder in Dana's apartment last night?"

"Ah, yes. We had some agents check it out with local law enforcement. They've dusted for prints, and there's an investigation. Sadly, he was long gone before they got there. But I think there's a connection between the attack and your work overseas, so this is a high-priority case."

He nodded slowly.

"If there's anything useful that comes to mind regarding Jabar, call me." She said goodbye and disconnected.

Zain tossed his phone to the couch cushion next to him and looked at the bedroom door.

Dana leaned against the doorjamb, her arms crossed in that damn robe he wanted to tear off her. "I didn't mean to eavesdrop, but that didn't sound good."

"It sucked." He reclined on the couch and

opened his arms. She glided across the bronze-colored carpet, and when she went to sit next to him, he pulled her onto his lap. "How's your arm?" He pushed up her sleeve and inspected the bandage. A scab had formed, and there was no sign of infection.

"Sore but okay." She sat across his thighs and leaned her shoulder into the crook of his arm. "I'm sorry about your phone call. They should have told you how incredible you are. Most people wouldn't have survived as long as you did, let alone escape and rescue a civilian."

He chortled. "I don't think they give a shit about either of those things."

Her palm cradled his face, and her ardent, glistening eyes shook him. "I do." She brushed her lips over his, and he deepened the kiss.

Slowly, he pulled away and held her chin with the crook of his finger. "I'd do it all over again." He dropped another kiss on her lips and pulled away before he got lost in her. "I told Rami I'd swing by the office today. Want to come? After I call my mom, of course. She's probably worried after I left so abruptly last night."

She smiled. "Sure."

CHAPTER 17

D ANA WALKED THROUGH the familiar building—glass walls, marble floor, sleek lines—
with Zain's arm brushing hers. It felt as if she'd
been away for an eternity, even though it'd been
only days.

She stepped into the elevator. Before coming
downtown, they'd stopped at her apartment so she
could change clothes. She'd dressed in jeans, a
pale-blue blouse, and flats. Every muscle in her
body hurt after the attack yesterday, and comfort
was all she was going for right now.

That was a lie.

If Zain weren't here checking her out as often
as he did, she'd have worn jogging pants and a
tank top.

Just walking through the door of her home had
made her sick to her stomach. The air had still
been charged with the attacker's energy and the
room tainted with Dana's fear.

She didn't know if she could ever live there

again.

A place that had once been so safe and comforting was now the setting of a sordid nightmare come to life. She'd feel his presence in the walls forever.

"Which floor?" Zain hovered his fingers over the buttons.

"Um, twenty."

He jabbed the number with a thick, long finger. And good lord, that action alone made delicious heat crawl up her neck, sparking the memory of how capable his fingers were. His gaze met hers as if he'd read the direction of her mind.

"What?" She wet her lips to offset the blush warming her cheeks.

A slow smile curved his mouth, and he tugged on a chunk of her hair. "You, that's all." His smile faded.

"What about me?" She poked him gently in the abs but didn't move away from his closeness. A dark cloud of worry, or maybe it was regret, always hovered near Zain. So if she'd done something to make him smile, she wanted to keep doing it.

He brought his arm around her waist, covering the small of her back with his palm. "You made leaving everything I worked so hard for easy." The words drifted from his lips like leaves in the wind. Soft and wistful. "And I don't understand that."

"I don't know if that's a good thing or a bad

thing."

The elevator dinged, and a smile returned to his lips, this one more generous than the first. "It's a good thing, babe." The doors whooshed open, and they were greeted by the expansive space of Backcountry Protection Services.

Black walls with wainscotting and white marble counters and accents made the ambiance modern yet comfortable. Oversized cream-colored chairs opposite a coffee bar sat adjacent to the floor-to-ceiling window, creating a cozy waiting nook.

The *click, click, click* of Micha's nails on the hardwood floor brought a smile to Dana's lips. "Hiya, girl." She patted the dog's head then reached for the treat jar on the counter. Knowing the guys, Micha had probably already had her daily walk and treat, but she always snuck a little extra for Rami's sweet dog.

"Nice to see you again." Zain held out his hand, and Micha sniffed it excitedly, her tail wagging.

"She likes you. Did Rami tell you she was rescued from the cartel that took Gigi a few months back?"

"No, he didn't. Poor thing." He scratched behind Micha's ears, and the dog's tongue hung out of her mouth as she squirmed with ecstasy beneath his touch.

I hear ya, girl. He has that effect on me too.

The receptionist, Pearl, stood and rounded the front desk. Her gray hair was styled in corkscrew curls, and her black-framed glasses sat low on her nose. She ran the office like a stern grandmother. "Dana, we're so glad you're home safe."

Dana gave Pearl a hug and thanked her. "This is Zain," she said, pulling away. "I'm sure that's the only introduction needed. Zain, this is Pearl. She's pretty much the boss here, so you'll want to stay on her good side."

Pearl covered her mouth with her hands, and tears shone in her milky blue eyes. "Oh, dear. I told myself not to cry. I'm just so happy you're here." She sniffed. "You look so much like Rami."

Zain smiled awkwardly and reached out to shake her hand. "It's my pleasure, Pearl. Thanks for keeping my brother on the right track while I was away." He glanced around with a hint of awe in his eyes.

"Well, I hear the boys are hiring, and I bet you'd be the perfect fit." Pearl winked. "Rami's nine o'clock just left. He's conversing with the others, but he told me to send you in when you got here." She looked at Dana. "Boardroom A, love."

"Thanks, Pearl." Dana pulled Zain's hand and steered him down the hall. Stopping at the boardroom door, she knocked.

Several of the guys glanced at her through the window, and then the door opened. August stood there beaming. "Hey, glad you made it home." His friendly green eyes flashed with curiosity as he reached his hand toward Zain.

"August is the one who practically insisted I take on your case," Dana explained. "If it weren't for him, I probably wouldn't have had the urge to fly to Afghanistan."

"*You* suggested she go?" Taschen bolted up from the far end of the table.

Dana closed her eyes to steady her breath. Of course Taschen would be here. She hadn't seen him before opening her mouth. He'd been working last night and hadn't made it their parents' house, so this was the first time she'd seen him since getting back.

He looked just as menacing as always, the jagged scar on his cheek announcing he'd faced a knife a time or two. Not to mention the chunk of hair missing from the side of his head. He kept that area shaved. A bullet had grazed his skull while he was protecting Gigi a few months ago. Thankfully, he'd recovered and wasn't suffering any serious long-term problems other than being a major pain in her ass.

"Let's give Zain a warm welcome, shall we?" She glared daggers at her brother but to no avail. Taschen's wrath was locked and loaded on August.

Dana entered the room and sat in one of the rolling black leather chairs as Zain shook hands with everyone.

"And you already met Brick," Rami said.

"Toth here is my business partner, and Ghost only works select cases for us."

Toth smiled, and his gray eyes sparked with welcome. "Happy to have you back, dude. We've heard a lot about you."

"Thanks," Zain said.

Ghost reached across the table to shake Zain's hand, his arm long and sinewy. Tattoos embossed his skin from his knuckles to his short sleeve and disappeared beneath his white tee. He didn't smile at her or Zain. She didn't think she'd ever seen him smile.

His smoke-colored eyes made unease shift inside her. There was something cold and detached about the man. If she didn't know any better, she'd expect to find him on America's Most Wanted list. His black hair and rich, thick, close-trimmed beard accentuated his perilous stare.

Taschen came to Dana's side and folded her into his embrace. She rested her cheek against his sternum like she'd done countless times. He'd always been so much taller than her. Funny thing was he seemed just as big to her now as he had when she was eight and he was eleven. "Sorry, sis. But please. Don't fucking do that again."

She patted his arm and pulled away. "For your information, nearly dying several times put a bad taste in my mouth. I have no intention of going back to Afghanistan."

"Good," he grumbled. He didn't back away.

"Thanks for keeping her safe," Taschen said stiffly to Zain. "I didn't give you the warmest welcome, but we're all grateful you're alive. Rami made sure we all worked to see you return."

Zain nodded solemnly. "I appreciate that. And if I have any say in the matter, Dana won't put herself in a similar situation again."

Taschen's gaze sparked with awareness, and he dropped his attention to Dana questioningly. Before she could squirm, August piped up.

"Rami said you were attacked at your place," August said, rolling out a chair for her. "What happened?"

She lowered herself into the seat and then waited for Zain and the others to sit before quickly recapping what had happened.

Toth leaned back, arms crossed. Taschen, Rami, and Brick all looked pissed. Ghost's expression didn't change, even when she described nearly being stabbed.

"Well, you've been back in the US for barely twenty-four hours," Taschen said. "Clearly the attack is related to Jaysh, but what the hell? How'd they'd find you so fast?"

"That's my question," Zain growled. He looked at Brick. "Did you tell them about the situation with Ali?"

He gave a curt nod. "Everything. Mind you, only Rami knows Ali, and not very well."

"We met once while I was stationed over

there," Rami said. "Didn't really like the guy."

Brick lifted a shoulder. "I doubted his business legitimacy, but otherwise I trusted him." The corners of his mouth turned down. "Not anymore."

"Obviously he was working with Jaysh," Taschen said. "So who put the hit out on my sister? Ali or Jaysh? Because both of them had reason."

"Ali probably has more connections in the US," Toth said. "My bet's on him. And I'm sure Jaysh was happy to fund the assassin."

The men talked, throwing around ideas about how to track down the assassin before he struck again.

There was too much masculinity in the room. Dana would rather be chilling with Pearl. She also didn't want to think about her attacker returning. Undoubtedly that was his plan, but she couldn't stand the idea of looking over her shoulder.

A cold sweat coated her palms, and she moved her hands away from the glass tabletop before she left prints. The reality was that the assassin had a job to do and wouldn't stop until it was accomplished.

Ten minutes later, Toth rocked forward in his seat. "Rami, Ghost, and August," he said, resting his elbows on the desk, "I want you guys to work with Zain on locating the assassin. Taschen and Brick, stick around. We've got a potential high-priority client we need to discuss."

Taschen swiveled his gaze to his boss. "Shouldn't I be on Dana's case?"

"Technically it's Zain's case, considering he's the one who pissed off Jaysh." Ghost lifted a shoulder as he looked at Dana. "No offense."

"None taken." Ghost wasn't wrong. The reason the assassin was after her was because she'd gotten involved in Zain's business overseas. But clearly Taschen saw only her in the path of a tornado.

"Someone tried to kill her last night," Taschen snapped. "Maybe it's best if she's with family."

Dana fought the urge to roll her eyes. Zain looked amused.

"Enough." Rami's command settled the room. "You heard Toth. Come on. We'll leave these boys the room. August, Ghost, Zain, and Dana, you're welcome to discuss this further in my office."

The three of them stood and went to the door, but Taschen caught her arm before she could leave. "I want you to stay with me until this blows over."

Dana let her arm hang loosely in his grasp. Discord palpitated in the air between them. Taschen was just as capable of keeping her safe as any man in this room. But she couldn't leave Zain. Wouldn't. Not even to appease her brother.

He must've anticipated her answer because that knowingness returned to his eyes, far too similar to hers. "Is that okay with you?"

Jerk. He had her backed into a corner, and he knew it. Stifling the urge to flick the scar on his head, she turned her attention to her right, where Zain stood. Although his focus was on August, who was speaking to him, the muscle jumping in his jaw told her he was listening to Taschen.

Moving her gaze back to Taschen, she smiled. "Thanks. I appreciate it. But I'm good where I am."

His eyebrow hooked. "And where's that?"

"At a hotel." She cleared her throat. "With Zain."

His head cocked a fraction. "We've got safe houses, Dana. Helluva lot safer than downtown." He tapped his index finger on his phone case, watching her.

She didn't want to let on that something was going on between Zain and her. It was no one's business, least of all her overprotective brother's. And she certainly wasn't going to broadcast their involvement in a room full of colleagues. "I'm well aware of my options." She flashed her teeth, but her muscles were stiff. "You just find the guy who tried to kill me."

He huffed. "I plan to. But if you change your mind," he said, lowering his voice, "let me know."

She patted his hand. "You don't need to worry. I'm fine."

"I wouldn't worry if you weren't always putting yourself in danger."

This time she chortled. "Not true."

His face hardened. "Just be careful."

She flattened her lips and turned her head back to the conversation. Taschen could grumble all he wanted, but she was staying with Zain.

★ ★ ★

ZAIN'S STOMACH GROWLED as lunchtime crept up. After more than an hour of sitting in Rami's office, they'd made a game plan. August had called his contact at the local police department and gotten the scoop on their intel so far. He and Ghost would access the footage from security cameras inside Dana's apartment building and surrounding businesses to get a lead on the assassin.

"How soon until we can have an ID on the guy?" Zain asked.

"Well." August twisted his face. "He's clearly a professional. My guy at the police department said not a shred of evidence was left behind. We're still waiting for prints, but since Dana saw him wearing gloves, I doubt they'll find any."

"Great," Dana mumbled.

"Doesn't mean we won't find him," Ghost said. "Everyone makes mistakes. It'll take only one little flaw to piece this together."

Zain cut his gaze to him. "Sounds like you've done this before."

A smirk appeared and then vanished on Ghost's hardened face. "Let's say I'm no stranger to finding idiots who don't want to be found."

A gentle knock made Zain glance over Dana's head. Ivy cracked open the door and smiled. Her long brown hair curled around her shoulders.

"Hey, babe. Need something?" Rami stood but Ivy quickly waved him down.

"No, I'm fine. Gigi and I brought lunch for everyone." She looked at Dana. "If you wanna leave this boring meeting, come with me."

Rami chuckled. Dana glanced at Zain, and he gave her knee a squeeze. "Go ahead. We're fine here." His hand lingered on her leg for a moment, and a blush deepened the color of her cheeks.

Everyone's eyes were on them. If anyone in the room doubted his involvement with Dana, they sure as shit knew the deal now.

Dana's expression pinched in a cute show of embarrassment. "Um, yeah. I'm kind of hungry. I'll make you a plate." She stood and went to the door.

Ivy paused before closing it. She flickered her gaze toward August. "My sister's antsy to see you. So hurry up." She waggled her eyebrows and shut the door.

Zain frowned and looked at August. "Her sister—Wait. You two are best friends and you're dating sisters?"

Rami's lip lifted with annoyance and August laughed. "That's not even the strange part. They're identical twins."

"Don't ask if they ever get them mixed up," Ghost said with a snicker. "That really pisses 'em off."

Zain chuckled. "Man, that'd be weird."

"It's only weird because it's August," Rami said. "Trust me, I've already tried telling Gigi she can do better than this oaf."

August snorted. "I know you don't believe that. Not after I saved your ass from getting shot *and* helped you save Ivy."

"If I'd known you'd still be holding that over my head, I'd have taken that fucking bullet," Rami said, his voice spiked with irritation and his hand balled into a fist. He shifted his attention to Zain. "And we've never once gotten them mixed up. Matter of fact, I could tell Ivy apart from ten identical twins."

"Well, those wouldn't be twins then, would they?" August crossed his arms over his chest, amusement lighting his eyes. "Twins means two, dummy."

"Settle down," Zain interrupted. "We've got more important things to do."

Ghost sighed. "Don't bother. They fight like ten-year-olds."

Rami and August's back-and-forth stopped as quickly as it had started, and Ghost began talking in detail about how they'd trace the assassin once they got a visual on him.

But Zain couldn't take his mind away from the

feel of Dana's knee in his palm. Never in his life had he thought he'd get turned on by a woman's fucking knee, but here he was with a rock-hard cock in a room full of dudes.

Damn, he'd have to talk to Dana about what she did to him, because this was nuts.

CHAPTER 18

I N THE LUNCHROOM, Gigi beamed at Dana and greeted her. Her brown hair was tied up in a topknot, and she wore a plaid apron over her coffee-colored floral dress. She immediately set down the stack of plates and pulled Dana into a hug.

Dana smiled and hugged her back. She was always a little surprised by how petite the twins were. Dana was on the short side, but Ivy and Gigi were even shorter. "Oh my god, lunch smells amazing."

Gigi pulled back and held Dana's shoulders. "Lunch is the least I could do after all you've done to bring home Zain." She hustled back to a platter stacked with foil cylinders.

Dana couldn't help but sniff to try to guess what was inside.

"I mean, he's not my brother-in-law, but he's Ivy's, so that makes his return important to me—and everyone." She handed Dana a plate. "I just can't believe how brave you are. Going all the way to Afghanistan and being captured by a terrorist group." Her hazel eyes rounded with disbelief. "You have to tell me everything."

Dana accepted the plate and pulled out a chair. "First you have to tell me what this is because I'm salivating."

Gigi grinned. "Chicken burritos. I hope you're hungry."

"Starving."

Ivy took a seat next to Dana and plucked one of the wraps from the platter. "These are amazing. She puts some kind of pineapple salsa on it. I dunno, it's to frickin die for." Ivy passed her some pico de gallo and sour cream.

Dana unwrapped the foil and the smell of chicken marinated in spicy tomato sauce made her tastebuds tingle. She took a bite, and the flavors of cheese and avocado buzzed on her tongue. She groaned and wiped her mouth. "Holy crap this is amazing."

Gigi beamed. "Thanks. It's a new recipe. August loves it."

Ivy rolled her eyes as she took a huge bite of her burrito. "You could make dog-shit cake and August would love it."

Dana snorted and Gigi scowled playfully. "Don't act like Rami doesn't dig you taking pictures. I can only imagine what he has you doing with your camera."

Ivy covered her mouth as she laughed. "You're terrible. And I'll never share what Rami and I do behind closed doors."

Gigi guffawed. "I know more about Rami than I care to, believe me."

"What's that?" boomed a deep voice from the doorway. Rami entered with a shit-eating grin, August beside him, his eyebrow cocked with interest.

Gigi's and Ivy's mouths fell open, and the identical expressions on their identical faces were comical.

Dana cleared her throat and handed each of the men a plate. "Gigi made burritos."

Excitement lit August's face, and he was immediately sidetracked. "Hell yeah. My new favorite. Thanks, babe."

Zain arrived next and picked up a plate and a burrito with all the fixings.

Rami finished filling his plate, too, and sat. He leaned down and whispered something in Ivy's ear that made the color return to her cheeks like a fire sparking to life.

"Ew." Gigi scrunched her face. "Please don't murmur sweet nothings in my sister's ear when I'm eating."

August caught the back of Gigi's head and kissed her lips. "Two can play their game."

Ivy laughed. "Stop. You're both so childish."

Dana couldn't help but inch her gaze to Zain's

face. He tethered his eyes to hers. Heat scorched her skin beneath his intense focus, and warmth spread through her loins. The need to be alone with him again almost made her chuck the delicious burrito and drag Zain back to their hotel room.

Suddenly realizing Ivy had asked her a question, she broke her focus on Zain. Embarrassment fizzled around her ears. "Sorry, what?"

Ivy smiled politely, but female knowing flashed on her face. "Oh, I just asked if you needed anything. Not sure if you were able to get things from your apartment or not."

Dana nibbled on her burrito then wiped her mouth. "We stopped on the way here, actually. I should be good for a day or two."

Gigi grimaced as she passed Zain a plate of chopped veggies and dip. "You think this will be resolved by then?"

He scooped up some cherry tomatoes, carrots, and cucumbers and mumbled his thanks.

Dana frowned. "Well, I hope so. We can't stay in a hotel forever, and I need to get back to work."

"Yeah, but finding a hired assassin isn't so easy." Gigi's voice rang with knowing. Only months ago, a Mexican cartel had found her while she was in witness protection.

August must have picked up on the strain in her tone, because he wrapped his arms around her shoulders and kissed her hair.

Gigi had a point. The assassin would keep trying until he finished the job. Nothing short of taking Dana's or Zain's life would suffice.

"If the bastard tries again, this will end really fucking quickly." The low, threatening timber of Zain's warning made pride swell in Dana's chest.

He glanced her way, and the hard, chiseled lines of his jaw screamed the need for revenge. His golden eyes flashed with murder, and his large hand balled into a fist on his thigh. She'd witnessed the wrath of those hands, had seen with her own eyes the trained soldier who'd killed more men than she could wrap her head around.

A shudder rippled down her spine. She should fear this man. He was aggressive, huge, and had emotions so pent up he could explode—something that both made her edgy and eager. Because lord help her, the quake Zain sent through her wasn't unease . . .

It was full-blown desire.

She wet her lips as his stare swallowed her up. Her heart squeezed in her chest. Zain captivated, allured, and fascinated her. A devastating mixture.

New fear swirled around her. Her attraction for Zain was either bound for destruction or heartbreak. There was no in between.

★   ★   ★

A DIFFERENT KIND of warmth spread over Zain as he sat next to Dana on the couch in their hotel room. They'd left Backcountry a few hours ago and had just finished watching a movie. Dinnertime was approaching, and despite the delicious burrito he'd had earlier, he wanted more comfort foods—foods he'd been deprived of the last three years.

Dana's calm, constant presence kept his blood pressure at a steady level. His mind never strayed far from Afghanistan, and this mundane existence, so unfamiliar to him, had him on edge. But being around Dana made that edge less maddening.

"It was nice to see everyone. Hard to believe I was gone only a few days."

"Mmm." He gave her a relaxed smile. "I take it you like working for Backcountry?"

"Yeah, I do. It's like working with a group of friends. I feel useful and appreciated." Sadness clung to her words.

"You weren't appreciated at your last job?"

She chortled. "No. Don't get me wrong, I loved working for the FBI. But the work atmosphere was stressful. My boss, Luis, was a prick. He hated it anytime I showed up Dustin."

"Who's Dustin?"

"An even bigger asshole than Luis." She sighed. Her gaze stayed fixed on the form-fitting light-gray sweatpants she'd changed into when they'd gotten back. "No matter how hard I tried, how much I succeeded, everything I did was a failure in their eyes."

"So you quit?"

She kept her eyes down and tucked in a corner of her mouth. "Not exactly. Dustin made a big mistake and tried to pin it on me. And it worked. But it was my fault for offering to help with the file he was working on. I thought I'd win them both over if I took on more work. Dustin had me sign off on something and I shouldn't have—turned out to be something very important he let slip through the cracks."

Anger pulsed through Zain. The fact that Dana hadn't been appreciated and had potentially been discriminated against for being a woman was one thing. That she'd taken the fall for something she hadn't done filled him with the fury of a nest of angry hornets. "He set you up."

Finally her blue eyes met his, and a half smirk tilted her lips. "Maybe, maybe not. He was certainly dumb enough to make the mistake that fell on my shoulders." She shrugged. "I spent months pissed about it. Actually, you're the first person I've told."

He reached over and pushed a strand of hair from her face. "I'm sorry you went through that. Bastards didn't know how lucky they were. After all, if it weren't for you, I'd still be in Afghani-stan."

She blinked and caught his wrist while he stroked his jaw. "If it weren't for me, you'd have completed your mission and protected a lot of people from a terrorist group."

"If it weren't for you," he said slowly, once again repeating the words so she'd understand the monumental impact she'd had on him, "I might be dead."

Tears filled her eyes, and she shifted until she straddled his lap. He let out a low growl as he captured her waist in his hands. She dragged her fingers over his scalp and knotted her hand in his hair before squeezing the back of his neck.

"Something came over me when August gave me his recent findings on your case. I can't explain it. I had this intense pull to go there, to do anything I could to bring you home. I know that screwed up a lot of things." She wet her lips, and tears fell on her cheeks. "But I wouldn't change it. Because if I hadn't gone there and risked my life, we never would have met." Her voice went high and squeaky at the end.

Longing clogged his throat. His mind grappled with words he hadn't used in so long. How could he explain to her how she'd changed the course of his life? "Dana, you didn't just bring me home. You reminded me how to feel."

He lifted his fingers to catch one of her tears on his thumb. "I'm still figuring out what all this means, but I know I want you to stick around when this is over."

Her lips parted, inviting him. He leaned forward and sealed his mouth over hers. She moaned and shimmied on top of him. Need amplified the pressure in his dick. Slipping one arm around her waist and placing his other hand beneath her perfect ass, he stood.

Dana didn't break away as he walked to the bedroom. Her little tongue darted between his teeth, and he nearly walked into a damn wall. The urge to bury himself deep inside her consumed every corner of his brain.

Striding into the bedroom, he lowered her to the bed and caught the hem of her shirt. Tugging the material over her head, he freed her bare breasts. Goddamn, he hadn't even realized she'd been braless all afternoon. Her pink-tipped flesh called to him. He groaned and caught both breasts in his palms.

Dana held onto his wrists as if to pull him closer. He swept his thumbs over the little buds until they turned hard. She let out a moan, pushing him to the max.

He couldn't hold out another fucking minute. He hooked his hands into her jogging pants. She gasped and squeaked as he stripped them off.

"Hold on, mister." She held up a hand before he could go for her purple lace panties. "I want you naked too."

His chest hammered. Blood pumped through his body with so much force it nearly blinded him. Would have blinded him if Dana weren't lying beneath him, her blue eyes like twin flames begging for him to touch her.

He leaned down and nuzzled her neck because he couldn't help it. "I'm going to get both of us off, but first I need to taste you." He kissed his way down her shoulder.

She dug her nails into his biceps, her back arching as he shifted between her knees. As if on cue, her legs fell open, allowing him to get closer to her center. Hugging her hips with his palms, he slid down so his knees hit the floor.

"Zain—Ohh."

He pulled her closer and yanked off her panties. Her feet rested on the edge of the bed, and her folds glistened in his face. Exactly where he wanted her. Zain pressed his mouth to the inside of her knee and slowly kissed his way down her thigh.

Dana shook in his hold. "Cold?" he asked.

She gasped. "Um, n-no."

He reached her perfect pink flesh and, with his tongue, licked her hood with a featherlight touch. She let loose a shuddering cry, and a smile pulled at his lips.

She already squirmed and bucked, and he'd barely even touched her.

"Zain?" His name came out on a whisp of air.

"Mmm," he replied, as he covered her flesh with his mouth. Her slick wetness coated his tongue as he licked and sucked leisurely.

"*Ohmigod.*" Her fingernails pinched the tops of his shoulders.

He went deeper, stroking her swollen lips. His cock ached and pulsed against the top of his thigh, needing release almost as much as Dana did. But he wanted to watch her come. Wanted her sweet taste in his mouth.

She tensed. Her body began gyrating in a gentle rhythm, her slight hips pulsing in his hands. He held tight, angled her pussy higher, and caught her clit between his lips. Swirling his tongue around her little nub, he applied more pressure and she detonated.

Dana's cries filled the room, and her breasts jiggled as she moved against him. Her orgasm dripped into his mouth, and he lapped it up, enjoying every agonized jerk of pleasure. Her body went lax, and she wiped her hair out of her face as he pressed one more kiss to her sweet center.

Crawling his way to lie on top of her, he caught her nipple gently between his teeth. She let out a haggard gasp and wrapped her arms and legs around him.

He brought his mouth down on hers and kissed her, letting her taste her own tantalizing flavors. It was erotic enough to make his head combust. Pulling away, he placed a kiss to her cheek.

Dana stared up at him, her breathtaking blue eyes heavy-lidded and sultry. Some of her mascara had smeared at the corners of her eyes, and her hair was splayed over the comforter in waves and tangles. She threaded her fingers through his hair again, and the gentle tug on his scalp undid something inside of him, pulled him closer to her as though they were opposite ends of a magnet.

She held her heart in her eyes as she dragged her delicate fingertips over his stubble. "I want more of you, Zain." Her voice grew soft. "As much as you can give."

Heat blasted through him like lightning hitting a dry, brittle forest and started a blaze he couldn't stop. Couldn't put out. Because goddamn, he didn't want to.

Her words changed the atmosphere from scorching hot to a slow simmer. It wasn't just unbridled need between them. It was so much more. A connection he hadn't known he needed but now couldn't live without.

"You've got all of me, babe. For as long as you want me." He reached for the condom in his wallet before he returned his lips to hers.

Right where they belonged.

CHAPTER 19

MOONLIGHT FILTERED IN through the window, sending large shafts of light over the floor. She should be exhausted. They'd stayed up late making love, then ended the night with a shower and tumbled into bed. She'd woken up a few minutes ago and couldn't get back to sleep. Dana lay facing the window with her head on the pillow, Zain's arm draped over her side and his breath warm on her neck.

Part of her wanted to stay in this hotel forever. To never return to reality. To forget that there'd once been a time without Zain.

But their days together were coming to an end. Once they caught the assassin and she was no longer in danger, Zain might not want her around. Dire circumstances often brought people together, and after that element dissipated, he'd probably move on.

Zain inhaled a ragged breath and stretched, his arm tightening around her waist and pulling her closer to his body. His lips found her neck, and he nuzzled her before a soft snore sounded from his nose.

A vibrating sound suddenly had her on alert. She turned just as Zain bolted into a sitting position. "The hell—"

He picked up his phone and was on his feet as soon as he answered. "Yeah?"

A male voice sounded through the speaker. The caller spoke fast, his voice loud and angry. Zain cursed a blue streak, and even in the darkness she could see how rigid his body was. Dana reached to the bedside table and clicked on the lamp. The clock read 3:57 a.m.

Zain stood buck naked. Thick, corded muscle stacked from his strained neck down to his calves. His glorious lines resembled those of Zeus, and his tattoos were as masculine as a Viking's. She let her gaze wander over his body like a lost person finding a lake in the desert. Her legs tightened at the sight of the large, throbbing dick hanging from his groin. All the delicious things he'd done just—

"*What?* Jesus Christ," he breathed, dragging his hand through his hair.

She snapped her gaze to his face. Worry clenched her stomach. Zain paced the room, anger vibrating every contour of his body. Even his tight rear end looked furious.

"I'll fucking kill them," he spat. "Where is she now?"

Ripples of unease shook Dana as she got to her feet and pulled on her clothes. He zeroed in his gaze on her and gave a sharp nod, seemingly indicating that getting dressed was a good idea. She ached to ask questions, to find out what had him so upset. But every instinct told her to wait. She made her way to the bathroom and brushed her teeth to give him some privacy.

A couple of minutes later, Zain appeared in the doorway. He'd dressed in jeans and a T-shirt. His scowl was even deeper than before.

"My mom's house is on fire." His voice was hollow. Grave. And so deadly her muscles quaked.

She gasped, then she flung her arms around him. "Oh my god. Zain, I'm so sorry." A ragged sob caught in her throat. "Please tell me your mom is okay." She wouldn't be able to bear seeing another ounce of pain on Zain's face. Wouldn't be able to watch him suffer more tragedy.

He didn't return her embrace. Instead, he cupped her elbows and pushed her away gently. "She got out."

"When did the fire start?"

His jaw hardened. "Someone started it."

She nodded quickly. "I know." He didn't need to tell her this was because of Afghanistan—because of her. The assassin hadn't gotten Dana, so he'd gone after Zain's mom. Disgust curdled in her belly, and tears misted her vision.

Rage sparked in his eyes. He appeared to be on

the edge of losing it, and she wouldn't want to be the monsters who'd done this to Greta. She also didn't want Zain wasting away in a jail cell for the rest of his life. She just had to pray Zain didn't find them—or that he wasn't caught for carrying out his own form of justice.

Zain ran his hand over his face. "Fire department got to her house a few minutes ago. Rami's on his way. I need to go there but I can't leave you. Are you all right with coming?"

"Of course." She followed him to the door of the hotel room, her heart high in her throat and her movements clumsy.

Zain's mother could have been killed. Whoever was behind this had to be stopped. And she'd make sure that happened.

RAMI'S VEHICLE WAS on the street, out of the way of the fire truck parked in front of their mother's house. Pressure sat heavily on Zain's chest, and for the tenth time since getting in the car, he rubbed the ache.

Dana sat in the passenger seat, quiet but comforting. He hated that he couldn't reach out to her. Couldn't reassure her. Not when he was so tied up in his own fucking head.

His mom.

They'd gone after her. Why? Christ.

He parked behind Rami's truck and got out.

Dana quickly came to his side. Her fingers curled around his biceps, and he caught her hand and kissed her fingers. "I'm sorry."

Her tear-filled eyes gutted him. "You don't need to apologize to me. None of this is your fault."

He shook his head. "They came after you. My mom. It's completely my fault, Dana." The words came out rocky and uneven. As much as he wanted to continue the conversation with her—she had a way of soothing his jumpiest nerves—he couldn't.

His mom stood on the front lawn, her shoulders shaking and Rami's arm around her.

"Go," Dana urged.

He broke away and strode across the lawn. "Mom."

She turned at the sound of his voice. He pulled her into his arms, shielding her eyes from the blaze. Flames licked around the front porch, and the scent of smoke thickened the air. "How'd you get out?"

She sniffled. "My neighbor saw the porch on fire. He came with a fire extinguisher while his wife called 911. If he hadn't, I'm sure the fire would've spread faster. All the racket woke me up, and I got out through the back. I don't understand how this happened." Her voice was thick with worry and guilt.

Goddammit. More than anything, he hated that she thought she'd done something wrong.

He gently pushed her back and caught her shoulders. "It's my fault. Someone's after me, and they thought I was here last night." He flicked his gaze to the charred white porch he'd walked down only hours before. "It wasn't an accident, and it sure as hell wasn't your fault."

Concern softened her eyes. "My god. Why would someone be after you? What happened, Zain?" The sadness in her voice made him lower his head.

He'd done everything wrong, that's what'd happened. But he didn't say those words. He couldn't.

Since getting Rami's phone call, Zain's mind hadn't stopped moving. Anyone working for Jaysh could've been sent to kill him, and Dana by default. Then there was Ali. He had unlimited funds, friends in high places, and the power to make an assassination happen on US soil.

The question of who wasn't a huge mystery. But finding them would be a bigger problem. Which was where Ghost came in.

Rami approached. "Ma, why don't you come stay with Ivy and me? I'll help you call your insurance company, and we'll figure this out."

Zain gave his mom another hug and watched her walk to Rami's truck. Dana hovered near the sidewalk with a crinkle in her brow he wished he could kiss away. She hugged and spoke briefly to his mom on their way to Rami's car.

Pulling out his phone, he hit his colleague's number. Rami had added him to the Backcountry group chat, so he had the numbers of all the guys now. Inhaling the cool, smoky air, he stared out at the large lots of the neighborhood. The sun had begun its ascent, and the pinkish purple hue of the sky promised a beautiful day. Nature lied.

"'Lo?" Ghost's groggy, irritated voice rumbled in Zain's ear.

"I need your help."

He grunted. "Figures. The morning I try to sleep in for once. What's up?" The rustling of covers echoed over the speaker.

Zain paced the lawn and explained what'd happened. Firefighters shouted as they moved over the property. Police showed up a minute later. The place was a buzz of activity.

He flicked his gaze back to Dana. She now stood with one arm drawn around her ribs and her head tilted down toward the phone in her hand. Her concerned eyes met his, and she gave a tight smile. He lifted one finger to tell her he'd come to her when he was finished on the phone.

"Shit. I'm sorry to hear that." For once, Ghost had expressed an emotion.

Zain cleared his throat and paced another wide circle in the grass. "I know you've been looking into Ali and who he might have in the US. Any luck?"

"No, man. Guy's squeaky fucking clean."

Zain grunted. "Bullshit."

"Hey, I don't believe it either. But I couldn't find a single connection to any known criminals. Doesn't mean he's not behind it. Just gonna be a lot harder to narrow it down."

He pinched the bridge of his nose. A deep pounding sensation started behind his eyes. It was too early for headaches. And worrying about Dana and his mom would be an even bigger one.

"Had a bit of luck with the security camera in Dana's apartment though."

Zain lowered his hand. "Yeah? Why didn't you say anything?"

The gently tapping of fingers on a keyboard sounded in the background. "Well, I started running the scans yesterday. It was tedious. Found a shot with a glimpse of the guy's profile. Plugged that into the system to run while I slept, and I just got the results now."

"You got a name?"

Ghost snorted. "Nah, it ain't that easy. I've got some matches—a lead. I'll make it a priority to have a name by lunch."

Zain didn't need to look at his watch to know that was hours away, but what more could he do? "All right. Thanks, man. We'll touch base soon."

A firefighter jogged forward. Early morning shadows and large headgear concealed his face. "Are you Mrs. Mitry's son?"

He pocketed his device. "Yeah, what's up?"

235

"Police want her statement. Is she still here?" He lifted his head an inch to glance over Zain's shoulder toward where Dana stood on the lawn close to the sidewalk. He had a scar through his eyebrow.

"No, she left. She went with my brother. I'll give the police his info."

The firefighter thanked him, and then Zain made a beeline for Dana.

"Everything okay?" she asked. Her gaze hovered on him for a moment then drifted to the hustle and bustle around them.

"Yeah, I just need to speak to the police for a minute. I'll be right back and then we can take off."

She gave a tight smile. "Okay."

He nodded and ducked in the direction of the cops. Some of the smoke had dissipated, and people now milled around on the sidewalk, gawking at the mess and chaos. At least the fire was under control and hadn't consumed the whole house. If that was any indication, things might look up for them.

Plus, Ghost was onto something. They had a bite, and Zain wouldn't let go until the bastard paid for everything he'd done.

★   ★   ★

DANA WATCHED ZAIN cross the lawn to speak to the police officers in the driveway. A sense of uncertainty crawled up her spine. The fire seemed contained now, and hopefully there wouldn't be too much damage. But the fact that someone had targeted his mom's house in hopes to hit him made anxiety sit heavy on her chest.

Zain might feel this was all his fault, but she was the one who'd set this whole thing in motion. She'd gone to retrieve him. She'd put him into the position of having to kill many of Jaysh's members and then Ali's bodyguard.

She bore an equal amount of responsibility, and she'd help get to the bottom of things. It was too early to call any of her old colleagues, but she'd sent an email to Suzanne, a woman she'd worked with at the FBI. How much she'd be able to help was yet to be determined, but it was something. She just hoped the woman got back to her before it was too late.

"'S'cuse me, ma'am?" A firefighter approached. Ash and soot covered his suit and face, and his helmet concealed is eyes.

"Yes?" She tucked her arms close to her ribs.

"Police need to speak with you. Please come with me." He gestured to the sidewalk.

Dana furrowed her brow but took a tentative step in his direction. "Oh, I didn't see anything, unfortunately. I don't think I'll be of any help."

"You can explain that to them. They need to talk to every witness."

She blew a breath through her lips and followed the man. A cruiser sat at the end of the driveway, bubble lights flashing and the siren off. A couple of other cars were parked along the curb. A lot of the spectators had left, and the street was quieting down.

The man turned, stopping Dana in her tracks.

She stumbled. "What—" She jerked up her head. The angle and close proximity allowed her to see beneath the man's visor. A silvery scar cut through his left eyebrow.

All the oxygen left her lungs, as if a bowling ball had hit her diaphragm. She opened her mouth to scream—

Something sharp pierced her side. A sizzling sound crackled in her ears. Her body jolted. Panic and pain combated inside her. A ragged, barely audible gasp escaped her throat.

Heat scorched her side as the man shoved her into the back of a car. Her body slumped against the seat, and spasms overtook her muscles. Her eyes rolled back, and darkness came crashing down.

CHAPTER 20

ANNOYANCE PUCKERED ZAIN'S skin.

The cop scratched his head. "We already took Mrs. Mitry's statement. Sorry, not sure who you were talking to." He shrugged and sidled around Zain to return to his car.

Zain grumbled and pivoted away from the driveway, heading to where he'd left Dana only moments before. The space near the sidewalk was empty.

What the—

He scanned the property, spinning toward the house. Some of the commotion had dwindled. Where the hell had she gone? "Dana!" he called.

No answer.

Angst fisted his esophagus. "Dana!" He moved across the lawn. Police cars still filled the driveway, and a firetruck was parked at the side of the road. A deflated hose was stretched across the grass. Had she wandered off? Stopped to speak with someone?

Every step he took told him Dana wasn't there. Panic climbed rapidly up his neck. He jogged to the cop he'd spoken with a moment before, who was now chatting with another officer. "Hey! My girlfriend's missing. Did you see her? She was standing over there." He pointed to where he'd left Dana.

The man removed his hat and wiped a line of sweat from his forehead. "Uh, yeah. I saw her a minute ago. She was talking to one of the firefighters when you approached."

His gut clenched. "She's gone."

"I'm sure she's not far. I'll ask some of the other officers." He strode away much too fucking leisurely.

Zain muttered a frustrated thanks and jogged to the firetruck. Men in heavy gear ambled around, loading up to head out. Zain searched each man's face—there were six of them. None of them was the guy who'd told him the police wanted to speak with his mom.

He stopped one of the men. "Was there another guy here? Heavyset with a scar on his eyebrow?"

The man shook his head slowly. "Sorry. We don't work with anyone who matches that description."

Pain spread through Zain's chest, but it wasn't just crippling fear seizing his muscles. Not only was this his fucking fault—he hadn't seen the signs. The assassin had walked right up to Zain, and he'd been too blinded by the damage to his mother's house to put the pieces together. Dana had told him about the scar on the man who'd attacked her.

Christ.

Zain dragged his hand over his face and pulled out his phone. His first instinct was to call Rami, but since he'd just left with their mom, he dialed Taschen instead.

"Hello?" he answered, sounding half asleep.

"It's Zain. Dana's missing."

"What?" Dana's brother's shrill yell rattled against Zain's eardrum.

He pulled the phone away from his ear an inch. "We're at my mom's. There was a fire this morning. She was with me and—"

"Don't move. I'll be there in a few minutes. Text me the address and call the others." Taschen hung up.

The pressure in Zain's head multiplied. His fingers shook as he forced himself to follow Taschen's instructions. Standing in one spot would drive him to insanity. He needed to move. To drive or run. Something. Anything but be useless when Dana was in danger. After sending the address to Taschen, he sent a group text to the team.

He needed to call Maxine. He stalked back and forth across the lawn as he dialed her office number. No answer. He muttered a curse and hit her private number. She'd be pissed he was calling it, but to hell with—

His eye caught something shiny on the sidewalk. He bent down and picked up the device. Dana's phone. Agony pulsed against his temples as the realization hit full force. He dropped to his knees. Desperation ravaged him.

He hadn't kept her safe.

"Hello? Zain?" Maxine's earnest voice punched through the halo of grief circling his head.

He brought his phone to his ear. "Maxine. I need your help. She's gone." He spoke rapidly, describing everything that had happened to the cold, emotionless woman on the other end.

"I'll do what I can. Just—Just don't draw any attention to yourself, all right? There's a lot of heat from higher-ups about how things were handled in Af—"

"I don't give a fuck about Afghanistan!"

"Zain," she said, cool and calm, her I-don't-give-a-fuck rivaling his. "I understand you're upset. Believe me, we don't want this story getting out. Finding Ms. McAvery is my number one priority right now. I'll get back to you in an hour."

He hung up and nearly threw his damn phone. Only common sense made him shove it in his pocket. Just what was he supposed to do for a fucking hour? Take up knitting?

He'd given the police on the scene a rundown of the attack on Dana and explained that she had an open file, but the effort had surely been a wasted one. If Backcountry hadn't been able to find the guy by now, the cops sure as hell wouldn't.

Taschen pulled up and leapt out of his vehicle. His gray complexion told Zain that he was at his breaking point. "What do you have?" he demanded, as he strode toward Zain.

Zain quickly explained what'd happened. Taschen uttered a curse but didn't pin any blame on him.

"We need to find out what vehicle he was driving."

Zain nodded. "I didn't get a good look at the cars on the street. I was too distracted. He probably would've parked close, though." He gestured to where Dana had been standing.

"Does your mom have outdoor cameras?"

"No. None." Sweat dampened the back of his neck. Minutes were ticking by. If they didn't locate Dana within the next few hours, she probably wouldn't be found at all.

He couldn't let that happen. He also couldn't stand outside his mom's house a minute fucking longer.

"What about witnesses?" Taschen's eyes shimmered with worry.

For a flicker of an instant, Zain was struck with what it must feel like to have a sibling missing. Rami had suffered. Zain had known that all along but had been helpless to do anything about it. Seeing the pain in Taschen's eyes reminded Zain once again what he'd put his family through.

"None that I could find." He measured Taschen for a moment. At this point, hiding that he'd worked with the CIA wouldn't help Dana. Maxine would be pissed, but Taschen had a right to know everything. Resistance swelled on his tongue.

"What is it?" Taschen demanded. "You're hiding something."

Zain hung his head as paralyzing shame pulled at his knees. "Not what you think." He cleared his throat and met Taschen's furious stare. "I wasn't held prisoner in Afghanistan. I was working undercover. For the CIA."

Taschen's head jerked back. "Huh?"

He shifted his weight and gave a brief explanation of his mission. "I reached out to my CIA contact, and she's doing everything she can to help find Dana."

Taschen scoffed. "How the hell's she gonna do that from Virginia?"

"I dunno, man. Same way they find terrorists overseas. Surveillance, I'd imagine."

"And you think they give a shit about Dana?"

A knot formed in his gut, and an undeniable, instinctive response rushed forward. No. They didn't. He clamped his teeth down before he uttered the syllables.

They were fucked.

★ ★ ★

NAUSEA BUBBLED IN Dana's stomach as she came to. She squeezed her eyes tight against the vomit rising to the back of her throat. Fire licked along her side, and every muscle screamed. Pain enveloped her body.

She carefully opened her eyes. A dim room filled her vision. Even the low light streaming in from a high window made her temples scream. She closed her eyes and breathed through her nose to steady the swell of anxiety and the roiling in her stomach.

Damp, musty air touched her nostrils. She shivered and squirmed. Her hands. She couldn't move them. A rough material held them together.

Memories hit her like the bruising balls of a paintball gun. Flames. Zain's mom's house. A firefighter. Pain and darkness. Being shoved into a vehicle and—

Oh god.

The silvery scar through the man's eyebrow.

She whimpered and forced her eyes open again. Garbage and stains covered a cement floor. She lay on a small, thin, scratchy blanket. At one point, the concrete walls had been painted blue, but now they were chipped and peeling. Her eyes landed on a door across the room.

Instinct told her it'd be locked.

Determination told her to hell with that.

She pushed herself up to her elbows. The room spun. The nausea intensified and she retched. Her arms and legs shook as she vomited. Water and bile splattered the floor feet away. She gasped and wiped her mouth with her shaking, bound hands.

Inhaling rapid breaths through her nose, she waited for her heart rate to slow. Some of the nausea settled, and the room gradually steadied.

She refocused on the door. Whoever had taken her hadn't chained her up, nor were her feet tied. She turned her wrists over as she examined the rope around her arms. He'd done a number on the knot, but the binding wasn't overly tight. Just enough to be irritating.

She got to her feet, and her legs shook like wet noodles. She forced her feet to cooperate as she took one step after another to the door. Her pulse thundered in her ears. The wheezing of her breath was almost as loud as thunder on a quiet night.

If he was close, he'd hear her.

She didn't give a damn. She closed her fingers around the cool doorknob and turned. It didn't budge. A sob escaped Dana's chest. She seized the handle harder and shook, twisting with all her strength.

Nothing.

She jammed her shoulder into the wood. It shook but didn't give away. She slammed her body against it again, to no avail.

Footsteps sounded above her. She tilted her head back and watched as dust fluttered down with every stomp of her captor's feet.

Terror clamped around her bones as she backed away from the door.

MEET YOU ALL *at the office in 10.*

The message in the group chat had come from Toth. As much as the guys' willingness to come together touched some deep part in him, something else took hold of Zain's hope. Something sinister.

The assassin didn't want Dana alive. He just hadn't been able to kill her right there with firefighters and cops so close. Zain didn't want to acknowledge that she could already be dead. Because if he did, he'd break in two.

Taschen elbowed him. "That the neighbor? Maybe he's got footage of Dana."

Next door, a man was getting out of his car. He paused to stare at Zain's mom's house. Zain quickly walked toward him.

"S'cuse me. Do you have security cameras? Someone went missing just a little while ago."

The man jerked back his head. "Oh my. Yes, yes, I do." He moved the bag he was holding to his other hand and pulled his cell phone out of a pocket. His eyes held the fatigue of someone who'd just worked all night. "Let me pull up my app."

Zain watched as the guy tapped on his screen, and a minute later, he handed over his phone. "Looks like there was a lot of commotion this morning. The sensors turn on with any activity. Go ahead and see if you can find anything useful."

Zain swept through a handful of videos of firefighters and people milling about on the street. There was nothing that indicated who might have started the fire.

In a more recent video, there were a lot fewer people. For several seconds, there was just grass and sidewalk on the screen.

Taschen huddled in next to him.

Dana's body entered the screen. Zain caught her profile before she turned her back to the camera. A look of confusion had been etched on her face as a man approached. She followed the guy a few paces down the sidewalk, and then he turned and she bumped into him. He jammed something into her side—a Taser.

Jesus.

The phone burned his fingers as he watched Dana get pushed into the back of a car, unable to do a damn fucking thing. Rage ricocheted through his brain. Fast and pounding. A heavy weight sat in his gut. His sinuses pulsed with unspent emotion.

The guy was large and swift; the abduction had been quick and concealed. Less than five seconds after tasing her, he had her inside the vehicle and was rounding the car to get in the driver's seat.

As the car took off, the license plate filled the screen. Zain hit the pause button.

"Plate number," Taschen hissed.

Zain grunted. "It's pretty grainy."

"Send it to me and I'll see what we can do."

Zain took a screenshot of the image then looked at the neighbor. "Mind if I text this to myself?"

He waved his hand. "Please." The guy rocked back on his feet. "Anything I can do to help. Such a tragedy. First a fire, now this." He shook his head sadly.

"Yeah, no kidding." Zain didn't hide the dryness in his tone. "Thanks for your help. Appreciate it. If you happen to see or hear anything else, you have my number."

The man nodded emphatically and pushed his wire-rimmed glasses higher on his nose. "Yes, yes. Of course. Good luck."

Zain turned and headed back to his truck. "I'll follow you to the office."

"Yup." He clapped his hand on Zain's shoulder. "We'll find her, man. If we've got a plate number, that makes this a helluva lot easier."

Still, the crushing force of fear sat hard on Zain's shoulders. Having the plate number wouldn't do a goddamn thing if Dana was already dead.

CHAPTER 21

D ANA WENT TO the wall and dropped herself back down on the blanket. She landed with a thud that shook her bones, but nothing could rattle her more than the sound of the hurried steps coming down the stairs.

Every footfall was harder and angrier than the one before it. Her breath hitched. She scanned the floor for a weapon but saw nothing other than the yucky blanket, magazines, and food wrappers.

Panic flooded every cell in her body. Someone stopped outside the door, and the rattling of keys reached her ears. She drew her knees to her chest, a prayer on her lips.

Please, God. Don't let me die here.

Tears wanted to rush forward, but she held them back. She had to glean as much information as she could if she wanted to get out of here. She was in a basement. The high window and the cold dankness of the room revealed that much.

Too bad there were a zillion basements in the

Seattle area.

The door banged open and a man breezed into the room sans firefighter gear. He wore jeans and a red T-shirt that hugged his thick middle. Black combat boots covered his feet. His hands hung at his sides. There was no weapon that she could see, but he'd had a knife when he attacked her.

He wasn't wearing a ski mask or a helmet this time, so she could study his face a bit more. The lack of lighting made identifying details tough, but his head was shaved and he had a tattoo on his forearm. A skull or something. *Real original, dude.* A scar chewed through his eyebrow. This was definitely the man who'd attacked her in her apartment.

He stopped a few feet away and tilted his head to the side, and the sudden movement made Dana cringe. Her spine instinctively straightened against the cement wall. He stalked forward, his expression cold and methodical. He opened and closed one hand and held a set of keys in the other. "Dana McAvery?"

She curled her lip. Just the sound of her name coming from his thick, slimy lips made disgust unravel inside her. "And you are?"

The corner of his mouth twitched. "Your worst nightmare."

She snorted. "You might be *my* worst nightmare, but Zain is yours."

The man laughed, a loud, pealing sound that

reverberated off the walls to beat against Dana's eardrums. He waggled his index finger. "This is gonna be fun."

"Fuck you."

His smile fell. "You're going to learn some manners, bitch."

"You took me, asshole. Why?"

He slid his gaze over her face, and the motion made her feel as if there were slugs on her skin. "I was given a great deal of money to do so, that's why."

She swallowed. His honesty stole some of her bravado. "Who hired you?" The words came out soft, hesitant. Part of her was desperate to hear the answer. The other part wanted to run from it.

His mouth quirked again. "I can't tell you that. But I can tell you they want you dead. Just as soon as you tell me everything you know about Zain Mitry."

Her heart pounded frantically. Misery wormed through her chest, and she fought the scream that wanted to be unleashed. Zain. He'd be looking for her by now. Worried. Scared.

Probably assuming her dead.

I'm not, Zain. I'm here. I'm alive, and I'm waiting for you.

But her thoughts were useless. He couldn't hear her. Couldn't find her. Not when she'd vanished without a trace. He'd have nowhere to even start. The gripping truth was that she was on her own.

She didn't even have a weapon to fight her own battle. All she had was what she'd been born with: her mind.

He wanted information about Zain. The longer she kept her knowledge to herself, the longer she'd stay alive. But she had to play his game before he got any sick ideas about how to get her to talk. She wet her lips, her thoughts working a mile a minute. "What do you want to know?"

"Everything about Afghanistan."

THE ELEVATOR UP to the Backcountry offices moved at a snail's pace. Zain pinched his brow. Taking the stairs up the twenty-something floors would've been faster.

"Send me the screenshot of the plate," Taschen ordered.

Zain opened his phone and sent the image. A ding sounded, and the elevator doors opened. He got out first and strode down the hall.

Behind the front desk, Pearl stood up, her lip quivering. "Oh, Taschen. I'm so sorry to hear about Dana."

Her words hit Zain harder than a stream of bullets. The apology sounded more like condolences.

Taschen cupped Pearl's shoulder. "Thanks, hon."

Pearl must have read the grim look on Zain's

face because she quickly sputtered, "D-Don't worry. We've got the best team this part of the country. I just know she'll be found."

He forced a smile but couldn't muster any words as he continued to the boardroom.

The other guys were already there, in front of a large whiteboard. The fact that they all seemed as buzzed with urgency as he was pacified him somewhat.

August moved toward Taschen first. "Man. I'm so sorry this happened." His green eyes flashed with worry. He shifted his gaze to Zain. "She'll be okay. Dana's smart as a whip."

Rami didn't approached Zain, but his face reflected every vicious emotion spiraling through him: concern, fear, and enough rage to light the room. "We're on it, brother."

Zain swallowed and stepped into the group. Brick patted his shoulder, and Ghost gave a curt nod of understanding. Zain cleared the gravel from his throat. "Thanks for being here. I'm going to give you a rundown of what happened while Taschen uploads the surveillance video we retrieved from the neighbor's camera."

Taschen lifted two fingers in confirmation while he opened the laptop on the boardroom table.

"A man dressed in a firefighter's uniform approached me and said the police needed my mom's statement. Rami had already taken my mom to his place at this point, so I sought out an officer to explain. Speaking to one, I learned they'd already gotten the information they needed from my mom. When I retraced my steps to where I'd left Dana, she was gone. In less than two minutes, the same firefighter who'd approached me had spoken to Dana and led her down the sidewalk, presumably with a similar story. Once he got close to his vehicle, he tased her and put her inside. That's the last she was seen."

Rami shook his head angrily, and Brick looked ready to put a hole in the wall.

Ghost narrowed his eyes. "You got a look at the guy?"

"I was too distracted to really pay attention, but I'm certain he had a scar on his left eyebrow, which matches Dana's description of her attacker." He returned Ghost's questioning glare. "Did you have any luck tracing the guy through the security cameras in Dana's building?"

Ghost crossed his arms, a smug expression flashing in his gray eyes. "Yeah, I got something actually."

"What?" Zain demanded.

Silence fell around where they stood. All eyes turned to Ghost.

"I was going to phone you this morning, but that's when Rami called everyone to the office. I found out who the asshole is. Drake Lambert."

Zain's heart stalled. His brain worked at

breakneck speed to fit the name to a face, but nothing came forth. "I don't know that name."

"Nah, you probably don't. He's not from around here."

"Who the fuck is he?" Rami snarled.

Ghost sighed. "Honestly, I didn't get that far. But a name's a pretty big fucking start. I've got a colleague working on it. The best in the biz." He reached into his pocket and pulled out his phone. "This the guy you saw talking to Dana?"

He turned the device toward Zain. A driver's license image filled the screen, and it lit Zain's last fucking nerve—shaved head, lifeless blue eyes, and scar across his left eyebrow. "That's him." The confirmation came out on a constricted breath.

"Good. From what I can tell, he's a professional. Not a surprise. We suspected a hitman. Finding out who paid him will be the hard part."

Rami nudged Ghost with his elbow. "That's your job. Find out who hired him and follow that trail. We'll work a different angle."

"I'll be in my office." He sliced through the guys and out the door.

"Video's almost ready," Taschen announced.

Zain moved closer to his brother. "Where's Mom?"

Rami's face softened. "She's safe. I took her, Ivy, and Gigi to Toth's house. They're there with him, Savannah, and the baby."

"Good. Should we send anyone else there to be

safe?"

Rami shook his head. "Toth's got it covered. Besides, our guy was likely trying to get to you by setting the house on fire."

Zain nodded gravely. Now that the killer had Dana in his grip, his focus had shifted.

When Zain got his hands on Drake, the bastard would wish he'd never gone after Dana.

"Ivy and Gigi are worried about Dana. Just beside themselves." He shook his head. "I should've called the guys out to help at Mom's. Shouldn't have left you."

Zain met his brother's eyes, and for a moment time moved backward. As a kid, Rami had been the wild one. Always in trouble and making their mom worry. Zain had been the one to ease their mom's fears. As a teenager he'd stayed closer to home, only occasionally joining his older brother in shenanigans.

Rami wasn't the same man he'd been when Zain left. He'd changed. It wasn't just the eye tat. There was a bold and glaring difference. Rami carried more weight now—not only on his heart but also on his conscience. The shimmer of regret and responsibility shone in his eyes.

And if Zain had known how much guilt Rami would shoulder regarding his disappearance, he'd have done things differently.

Somehow, he would've found a way to spare Rami that burden. He placed his palm around

Rami's shoulder and met his eyes. Hell, he even seemed taller than he had three years ago. "None of this was your fault," he said, his voice gruff. "It's mine, brother. All of it."

He cleared his throat before he wasted any more time. "I know I said this, but I'm sorry. I should've done things differently. But I'm proud of the man you've become."

Rami gave him a half smile. "You too, man."

"Aww aren't you boys cute," August sang.

Zain dropped his hand from his brother's shoulder and rolled his eyes.

"Yeah, real cute," Taschen piped up. "Let's find my fucking sister, though. Save your brofest for later."

"If you'd get that damn thing runnin' we would," Rami shot back.

Taschen gestured at the screen. "Watch."

They all stared at the large white screen on the wall. Zain rewatched Dana's kidnapping, and it was like experiencing painful déjà vu. He folded his arms, his stomach clenching.

The whole thing was over in seconds. The energy in the room shifted. Unease charged the atmosphere.

"Anyone run the plate?" Brick asked solemnly.

"Haven't tried to enlarge it yet. Not sure if we can." Taschen rolled out a chair and sat. The others followed suit, but Zain couldn't do more than pace.

Rami snapped open his laptop and punched the keys. "Send it my way."

Taschen must've obliged because after a few minutes Rami spoke. "A bit grainy, but I think I've got something legible. Anyone else want to try?"

"Me." Zain placed his palm on the table next to the computer and looked at the image Rami had enlarged. Grainy was an understatement.

The pixelated navy-blue letters and numbers were difficult to make out on the white background, and the angle of the shot and the movement of the vehicle heightened the complexity. Zain rattled off the letters and most of the numbers but stopped at the last one. "Is that a three or an eight?"

"I say three," Rami said.

"Lemme see." Brick stepped in and leaned forward. "I agree."

Zain nodded. "I was leaning toward that too. Let's run it."

With a registered plate and the name Ghost had found today, they might just find an address for this motherfucker.

Problem was, even if they were lucky enough to find the plate registered under Drake's name, a professional assassin wouldn't take Dana to his house. But it was something.

It was all they had.

In minutes, Rami was inside the DMV database. Zain watched his brother's fingers tap against the desk as they waited for results. A low ding sounded from the computer. Rami grunted. "It's a stolen plate."

"Fuck," Zain ground out.

"Not only that, but there's no vehicle registered under Drake Lambert. It's hard to say if that's an alias or not."

The office door swung open, and Ghost stormed inside. "I've got something." He slapped a piece of paper on the table.

Zain snapped out his hand and dragged the sheet across the laminate surface. His heart rate soared into dangerous territory. He stared at the words, his mind tripping over every character, unable to piece them together. "What's this?"

"From my colleague. He's a hacker. I called him after Dana was attacked, and he's been on this since then. It wasn't Jaysh who hired Drake."

"I don't understand." His throat clenched. He didn't want to believe the words he'd read—the words Ghost had confirmed.

Rami took the paper from Zain. "Holy shit." His voice booming, he ordered everyone out except for Zain and Ghost.

The room spun. Zain's heart pumped wildly while the walls closed in around him. He'd known all along that he'd endangered Dana. That his mission was too risky. That he was wrong for her.

Wrong to get involved. Wrong to fall so fucking hard.

But this was so much worse than he'd anticipated. The damning statements verified the
whisper of suspicion that'd plagued him over the
years.

His breath hissed out. Numbness inched over
his skin, bringing with it a freezing chill that
touched his bones. He hadn't just walked Dana
through hell—he'd hand-delivered her to the devil
himself.

CHAPTER 22

D ANA FOUGHT THE urge to spit in the creep's eyes. She'd give anything to take a knife and drag that scar down the rest of his face. He knelt with his forearm resting on his knee and flexed his hand as though he wanted to jab her with it.

In her head, she gnawed over an explanation as though carefully laying out a Tetris puzzle. She'd never been good at that game. The last piece always screwed her. "Considering I was in Afghanistan for two days, I really don't have much to share."

His mouth twisted. "Come on. You saw a lot. Your boyfriend killed several people. Start there."

She swallowed. "Even if I could tell you how many lives he took, I wouldn't know their names. I didn't ask a lot of questions, and he didn't offer information."

"Bullshit."

She tried again. "I went there under the impression he was being held against his will," she said carefully. "If the situation was any different, I don't know the details."

"He didn't tell you who he worked for?"

"No," she blurted, without missing a beat. If she died here today, she'd make sure whoever had beef with Zain didn't know he'd been undercover. No matter what, she had to keep that to herself. And she'd gladly accept death over whatever torture tactics her scarred-up friend had in mind.

He reached into his pocket and pulled out a knife—just like the one he'd used in her apartment. Lovely.

She brought her gaze back to his face, summoning whatever bravado she could find. "By the way, I think you broke my lamp. You owe me a new one."

One vicious blue eye narrowed.

"How's your head?" she taunted.

He lunged forward, jamming his fist into her jaw. A labyrinth of stripes blinked in front of her eyes, and pain exploded across her cheekbone. She wiped a dribble of spit from her lips as the taste of blood filled her mouth. Pissing him off wasn't smart. Buying time would be harder than she'd anticipated.

"We can do this the easy way or the hard way," he hissed. "You answer my questions without wasting my time and I'll kill you quickly. Fuck around and I'll slice out your pretty blue eyes. Got it?"

She blinked away the tears blinding her. "Neither option is very appealing."

He flicked open the blade. "How about I start with your fingernails then, hmm?"

Curling her hands into tight balls, she hunkered closer to her knees. "I have nothing to hide. I was only with Zain for a couple of days. It's not like we sat around spilling our secrets."

He snagged her wrists, dragging them away from her knees. Anxiety contracted across her chest. She held her arm firm, refusing, but he was too strong.

"Stop." Her command came out brittle.

He smiled, revealing crooked discolored teeth. Feeling as if she might pass out, Dana forced a breath in through her nose. Part of her wanted to depart from this moment, to slip into a blissful state of unawareness, but the crippling fear of what he'd do to her kept her alert.

"Just cutting you free, princess." He fit the knife beneath one of the ropes, and the twine fell away with sickening ease. If that knife made rope fall apart that quickly, her skin would peel back like hot metal through butter.

She shook her hands, getting blood flow back. He recaptured her wrist and had her arm locked straight before she could even squirm.

He flashed the knife in front of her. "Answer my questions and you can keep your fingernails." He brought the knife to her closed fist and pressed the tip of the blade against the edge of her palm.

Dana jerked her hand, and the movement caused the knife to slip deep. She gasped, but he didn't release his hold. Blood oozed from her flesh. The cut smarted, but she didn't make another sound.

"Tsk tsk. Making a mess already."

She met his bottomless eyes. He was going to hurt her. If not now, soon. And he'd enjoy every minute. All she could do was play her hand and hope God would grant her a window of opportunity. "What do you want to know? I can't confirm he's CIA, but I don't see how that's true."

His thumb dug relentlessly into the inside of her wrist. Impatience danced across his face, tightening his clean-shaven jaw. "Here's what we're going to do. I'm gonna ask you questions and you're gonna answer quickly. If you don't play right, you lose a fingernail. Got it?"

Sweat collected at her hairline. Her heart beat frantically in her chest. "I don't—"

"Did you ever hear Zain speak about Jabar?"

She exhaled rapidly. "No."

"Did he talk about a hospital bombing?"

"A what? N-No."

The asshole drilled her with his gaze. He pried her pinky away from her palm and placed the blade beneath the ridge of her nail.

"I said no!" she shrieked.

The blade pierced the sensitive flesh beneath

her nail.

Tears stung her eyes. She didn't flinch for fear any movement would drive the knife into her nail bed. Gnashing her teeth, she glared at him. "I'm cooperating."

"You're denying everything," he said coolly. But the current of evil running through his eyes struck her. "Last question to see if you're lying."

Dana's pulse roared in her ears. What the . . . ? How—

"How close are you and Zain?"

She frowned. Moisture rolled from her brow to sting her eyes. "I don't know what you mean."

"Are you fucking him?" he demanded.

Confusion held her tongue in its grasp. What the hell did her relationship with Zain have to do with anything, and how would he know if she was lying? He could be bluffing. But if he wasn't and she lied, he'd rip off her fingernails—and then worse.

Her chest squeezed out a breath. Indecision momentarily paralyzed her.

He drove the knife beneath her nail and lifted. She let out a scream. The sharp metal peeled back her delicate nail, and hot, throbbing pain followed. He stopped, her nail half lifted from her flesh.

"Stop! Please, just stop." Dana withered in his hold, her body limp and sweating, her chest heaving.

His mouth curved in a satisfied smirk. "Answer

me."

Tears spilled onto her cheeks. Every instinct told her this wasn't the question to lie about. But for some reason, whether she'd slept with Zain or not was important. And if that detail could hang Zain . . . She wouldn't take the risk. Not with his life. "No. No, I didn't sleep with him." She practically whispered the words, damn near begging her captor to believe her.

The man's gaze darkened. "That's a fucking lie." He ripped the knife back, tearing the nail from its bed. Pain spread through her body like fire. Black-and-white lights blipped in front of her eyes. Her bloody fingernail danced across the cement.

He dropped her fingers, and she covered her injured hand, rocking and howling, her cries pitiful and deranged. He grabbed her arms again, and she screamed from the depths of her soul before kicking and thrashing, but the fight was no use. He had her wrists bound again in seconds.

He let her go, and she collapsed onto the floor, her senses overloaded. Dana was barely aware that he'd stood. Was barely aware of the sound of the door locking behind him.

With her body folded over, she closed her eyes and dragged in mouthfuls of oxygen. Each breath was excruciating. Bile sat at the back of her throat, hot and filling her mouth with acidity. She squeezed her fingers until she feared her bones might snap. Only the intense pressure lessened the pain.

She stayed like that for minutes or hours. Time grew legs and ran away from her. When her heart rate returned to a normal-ish level and she was able to hold up her head, she sat.

A fog settled around her as she stared at the empty room. He'd caught her in a lie, but before she could attempt to piece together what that meant, she had to do something about her finger. She'd need the use of her hands to escape or fight.

Lifting the hem of her shirt, she brought the material to her teeth and bit down. She gnawed until she managed to get her canine tooth into the fibers of the clothing. With a small hole made, she tugged the material. The shirt ripped. She worked quickly to pull off a strip along the bottom.

Sitting against the wall she took several deep breaths. She'd have to look at her finger to dress it, and the thought of seeing her nail missing made her head swim.

You can do this. You have to.

She trembled as she lifted her hand and un-locked her fist. Pain blasted though her nerve endings. She bit back a scream as she examined her pinky. Blood coated the end of her finger where her nail should be. The exposed flesh was raw and pulsating. A barely audible wail sounded from her lips as she fought to wrap the injured extremity. She needed something to prevent infection, but there was nothing else she could do.

As it stood, she'd be dead before infection set in.

She had to push that thought from her mind. If she crumbled now, she wouldn't have a shot at survival. Closing her eyes, she pictured Zain's face.

His eyes. Those amber hues had stolen her heart the moment she saw his case file. Their depths were so raw and dangerously inviting that even in an image she'd been drawn to him.

The picture was one thing; the real man another. When he'd rescued her in the cave, she'd both feared and pitied him. He'd been so withdrawn, so achingly lost that all she'd wanted was to unravel his suffering. To shoulder some of it. To hold this mammoth of a man who'd appeared to have lost his heart.

She couldn't have been more wrong. Zain wasn't a man to pity. He'd struggled. There was no doubt about that. He'd seen and done things that the average person wouldn't survive—but that's what made him the unyielding force he was.

The man who, once again, would come through for her. He hadn't let her die in the cave, had shielded her from a bomb, had protected her with his life without question. Wherever Zain was now, he was moving heaven and earth to find her.

She had to do everything possible to help him succeed. Because she wouldn't allow Zain to carry another ounce of guilt or pain.

All she had to do was stay alive and make it easy for him to find her.

To start, she had to figure out who was behind this in the first place. She replayed her captor's questions about her relationship with Zain.

Why would that matter? What piece did their involvement hold in this puzzle?

It shouldn't matter if they'd slept together, but for some messed-up reason it did . . .

Her brain raced, trying to make sense of the mess, just as it had when Zain first kissed her. She'd thought he'd fallen for her, but he'd only wanted to fool Ali into—

"Oh my god," she whispered. Ali was involved. Had to be. He was the only one who had a shred of proof regarding her intimacy with Zain.

That was how her captor knew she'd lied. He'd tested her and she'd failed. But what did Ali want with her? He wanted to kill her, of course. But what information did he want about Zain's mission?

Considering she knew very little about Zain's objective overseas, she wouldn't figure that out. If Zain didn't piece together Ali's involvement, he wouldn't find her. She had to secure her escape.

And fast.

"HANG ON A fucking minute," Rami cautioned. "You're gonna blow this."

But Zain couldn't contain his fury. Heat, scalding and lethal, burned his extremities. He'd been lied to. He'd been used. And now, those same cocksuckers had gone after Dana.

An innocent person in all this shit.

Zain paced the boardroom. The space was too small, and the walls and ceiling moved closer and closer to him, containing him in a box no bigger than a prison cell. He pressed his forefingers to his temples and closed his eyes over the roaring of blood against his eardrums. "Where'd you get this information?" he asked Ghost.

"Well, you're not going to believe this, but Ali is an informant for the CIA."

Zain blinked. "What? How do you know?"

Ghost sat and laced his fingers behind his head. "I have an intel guy in Afghanistan—"

"Who?" Zain demanded. He wanted names and he wanted answers.

"He's the same colleague I called when Dana was attacked. He's the best of the best. Hacker extraordinaire. He worked government-level jobs until they couldn't afford him."

"So how'd he find out about Ali?"

"Ali's phone records can be traced right to Langley."

Zain snorted. That was pretty fucking damning. The revelation sat like battery acid in his stomach. He couldn't piece shit together fast enough, not when he needed this information yesterday and his mind couldn't get over the fucking shock of how royally he'd been fucked.

"Ali was ordered to arrange the bombing of your SUV on the way to the airport. No surprise. But Maxine ordered the hit."

Rage prickled in his eye sockets. He balled his hands into fists. That fucking bitch. She'd lied about everything. Tricked him. And gone after Dana. "I don't understand," he growled. "Why do this? Why go after her? Dana knew nothing. Hell, I fucking knew nothing other than that they wanted to get to Jabar. Hardly something to kill a civilian over."

Ghost's hardened face was unreadable. "There's more."

Zain continued pacing. He couldn't keep still. Couldn't contain himself another goddamn minute let alone listen to facts that were tearing his life apart. But he had to. He'd walk through a mine-field and back if it meant they'd find Dana. "Tell me."

Ghost rocked forward in the chair and the metal squeaked. He rested his arms on the table. "This is gonna be hard to hear, but you need to know."

Zain froze. A low buzz of warning sounded in his ears.

"Before the CIA recruited you, a hospital in Afghanistan—can't remember the city name—was bombed. A lot of innocent people died."

Zain's head bobbed with a mind of its own. "I

was there. We saw the bombing. The news reported that Jaysh issued the attack . . ." His throat became scratchy as memories assaulted him. "It was the CIA. But it was an accident."

Slowly, Ghost shook his head. "It wasn't an accident. The hit was planned, and that's why your entire crew was killed."

Zain bolted toward Ghost, and Rami's hand caught his shoulder. He shook off his brother's hold and refocused on Ghost. "What the hell are you talking about?"

Ghost's emotionless eyes met his. "Think about it. What's the likelihood only one of you would survive? The CIA needed you. Only you had the capabilities to infiltrate Jaysh."

Zain shook his head. "I don't understand what you're saying."

Ghost sighed. "My guy dug up classified CIA documents detailing the attack on your unit," his voice lowered, as if the details were too heavy to speak boldly. "They made sure every single one of 'em died but you. Fed you the story that Jaysh hit you with an IED when it was really them."

Reality crushed Zain down. He brought his knuckles to his chest to erase the burning sensation, but it didn't help. Like ash falling from an inferno, memories fluttered into place.

His fellow soldiers had asked a lot of questions about the hospital bombing. Zain had been on the ground but hadn't witnessed it as closely as the others. A few days later, their trucks were hit with the IED.

And Zain had been rescued.

In his mind, the horrific scene had mostly been filled with blank space, but he remembered certain clips. Remembered the shrill, piercing pain. He'd wanted to die just to escape the noise.

He'd suffered a head injury and had been in and out of consciousness until medics arrived. In his moments of consciousness, he saw deceased soldiers. Some were so severely mutilated that death was imminent.

But George . . . he'd been alive. Seemingly un-scathed compared to the others. In the hospital, when Zain asked doctors about George, he was told he'd suffered a bullet in the lung and hadn't survived surgery. Maxine had given Zain the same story.

But that's not how he remembered it. George's death had sat like cement on Zain's mind. It just hadn't fit.

Now it fucking did. "George Harrow. Was there any mention of him?"

Ghost's eyes narrowed. "George's records stood out to me. His file was missing a lot of documentation about his medical state when he was found, and about the efforts made to ensure his survival. I'd bet anything his files were fabricat-ed and he was murdered in the hospital."

His senses tilted. Zain hung his head, his hands

still braced on the tabletop. Shudders shook his shoulders. Trapped emotions rose from his gut. Hate burned his eyes. He'd fucking kill them all—after he exposed them.

His brother's hands landed on his shoulders, firm and intrusive. "Dude. Listen to me."

Zain's breath came hard and heavy through his nose, almost drowning out Rami's voice.

"Come on. Work with me here."

Zain lowered his hands and met Rami's gaze. "They're going to kill her." The words came out weak. Broken. Emotion pressed against Zain's sinuses, and he blinked away what moisture came forth.

Rami didn't blink. His brother's blue eyes, so damn much like their father's, were like a balm around Zain's shredded heart.

"She doesn't deserve this," he continued.

Rami nodded. "I know. I know." He gripped Zain's shoulders harder. "You need to stay strong. We're ahead of them. They don't know we figured it out. We've gotta play this right."

Zain pressed his tongue to the roof of his mouth. He couldn't play this game when his head was about to explode. Not when his world teetered. Not when the very ground he stood on was falling beneath him.

Zain shook off Rami's hold. "If I call Maxine and tell her I figured it out, she'll just deny it and hide Dana's body."

A cold, bitterness filled Rami's eyes. "She won't get away with this. I fucking promise you."

Whether she got away with it or not didn't matter right now. He didn't want to avenge Dana's death—he wanted to take her home.

"When were you going to tell us you were CIA?" Ghost asked, his tone chilly.

"Dude," Rami said. "Fuck off and just work on finding Dana."

Ghost scoffed and left the room.

"Ignore him," Rami said calmly. "We've got a lead now."

Zain rubbed the back of his neck and leaned against the wall. As far as the CIA was concerned, Dana was a liability. A loose end. She'd seen too much.

All along he'd been worried the terrorists had Dana, but the real perpetrator was even more terrifying. He shook his brother's arm. "The CIA can't be bought, but they can be blackmailed."

CHAPTER 23

D ANA KEPT HER back against the wall and her knees pulled into her chest while she searched the ceiling and walls of her basement cell. Tremors took hold of her body. Her teeth chattered. But she couldn't fall apart. Her captor would be back. He hadn't gotten the information he wanted, and he'd do far worse to get her to talk.

She refocused her attention on her surroundings. She was almost certain there weren't any cameras. Either way, she had to be careful. The guy likely assumed she was incapacitated. But now more than ever, she was fueled to fight. She had training. She could take him.

He'd bound her hands again, but she'd been a shaking, screeching mess when he'd done it, so the rope wasn't as secure as it'd been before. Until she found a weapon or a way out, she'd keep her hands tied in case he came back.

Dana got to her feet and the room swayed. She

leaned against the wall to prevent herself from toppling over. Just standing made her leg muscles scream and burn. She closed her eyes and took several deep breaths until the ache in her limbs abated. Pushing away from the wall, she moved around the perimeter.

The cement walls were bare, and the odd chunk was missing. Even if she found a tool, trying to dig through cinderblock would be useless. She cast her gaze toward the window just above her head. It was now midmorning. If it weren't for a piece of plywood against the glass, the sun would shine through brightly.

Dana inched closer to the window and examined the plywood. It wasn't nailed to anything, just rested against the glass. She turned around. There wasn't any furniture in the room for her to stand on. She stifled a growl of frustration. Then she spotted a bucket in a corner.

She crossed the room and peered into the bucket to find it empty. Thank god. Her overactive imagination had envisioned all kinds of horrors that would have haunted her for the rest of her life. She stalked away from the corner, gaining more clarity with every step.

This was what she needed. To move her body and stimulate her muscles to push out the shock. She sucked in a long, deep breath. The thick, damp air made the back of her throat itch, but she couldn't think about the mold and mildew she was inhaling. She reached a small closet—more like a nook, as it didn't have door.

Inside was a wet/dry vacuum—as if anyone had ever cleaned the place—and a pile of towels. Perhaps there'd recently been a leak. That would explain the wet towels and floor.

She knelt and grabbed the material awkwardly with her bound wrists. A sheet of plastic was crumpled beneath. What the heck? She unfolded the plastic and her heart stopped.

A burnt-red color stained it. Her heart slowed, and the sheet fell from her fingertips. She backed away from the closet, her heart hammering. The plastic had been used to catch blood. The water to mop up the mess.

Oh god. Oh god.

Someone had died here.

Panic kept her on her knees on the cool, hard floor. The muscles in her chest squeezed tighter and tighter, as if a boa constrictor circled her. Her pulse beat relentlessly against her forehead, and the sound was deafening.

Get a grip. If you don't escape, your blood will be on there too.

Tears leaked from her eyes, and Dana wiped them away with her fingertips. Okay, nothing of use in the closet. She steered herself in the other direction and studied the wall. There had to be something in here, dammit. Anything.

She turned her gaze back to the corner. The

bucket would be useful to reach the window. If she could wiggle out of the ropes around her wrists, she could escape. She wasn't going to find anything sharp.

Bringing the rope to the light coming in from around the plywood, she examined her restraints. The rope was wound around her arms a few times, and the loop on top seemed looser than the others. Using her teeth, she pulled at the slack piece and tried to work it over her hands. Her jaw screamed as she clamped down and pulled.

Minutes later, sweat trickled down the back of her neck. She stopped to catch her breath, panting heavily as she cursed the stupid thick material. Giving her mouth a break, she wrenched her arms apart. She twisted and turned her hands. The rope burned her skin but she didn't stop.

She let her arms drop to her legs, her chest heaving. Her pinkie screamed and the skin on her wrists stung. Lifting her hands once again, she gently moved her arms. The rope had loosened. A thrill raced through her.

Yes!

Once she had the bindings off—

Footsteps stomped on the floor above. Dana tilted back her head as dust particles fluttered down like tiny warning flags.

Her pulse skidded to a stop, and the frigid hands of fear circled her throat.

★　★　★

"HOLD ON A minute." Rami covered Zain's phone with his hand before he could dial Maxine's number. "What the hell are you gonna say?"

Zain shooed away his brother's hold and clamped his hand around the device. His gaze pulsed with ferocity. He'd once respected the oath of secrecy he'd taken, but that was blown to hell now. The CIA had killed innocent people, murdered his unit. And now they had Dana.

A week ago, he'd have known how to tackle this situation. But that was before he'd met Dana.

Before he'd endangered her. Before they'd fucking taken her.

Before he'd fallen for her.

Not only was Dana—a goddamn innocent in all of this—in danger, but he also had the moral responsibility of exposing the information Ghost had uncovered.

The CIA had murdered his fellow unit members, and he wouldn't stop until he'd avenged their callous deaths.

"I'll tell her if she doesn't give Dana back then everything I know will be on the news." He reached for the sheets of paper Ghost had brought in moments before and snapped pictures of each.

It might not be enough.

"Maxine told me Jaysh was planning a massive terrorist attack," he continued. "That's why I was supposed to locate their leader, Jabar. I was scheduled to meet him just days after Dana arrived. If I'd made it to the meeting and gotten the information they wanted, she'd have sent in a team to kill Jabar—and she'd have fucking murdered me along with him."

Rami's expression turned grave. "I'm sure that's how things would've gone. The mission would've been a success, the CIA heroes, and you a prisoner casualty. Easy out."

Zain nodded. "Right. Only I fucked everything up by leaving. Not only did they not find Jabar, but I'm alive to speak about the hospital bombing and the men in my platoon who survived the IED."

"Maybe you shouldn't show your hand," Rami said. "We've already got a name on the assassin who took Dana. If we can track his plates and find out where he took her, we could take this a different route."

Zain pinched the bridge of his nose. He couldn't fucking think. Inside his head a clock ticked, warning him that he was running out of time. "We're damned if we do and damned if we don't. If Maxine sees I'm a threat, she might let Dana go."

A cloud of worry crossed his brother's face. "Jesus, man. This is fucking dangerous."

He nodded. One wrong move and this whole thing could blow up in his face. He pulled up Maxine's private number and hit the call button.

The line rang in his ear, the strident tone enough to make him want to beat his head against the wall.

"Zain, why are you calling me?" Maxine's voice was low, her irritation clearly high.

"I think you fucking know why."

A long pause. "I assure you I don't. Nor do I appreciate your tone. I'm doing everything I can to help find your girl—"

"You killed my unit." The resolute accusation fell like lead from his mouth.

Maxine's sharp breath whistled in his ear. "I don't know what you're talking about."

"Don't deny it. You're wasting my time, and Dana's. I have proof the CIA hit the hospital. You admitted as much to me after my rescue, but everything else you said was a lie."

"Zain—"

"You killed innocent people. Recruited me and lied to me so I'd do your bidding. I'm going to expose you—unless you bring me Dana."

Silence.

Zain clicked the speaker icon and quickly sent Maxine a text containing one of the documents from Ghost.

"I want confirmation you have Dana. Now." He had her in a corner. The sooner she knew he wasn't bluffing, the better.

"How did you get this information?" she screeched, her tone obliterating any doubt left in

Zain's mind. He could practically see her stern exterior melting into a puddle of makeup and hairspray.

"I have my sources. You've got five minutes to give me proof you have Dana or this, along with several other documents, is sent to a reporter."

"You have no idea what you're dealing with. You think—"

"Four minutes." He hung up.

He set his phone on the desk and cradled his head in his hands. Despite his bluster, sweat trickled down his face and anxiety made his stomach roil.

Jesus.

He'd just thrown all his eggs in one basket in the hopes the damn thing wasn't already on fire. Lowering his hands he lifted his head. One look at Rami told him everything he needed to know. Rami's face had lost a bit of color, his brow was tense, and disbelief flashed in his eyes.

"That was one ballsy move, dude." Rami's tone lacked reproach. Instead, it held a hint of awe.

"I didn't know what to do. If we're wrong and they don't have Dana, then this shouldn't blow back on me. But considering the evidence, chances they're not involved are nil."

Rami gave a sharp nod. "Agreed. Given the circumstances I think you played this well. Better than I would've." He nudged Zain with his shoulder. "It's gonna be okay. We've got a whole team working round the clock. I bet they'll have something concrete in a few hours."

Zain curled his lip. "She won't live that long."

"You don't know that." He rocked on his heels. "I never told you about how I met Ivy."

Zain cocked his head. "Tell me."

"I rescued her from human traffickers. If it weren't for Gigi's insistence, though, I never would've taken the job. Backcountry was fairly new at the time. We were growing but nowhere near search and rescue." He wet his lips and swiveled his head toward the door.

When he looked back at Zain, his eyes were filled with sadness. "Had I not taken that job, no one would've found her. She was in Mexico being held by a cartel. Every fucking day I kick myself for what could have happened had I not followed my gut." He placed a hand on the back of Zain's neck and brought his forehead to rest on his brother's. "You'll bring her back, man. Have faith. You've got all of us behind you."

Desperation moistened Zain's eyes. If he lost his footing now, he'd fall to his knees in despair. No, he had to stay standing. "Thanks, Rami."

Ring, ring

Zain's phone vibrated on the boardroom table. A text lit the screen.

Holy shit.

★ ★ ★

METAL TINKLED IN the lock, and the door swung open before Dana could steel her nerves or summon an ounce of false courage. Her captor stormed into the room, his ominous eyes landing on her with disgust.

She scampered backward until her shoulders smacked into the cement wall. Her elbows flanked either side of her knees, and her bound hands hung in front of her. She wanted to scream and fight him, but she wasn't prepared.

That said, now she knew what he was capable of. And if he came after her fingernails again, or even a lock of her damn hair, she'd lose it. She'd rather die fighting than have her body parts ripped off.

He stalked forward and Dana began to shake. He lowered himself down to her level, only a few feet away, and her breath hitched in the back of her throat. She opened her lips to demand what he wanted but nothing came out.

She stared at this demon incarnate and clung to a prayer—surely only Jesus could banish something so evil.

He smiled. The lifting of his lips crinkled his eyes. "How's your finger?"

She squeezed her hands together. If he touched her, she'd strike. "About as ugly as you now."

His expression froze, and his blue eyes swirled

with ice. Then his face cracked, and he burst out laughing. "I'm going to enjoy breaking every bone in your body."

She glowered at him. "Why keep me here? What's the point?"

"The point is to cut out your fucking throat once I get the information I need from it."

"I told you everything I know."

He snarled. "Bullshit."

"So then kill me." She shrugged. Antagonizing him probably wasn't smart, but there was a reason he'd paused their little interrogation, and the more knowledge she gained, the better off she'd be.

"I want nothing more." He worked his jaw. "It's not my call, though. Not yet anyway."

She tilted her head an inch. "Who do you work for?"

His smile spread. "Powerful people, baby." He reached into his pocket.

A gasp lodged itself at the base of her tongue, and she lifted her arms in front of her face, anticipating the dreaded knife.

"Put your fucking hands down before I chop off a finger."

Vomit inched up her esophagus but she dropped her hands. This wasn't a man who didn't follow through.

Instead of meeting the blade of his knife, she found herself staring at the lens of his phone camera. "Say cheese."

He snapped a picture, glanced down, and tapped the screen.

"Who'd you send that to?"

He smirked. "None of your business. But guess what? That was the before picture."

Before Dana could grapple with his meaning, his knuckles slammed across her cheekbone. The blow sent her reeling to the floor. A low buzz sounded in her ears, drowning out the abusive words he spat.

She blinked away the crushing pain and lifted herself onto her arms. Slowly, her hearing returned, but vomit threatened to meet the pile of it staring at her.

"Got a present for ya." He opened his fist.

Her fingernail sat in his palm. He dropped it in front of her, and Dana threw up violently on the cement.

He shook his head and spat. "Nasty."

She cringed and lifted her hands, anticipating another blow, but only the sounds of the door slamming shut and the lock turning reached her ears.

They might as well have been dirt on her coffin.

CHAPTER 24

ZAIN PICKED UP his phone. Time slowed to the rhythm of his barely there pulse. The atmosphere in the room crackled with tension. The device sat in his hand like a grenade. Lighter but more lethal.

Only a few minutes had passed since he hung up on Maxine. He'd either have an unpleasant, threatening message waiting for him, or proof they had Dana. He wasn't ready for either.

Even Rami seemed to hold his breath while Zain opened the message.

He swiped to see the text. A small grainy image had been sent from an undisclosed phone number. But he'd recognize the face anywhere. Dana's drilling blue eyes struck him.

He enlarged the picture, and Rami leaned in. "Shit. Holy shit. They have her."

Believing they had her was one thing—seeing the proof was an entirely different ball game. Scalding pain spread through his chest, cinching around his heart. Dana's eyes were puffy and red, as if she'd been crying, and her skin was sallow and almost fucking translucent—she was so pale. Even her lips lacked color. Her wide, terrified blues screamed that she'd already endured too much.

The constriction in his chest intensified. He dropped his phone on the desk and tunneled his hand through his hair. "Fuck!" He paced, his mind whirring faster than an engine.

Rami's pained gaze followed Zain. "I know it's scary seeing her like that, but she's alive, man."

"I won't believe that until I hear her voice."

"Fair. But let's work with the information we have."

The shrill ring of his phone ripped through the air. Unknown caller. Without hesitation, he snatched the device and answered. "Yeah," he demanded.

"You have your proof," said Maxine. She was likely calling from a secure line. "Now I want to know who gave you that information and how."

"You're not in a position to make demands."

"Neither are you." Each word was punched out harder than the last.

"I'll tell you my source when Dana's safely with me. For all I know, you took that picture then killed her." A beat passed. "Why'd you do it? If you'd left things alone, I never would've looked so hard at the bombings. Never would have discovered what you'd done to my unit."

Silence stretched for miles. "This wasn't personal."

"It's very fucking personal."

Maxine sighed. "I'm just doing my job."

"Roger ordered the hit on Dana?"

She paused, seemingly weighing her words. "I don't make those kinds of decisions."

"But Roger does."

No response.

A few seconds ticked by. "If you want the woman returned in one piece, I suggest you send me every shred of information you have, as well as how you obtained it."

"I'm not negotiating until—"

"This isn't a negotiation. It's an order. And if we find out Dana knows more than you've disclosed, your entire family will suffer the consequences. You have thirty minutes to send me everything you have, including your source."

The line went dead.

"Goddammit!" Zain roared.

The door opened, and August and Taschen walked in. "What's going on?" Taschen's voice shook as if he feared the worst.

Zain couldn't respond. He couldn't do a fucking thing but pace. There was no way out of this. He wouldn't fall for Maxine's bullshit. They'd already tried to kill Dana twice—the likelihood of them letting her go *after* they'd kidnapped her and he had proof was zero.

If he gave Maxine everything Ghost had obtained, she'd still turn around and kill Dana. He had to find Dana without Maxine's help.

But Dana could be anywhere by now.

Grabbing his phone again, he brought up the picture of Dana while Rami explained to Taschen and August what had unfolded.

Their angry voices gave Zain a little peace. For some reason, knowing he had a herd of pissed-off alphas on his side gave him hope.

Staring at the image of Dana brought fresh emotion to his eyes. He wanted to reach through the phone and rip off her bindings. To pull her through the screen and save her from another second of agony.

I'm coming, baby. I promise I'll find you.

Dragging his gaze from her haunting face, he examined the room around her. She sat in what appeared to be a basement. There was a window about four feet above the ground and a piece of plywood in front of it. Cement walls boxed her in, and she sat on an ugly brown blanket.

There wasn't anything else in the picture except a filthy floor and cinderblock walls.

Come on, give me a clue.

Taschen strode up and leaned over Zain's shoulder. "Jesus." He snatched the phone and gazed down at the photo of his sister. "Those fucking bastards."

August appeared and he, too, looked at the

image. "Send that to Ghost."

Taschen downloaded the image and forwarded it. "I don't know what information he can get from this. It's just a basement."

"You'd be surprised," August said. "Not many newer homes in the Seattle area have below-grade spaces. I'd say this house was built before the eighties."

"Yeah," Zain said, "but I suspect a lot of houses were built before the eighties. I see where you're going with this, but it's not enough." He broke away from the group and made his way down the hall to Ghost's office.

The door sat partially open, and Zain knocked on the doorframe.

"C'min."

Zain entered the brightly lit space. A black wrought iron desk with a glass top was in the center of the room, and a large window ate up the wall adjacent to where Ghost sat behind his computer.

Two brown leather chairs were positioned in front of the desk, and a tall indoor plant was nestled in the corner—probably thanks to Pearl; Ghost didn't strike him as the type of guy who'd keep anything but himself alive.

"I got the text," he said grimly, and motioned for Zain to sit.

"Think you can find anything from the picture to give us a location?"

He lifted the corner of his lip. "Nah, not by itself."

Zain's shoulders slumped.

"But take a look at this." He turned his computer monitor in Zain's direction. "I've been tracing the vehicle. It entered a neighborhood in the northeast."

Zain straightened. "That's an older area."

Ghost's eyes flashed. "Exactly. I think we're onto something, but finding the correct house will be tricky."

"What about tracing the phone number?"

Ghost straightened. "Wasn't the photo sent from your lady at the CIA?"

"I don't know. She contacted me from an unknown number, and the text also came from an unknown number. But she wouldn't be with Dana. When I called her about ten minutes ago, I reached her through her private line at the office in Langley."

Ghost massaged his chin. "No shit."

Zain opened the text and handed over his phone so Ghost could analyze the sender. "Can you trace it?"

He swished his lips to the side. "It'll be tough. I'm sure they have the best firewalls in place, but I'll try." He glanced up, and Zain read hesitation in Ghost's expression. "Not sure if I'll be fast enough, though."

Zain encased his impatience. "Get started. This

is the only lead we have right now."

Ghost began tapping on Zain's phone. "And what are we gonna do in the meantime?" he asked, without looking up.

"Try to buy some time from Maxine."

Brick entered the room. "I think I can help with that."

★   ★   ★

DANA GULPED DOWN a mouthful of saliva and blood. The pain in her cheek pulsed across her head. With her hands braced beneath her, she scooched so she sat against the wall again. She was out of time and out of information. She grabbed the rope in her teeth and yanked until her jaw screamed. Panting, she stopped and jerked her arms apart until the loose loop of rope gave way some more. If she could stretch the loop over her hands, she could remove the rest a lot more easily.

Summoning strength, she caught the rope in her mouth again and tugged. Pulling her arms downward and away from her face, she had the loop over her hands a minute later.

She let out a shaky laugh. Holy shit. She was getting the hell out of here. Unraveling one loop after another, she shook her hands free. The binding dropped to the ground near the two puddles of vomit. She opened and closed her hands, pumping blood to her extremities.

She got to her feet, and her head swam. Steadying herself on the wall, she waited for the dizziness to pass. After a very early morning, being tased, vomiting twice with nothing in her stomach, losing a fingernail, and being hit in the head, she wasn't in very good shape.

But adrenaline warmed her skin. Even the pain in her head lessened as she crossed the room and snagged the pail from the corner. She kicked aside the blanket on the floor and turned the bucket upside down. Hanging tightly to the windowsill, she stood on the bottom of the bucket.

She grabbed the edge of the plywood, which was about ten by thirteen inches, took it down, and leaned it against the wall carefully so it didn't fall and alert her captor. As she stared out the window, the sunlight made her squint.

A large crack split the glass. If she tried to open the window, the whole thing would break, possibly causing a lot of noise—not to mention making getting out of the window difficult. She'd end up filleting her flesh.

She examined the old single-pane glass. Breaking it the rest of the way would be easy, but messy. She bent down, grabbed the blanket from the floor, and wrapped it around her fist. Carefully, she knocked along the crack. The glass split even more, and a long triangular piece fell onto the sill.

The sight of the jagged edge made her ripple with excitement. She had a weapon now. Carefully, she picked up the glass, stepped off the bucket, and unraveled the blanket from her fist. After laying the glass on the material, she got back on the bucket and returned the plywood to its position in front of the window. Finally, she took the bucket back to the corner of the room.

She swallowed and stared at the glass. Her only chance at escape was to strike him hard enough to kill. His throat would be the best spot, uncovered and delicate. She picked up the blanket and wrapped it around the wide base of the shard then held out the sharp end.

Oh, yeah. That could do some damage.

Wariness filled her. The moments ahead could determine whether she lived or died. Whether she ever saw Zain again. Her heart swelled as she brought up Zain's face in her mind's eye.

If she didn't succeed, she might not survive this. She'd never be held by him again. Never feel the comfort of his warm body or his gentle hands. He was everything her heart needed, and had she realized it days ago, she'd have told him that.

She'd have risked everything. She'd have even risked hearing he didn't feel the same way—because now she stared death in the face.

Now, she might never see him again. Never see her family, get married, or have children. Dammit, there was still so much she wanted out of life. Starting with Zain.

Swallowing, she gripped the wrapped end of the glass tighter and slammed her shoulder into the door. "Let me out!" she screamed.

Nothing.

Bang!

She struck the old wood again. The hinges jumped. Again, nothing. Great, the asshole had probably left her here to die.

"Hey, moron! I have to pee!"

Bang!

This time the door threatened to give way. Footsteps slammed on the floor above, angry and hurried.

Dana's lungs expanded and contracted rapidly as he came charging down the stairs. She stood behind the door, her breath coming hard and fast. She pictured his height, envisioned where to strike. If she missed, this could go very, very wrong.

Keys clanked. She gripped the glass, the sharp edges piercing the thin blanket. The door swung open and he stepped through. He came to a halt when he saw the empty spot beneath the window.

Dana lunged and let out a shrill scream, the cry of desperation shaking her vocal cords. He jumped and turned toward her as she drove the sharp end of the blade toward his thick neck. The glass moved across his throat, not penetrating.

Still, blood spurted from his neck, and he clamped his hand over the wound. "Fuck!" he howled.

Another scream wrenched from her throat as she dodged around him. He caught her arm before she made it through the door.

"Fucking bitch!" he spat.

She jammed the glass at him again, and this time the shard went right through the soft tissue near his armpit. He hissed in pain, spit flying from his mouth. She sliced downward and blood rushed forward.

His arm dropped, and he gasped and sputtered as he stared down at the glass wedged in his flesh. Dana turned and ran for the stairs. Her feet slapped against the wooden steps, and her heart pounded in her ears. The top of the stairs seemed to stretch farther and farther away.

She heard movement on the cement downstairs. A cry filled the back of her throat but she gulped it down, not wanting to waste an ounce of energy.

She slammed open the heavy wooden door at the top of the stairs. Her foot caught on the step and her hands and knees banged against the hardwood floor.

Her assailant's footsteps pounded behind her. She threw a glance over her shoulder. A menacing scowl folded his brow, and his eyes glittered with loathing.

The scream tore itself from her lungs before she could stop it. She hustled to her feet and slammed the door shut, hurtling herself away. She only made it a few paces before it banged open as her captor flung himself onto the main floor.

Dana scampered down the hall, her brain racing as she tried to locate a way out. The long corridor led her into a small kitchen. A back door waited at the bottom of two stairs. She rushed toward it and yanked it open.

Warm fresh air hit her face. Her feet landed on the concrete stoop. She opened her mouth—

A rough force dragged her backward by her hair. She gasped and twisted against the searing pain. Her tailbone smashed against the floor.

Her captor leaned down, his face inches from hers. "You're gonna wish you hadn't fucking done that."

Tears streaked her face. She clawed at the hand holding her hair, but he didn't let go. Blood oozed down his neck and poured from his armpit. He'd ripped out the glass. His top lip lifted to reveal his front teeth. "Time to send your boyfriend a finger."

"No!" Dana threw herself toward the door.

He slammed it shut in her face, nearly taking off her hand. His arm hooked around her waist and hauled her in the air. She kicked and bucked, but he carried her as if her strikes were no more harmful than a gnat.

Terror seized every atom in her body. She let out a shriek to shake the heavens.

The sound reverberated off the walls, echoing through the chambers of her hell.

CHAPTER 25

ZAIN FOLLOWED BRICK to his office. Staying mobile made him feel less out of control. "What do you have?"

Brick closed the door and motioned to his desk. Like the offices of everyone else on the team, Brick's held personal touches. The walls were painted black and had wood accents. A potted ficus stood near the window. Unlike Ghost's, this one appeared artificial. A large bookcase filled with books and artifacts sat behind the desk chair.

"I've been thinking. Maxine wants information. So give it to her."

He folded his arms. "If I give her what she wants," he said with annoyance, enunciating each word, "she'll kill Dana." Jesus, was this what he'd been called in here for? To be told to cave and lose whatever bargaining chips he had?

"I say we play offense. Tell her you got the information from a mole and if she wants it, she'd better produce Dana."

He twisted his lips to the side. Maxine would likely believe a mole existed, given that high-level information had been shared. She'd still want the proof, though. He'd have to find a way to make her hand over Dana first.

"What do you think?" Brick pressed.

He nodded slowly. He had maybe ten minutes before Maxine's time limit expired. She'd already refused to give him Dana—instead, she'd made more threats. He had to play this right and get Maxine where he wanted. Besides dead. That would come after Dana was home.

"I think she's going to agree to anything and then fuck us," Zain said. "That's what I think."

Brick smirked. "Did they pay you big money in the CIA to figure out simple shit like that?"

Zain chuckled. It was the closest he'd gotten to a genuine laugh all day. "Okay, brainiac. What's the drill then?"

"*The drill* is you get Maxine to agree to a phone call with Dana. Leverage whatever the fuck you can, but get on the damn phone with her. I'll do my best to trace the call. Maxine knows we've got intel, but she doesn't know the skills Backcountry has at their fingertips."

"How long do I need to keep Dana on the line?"

"A minute, give or take."

He exhaled sharply. "I sure hope you can work with less than that."

"Not by much. But Dana will know what we're trying to do. She's familiar with our equipment and software. She'll keep the call going as long as possible."

Zain nodded. All along, he'd been thinking about how scared Dana must be. How alone. Hurt. He hadn't given her enough credit.

She was incredibly strong. Even in the face of terrorists, she'd kept her wits. Her smarts alone could keep her alive for a while. He just had to meet her halfway—and he'd do that if it was the last thing he did.

He pulled out his phone. "Can you tap my line and record the call?"

Brick made a face. "Toth doesn't like us to record calls. Says it won't hold up in court."

"I know we can't use it in court, but I want to make sure I can replay what she says, in case there's any indication of where they're holding Dana."

"I'm game. What Toth doesn't know won't hurt him." Brick took Zain's phone and copied some information into a program. Then, using his own cell phone, he called Zain's number and conducted a test. "There we go."

"Perfect." He called Maxine.

She answered immediately. "I see you're cooperating."

"Of course." He balled his hand into a fist at his side. "All I want is Dana. And I'm sure you want this over with too."

"I want to know your source." Her heartless tone beat through the speaker.

He paced in a small circle, his pulse pummeling against his temples. "You've got a mole, Maxine. Someone high up."

Her breath caught. "You're full of shit."

"Think about it. How would I know about the attack on my unit? I imagine something like that would be kept under tight wraps." He had to force the memory from his mind so he didn't lose his shit. He couldn't help the murdered soldiers, but he could damn well save the one person who mattered to him now—Dana.

"Who?"

"I know who, and I can prove it. But I'm not doing a damn thing until you bring Dana to me."

Silence stretched out.

"Maxine, I have enough evidence to put you away for life. You know the crimes you've committed. Give Dana up and all this goes away."

She smacked her lips. "Fine. Let me call my guy, and I'll see where he wants to meet you. But you need to give me everything. Have it all on a drive and ready to hand over when you see your girlfriend."

Excitement fissured through him. "I need to talk to Dana first. I have to be sure this isn't a setup."

She let out an exasperated sigh. "You'll receive

a call in a few minutes."

The line clicked off, and he bowed his head. Holy shit. They might just have a chance.

One minute. God, please just give me that. I'll figure out the rest.

★　★　★

DANA REACHED OVER her attacker's shoulder for the railing, and her fingers scraped the old wood. He yanked her arms away and buckled them against her side as he pounded down the stairs with her in his hold.

"Let me go!" she yelled.

He descended quickly, and the basement loomed before her. Panic frothed over her senses. She twisted and lifted her knee into his injured armpit.

He screamed and cursed, stumbling. They both slammed into the concrete, Dana landing inches away. She scrambled to her feet, but he caught her ankle before she could escape.

Her head banged against the stairs. Fingers of darkness danced in front of her closed lids, but adrenaline was quick to dispel them. Heat singed her face as she kicked at her captor.

He was too fast. Too strong. He had her in a chokehold as he hauled her to her feet. Then he shoved her toward her cell.

She gave a wail of despair. Fear electrified her senses, shutting off her awareness of the heinous words he spat against her ear. Nothing he said could make her more terrified than what she already knew—he was going to torture her.

Time to send your boyfriend a finger. His earlier promise rang in her head, and she instinctively curled her fingers into her palms. His rough hand shoved the back of her head. Dana landed against the cement wall, her shoulder taking the blow.

She sank to her haunches and watched the monster in front of her radiate with fury. Blood continued to run down his neck. The gash was thin and wide. Not deep enough or he'd be dead. But the gaping wound beneath his ripped T-shirt promised more blood loss.

Ire sparked from his hollow eyes. He still had enough energy to inflict a whole lot of pain on her.

His chest heaved, and he took a step forward.

Dana shuddered and shielded her face. Any minute he'd strike her again. He'd rip off her fingernails and then her fingers—god, maybe even her eyes.

Her body shook in waves.

"I'm going to take you apart piece by fucking piece. Then I'll soak you in acid, and nothing will be left."

Ring, ring

The screech of his cell phone made Dana jump. The loud noise was eerily familiar in such a foreign situation.

He huffed then pulled out his phone. "What?"

he snapped.

A voice drifted through the air—a woman's. Dana lowered her gaze and focused on trying to decipher the words, but they weren't clear.

"And then I can finish this?" he asked.

More chatter on the other end.

"I don't want to fucking wait," he spat.

Dana's skin burned, warning her that his gaze was still on her. She tried to make sense of what was happening.

He wasn't happy. That was obvious. Maybe this was over. Maybe Zain had come through and they'd reached an agreement.

That little glimmer of hope shone brightly, and she whispered a prayer.

He clicked off the phone. "It's your lucky day. You get a phone call."

Dana surged forward. A phone call? *Zain.* It had to be. She scanned the room, looking for some kind of clue she could give him so he'd be able to find her. But all she saw was a dank basement. Plus, if she told Zain anything specific, she'd likely be moved to a different location.

Her captor tapped his screen then spoke into the receiver. "Your request is granted. Make it quick." He passed Dana the device.

She greedily brought the phone to her ear. "Zain?"

"Yeah, baby. It's me." His smooth words rumbled through the speaker, so deep and authoritative.

She closed her eyes as she savored the sound of his voice. Tears spilled onto her cheeks, but she didn't dare waste a second to dash them away. Not when this could be the last time she ever spoke to him.

Hearing his voice made something quake inside her—a longing and desperation so strong she just wanted to disappear into it. "I'm so sorry," she choked out.

For what, she didn't know. Sorry she hadn't been more careful, maybe. Sorry she'd never told him how deep her feelings for him ran.

Sorry she wasn't coming home.

"Can he hear me?" Zain's question was low, barely audible.

"No." She glanced up at her captor. He stepped forward as if to intervene. "I'm okay. He hasn't hurt me," she quickly said. Just in case he suspected she was giving Zain clues.

She clung to the phone as though it were a lifeline. He'd have to tear it from her cold, dead hands.

"We need to keep the call going as long as possible. Do anything to make that happen, okay?"

Hope flared inside her. He was working on finding her. She just had to help him. "I miss you too." She wet her lips.

"All right." Asshole swirled his finger in the air. "Wrap it up."

"Are you okay?"

Zain's heavy tone made her lips tremble.

"I want to come home," she wailed. She flicked her gaze to her captor's bored face. "Please tell my family I love them."

"You'll tell them yourself. I promise."

She closed her eyes, holding that pledge close to her heart. "I—"

"That's enough." Asshole moved forward and reached for the phone.

Dana dodged out of his grasp. "No! I'm not done. Zain—"

He seized her arm, and his fingers bit into her flesh. She cried out. Zain's furious shouts bellowed through the phone. She needed to do as Zain said—keep the call going.

Grabbing the device from her fingers with her free hand before he could tear it away, she slid the phone as far as she could.

The device skittered across the concrete floor and into the hallway. "Christ!" He shoved her toward the ground.

She flung herself at his ankles, taking him down to the floor. "Sonofabitch!" He flung his hand backward, and his knuckles caught her mouth.

Pain exploded across her cheek. Her head shook with the force of the blow, and a high-pitched ring sounded in her ears.

Her captor pushed himself to his feet. "Fucking bitch."

She watched as he limped across the room and into the hall. He slammed the door behind him. He'd make her pay for that stunt. She just hoped to hell she'd given Zain enough time.

★ ★ ★

PRIDE COUPLED WITH fear arced through Zain. Hearing the bastard hit Dana had nearly made Zain's head explode. The whack of knuckles on skin and her sharp cry of pain would live in his mind forever.

A blow to her delicate face that never should've happened.

He'd thought it was over. That surely the call had been too short to trace. But then the crackling on the speaker and distant voices told him she'd sent the phone across the floor.

Brilliant.

If the action didn't get her killed.

He swiped his hand over his face then stared at Brick and Taschen. "Was it enough time? Did we get 'em?"

Taschen looked up, his brows raised. "We got a location."

"Yes." Zain slammed his palm against the table, making the equipment shake. He let out a loose laugh and paced a few feet. "Holy shit." He wheeled back around. "Where are they?"

"A neighborhood in the northeast." Brick turned the computer screen in Zain's direction.

He studied the little red flag on the map and snapped his fingers. "Ghost got a reading of the license plate in the same neighborhood."

"Well, now we've got a house to ambush." Taschen was on his feet. "Let's go."

Zain was one step ahead of him.

"Hang on a minute," Brick said, chasing them. Zain already had the office door open. "We need a plan. Don't forget, Maxine is waiting for the information you promised. She wants to make a trade."

Rami and August entered the hall. "What's going on?" Rami demanded. Micha, likely sensing the shift in energy, trotted down the hallway, her nails clicking on the floor as she made her way to Rami's side. He patted her head, and she sat obediently.

Zain quickly explained what had unfolded, but every second he stood there was a second wasted. A second that could determine whether he found Dana alive or dead.

August's green eyes flashed with urgency. "Sounds like we've got the fucker, but Brick's right. We can't go in half-cocked."

Rami gave a stern nod. "Don't forget, we do this shit for a living."

Zain threaded his hand through his hair. "All right then, what's the deal? Because any minute Maxine's going to call and expect me to meet her guy."

Taschen shrugged. "When Maxine calls, tell her we'll meet. We'll split into two groups. One goes to the house, the other to the meeting point. If something changes, either group can head in for reinforcement."

Rami swished his lips. "That could work."

"It's our best shot," Brick added.

"Fine." Zain didn't really give a shit what the plan was as long as they had manpower where Dana might be. "I'm going to the house now. I'll call you when I hear from Maxine."

August caught his shoulder. "Maybe Rami and I should go to the house and you wait for Maxine's call. For all we know, they could be moving Dana right now. On the off chance Maxine follows through and brings Dana to trade, you're gonna want to be there."

Indecision froze him to the spot. The muscles in his neck knotted. August made a valid suggestion, but instinct told Zain he needed to go to the house.

He'd done nothing but lead from his intuition for the past three years, and it hadn't steered him wrong. Now everything was muddled because his heart was in the goddamn way. Every thought was second-guessed, every assurance reevaluated. "I'm going to the house," he declared with conviction.

"I'm coming with you." Taschen chimed in. "Gimme a sec." He disappeared into the office and returned with an assault rifle across his chest, another in one hand, and a Glock in the other. He passed Zain the second assault rifle.

He took it eagerly. "Let's go."

"Wait," Rami called. "Take Micha."

Zain hesitated. The dog was highly skilled, but the last thing he wanted was for the sweet girl to get hurt. "Are you sure?"

"Hell yeah." Taschen grabbed Micha's leash from the wall. She immediately stood and wagged her tail. "Who's a good doggy?" he crooned. "Let's go eat some bad guys."

Micha responded with an excited bark.

They stormed through the office to the elevator. As they passed Pearl, she firmed her lips and met his stare. "Bring our girl home."

"I will," he vowed. Emotion prickled the corners of his eyes. Pearl was as sharp as a tack and had likely picked up on his connection with Dana.

Taschen jammed his finger against the button, and the elevator doors whooshed open. Micha beat them inside, and Taschen pressed the button for the garage. The cart descended.

Fire singed the back of Zain's neck. He'd been utterly useless the last couple of hours. Helpless. If it weren't for Backcountry, he wouldn't have had the resources. He would've—

He gave his head a shake. He couldn't go there. Couldn't think about how bad things could have— or would have—gotten. Right now, they had purpose. He was ahead of the fucking bastards.

A sharp ring from his pocket seized his muscles.

The elevator door opened, and he pulled out his phone as they crossed the threshold into the concrete area housing Backcountry's vehicles. According to signs throughout the space, the entire garage was for their parking alone.

"Is it her?" Taschen asked, just as Zain looked at his screen: UNKNOWN CALLER.

"Yup."

"Stick with the plan."

"No shit." He swiped to answer. "Yeah."

Taschen opened the back of a large SUV, and Micha hopped in, tail wagging ferociously. He gave her a pat on the head and she lay down on the dog mat.

"Well, you have your proof. Your girlfriend's okay."

He grunted. "Sounded like she was fucking hurt when I spoke to her."

Taschen closed the liftgate, and they stashed their guns in the back seat. "Stall," he mouthed.

He nodded. The longer it took him to agree on a meeting point, the more time they'd have to get to the house before Maxine attempted to move Dana.

"She's in one piece. I promise you that." Maxine's chilly words weren't very fucking reassuring.

Zain's temper knocked against his forehead. Fucking bitch. He opened the front passenger door and settled in the seat while Taschen got behind the wheel.

"There's something I want to know," he said, slowly, while Taschen navigated through the parking garage. He had to keep her talking as long as possible. "Why take her in the first place? Why not me?"

"That's very simple. We suspected you knew more than you let on. It's unfortunate, but loose ends can't stay loose."

"I was the loose end?" He'd never considered himself close with Maxine, but over the last three years, she'd become someone he trusted.

That's why he'd reached out to her for help at the airport in Pakistan. Why he'd called her after Dana was attacked and then taken. All the while, he'd been playing with a goddamn viper.

"It's just the way things ended up."

"You would've killed me regardless."

"Not true. When you went rogue during the mission, we suspected you'd already given up classified information."

"And Dana? You still haven't told me why you took her." It had all been spelled out for him now, but Maxine seemed to want to talk. Which worked for him.

Taschen held his phone in his hand, map open but silent as he steered through the streets.

"Really, Zain. You should understand all of this by now. We needed her to ensure your full cooperation."

"Well you fucking have it," he spat.

"Good. I'll have our guy bring her to a meeting point in an hour. How's that work for you?"

He rocked his jaw. She had no intention of delivering Dana. She'd use the opportunity to kill them all. But Maxine didn't know about the crew he had at his back. "Fine. Where?"

She rattled off a destination—a deserted path toward a waterfall forty minutes from the city. Perfect place to dump a few bodies. If only they could dump hers and not her hired help's.

"I want everything you have on a drive. And if there's any hard copies, those too."

"You have my word."

"Good. And Zain?" Her tone rang with supe-riority. "Don't cause any trouble. You know what will happen." The line went dead.

CHAPTER 26

DANA LAY ON the cold cement floor, the acidic scent of vomit close to her face. Sobs racked her shoulders.

She'd failed.

Inches from escaping and he'd caught her. She swiped the tears off her cheeks, but they kept coming. Every muscle in her body ached as her adrenaline drained away. She curled her knees tighter to her stomach. Any minute he'd be back.

Probably waiting on orders to finish her off.

She closed her eyes and replayed Zain's voice in her head. He was close to finding her. She had to believe that. If he was in contact with her kidnappers, he could have already negotiated for her freedom.

She snorted at her naivety.

These people didn't want anything but death. She was still alive only because they were using her to get to Zain. Then they'd kill him. Rivers of fear ran through her. It was a trap—the picture, the phone call.

She couldn't let them win.

As she pushed up from the ground, her elbows threatened to buckle. Inhaling a breath, she drank in courage. She'd faced worse obstacles. The cave in Afghanistan. The bombed vehicle. She could do this. She could escape a stupid basement.

The sickness in the pit of her stomach grew as she forced herself to her feet. Her face pulsated where he'd struck her, and her scalp throbbed. She swallowed and brushed away the almost-overwhelming agony. If she got out of here, she'd soak for hours in the hottest bath she could tolerate.

She moved across the room and inspected the door. He'd slammed it pretty hard, but she couldn't remembered if he'd locked it. He hadn't tied her back up, nor had he tried to find where she'd obtained the glass.

His face had looked ghostly pale. With any luck, he was struggling as a result of the wounds she'd inflicted. Had he even made it upstairs? She'd been too shaken to pay attention to his footsteps. With painstaking caution, she placed her fingertips on the cold doorknob and turned the metal.

Locked.

Dammit.

That hope had been too good to be true. Her gaze landed on the bucket. She picked it up and then grabbed the blanket. She placed the bucket below the window and removed the plywood.

The bright, warm sun touched her cold skin, taunting her with its rays. She leaned her face close to the pane and scanned the area outside. Dirt with scattered patches of brown grass filled her view. About five feet away from the window was a fence separating the property from the neighbor's. Craning her neck, she glanced to the left—more dead grass indicated that the backyard was in that direction. Looking to the right, she couldn't see much but weeds and a tree trunk.

Her best bet was to go right. That was probably where the street was. She lifted her trusty little blanket, folded it over her fingers, and carefully plucked and pulled off shards of glass from the pane. The window wasn't large. Probably three feet wide and less than two feet tall. But she could fit.

She removed only the necessary amount of glass. It'd take way too much time to get every piece, and with each movement, she risked making noise her captor would hear. Once half the glass was cleared away, she slid open the screen.

Anticipation swept over her. Warm air spiraled in to caress her cheeks. Then the clomping of boots on the stairs made her freeze in terror.

Shit!

If she tried to get out now, she wouldn't make it through the hole in time. She quickly grabbed the plywood and put it back over the window. His keys fiddled at the lock as she snatched the bucket and raced to the corner of the room by the door, where it'd been.

He flung open the wood and whirled around to catch her standing behind the door. His face pinched as he advanced on her. "Thought you'd hit me with the bucket this time?"

His hand caught her around the throat, slamming her to the wall. Her back connected with the concrete, sending jolts up and down her spine. She winced.

He dipped his face closer to hers. "You're really damn lucky, you know that?" Alcohol lined the stench of his breath, and she clamped her lips together to stop herself from vomiting a third time.

Dark bags hung under his eyes, and his face glistened. The skin beneath the sheen of sweat was chalky and nearly gray. Although the hand around her neck held a lot of strength, she suspected the force took a lot of effort.

She met his eyes. "I wouldn't consider myself very lucky right now."

The corner of his lip lifted. "You're still alive. That's something." His fingers slipped away from her throat. It was as if talking sucked his energy dry.

He straightened to his full height, and her gaze dropped to the grocery bag dangling from his hand. Apprehension hitched inside her. He slammed the door shut, then turned the bucket over and sat. "Sit," he commanded.

Swallowing, she sat on the floor in front of him. He opened the bag and took out a roll of duct tape and some rope, thinner than the kind he'd used before. "Turn around. Hands together."

No, no, no. If he tied her up again, she wouldn't be able to get through the window. She wanted to beg, but there was no use. This man didn't have an ounce of sympathy, nor would he fall for any excuse she came up with.

His eyes lifted to her face and flashed with cruelty. "I said turn around."

She inhaled a frustrated breath and obeyed. The sound of duct tape ripped. Rough hands bound her wrists tightly together. She squirmed. "You're going to cut off my circulation."

He yanked on her arms and her spine connected with his knees. Pain split across her shoulders. She cried out, but he only pulled harder.

"If this was up to me," he said slowly, his breath hot against her ear, "I'd cut off little pieces of you." With that, he pressed the tip of a knife to her chest and dragged the cold steel beneath the neckline of her shirt. Dana shuddered. "Starting here. Then I'd cut out your fucking eyes and your fingers and see if your boyfriend still wanted you then." He shoved her forward.

Her face hit the cement. Fire shot from her nose across her cheekbones. Her vision blurred. The scuff of his boots on the floor made her whimper.

Her consciousness flickered in and out. She clung to the terrifying scene—him standing over her, knife dangling at his side.

Warm blood oozed from her nose over her lips. She didn't move. Didn't breathe. Just struggled to keep her eyes focused on something so she wouldn't pass out.

His rough hands grabbed her biceps and hauled her up. The room spun, a kaleidoscope of cinderblock. She groaned and then landed with a jerk on her kidnapper's shoulder.

Before finally slipping into the dark abyss, she saw an image of Zain's golden eyes in her mind.

★ ★ ★

ZAIN SAT RIGID, his gaze fixed on the 1950s house set back from the street. The one-story home with a single attached garage looked cute with its white shutters and red front door. The yard was unkempt, full of wildflowers and weeds, but other than that the place didn't appear dilapidated.

The lot was wide and deep, which probably prevented people from hearing screams inside the house. Zain stretched his neck from one side to the other. After his call with Maxine, he'd texted Rami the location pin she'd sent him. Hopefully they'd be there waiting long before anyone from Maxine's payroll arrived. With any luck, Zain would have Dana safely in his arms before Maxine's people reached the meeting point.

Taschen parked on the street about twenty feet from the front of the house. "There's no car in the driveway."

No shit. Zain's nerves were as frayed as old electrical wire, and his patience was nonexistent. "Probably in the garage."

"We goin' in now?" Taschen asked.

Micha whined.

"We'll search the perimeter first. I want eyes on Dana before we go in shooting."

"In the picture, it looked like the basement window had plywood over it, if I remember correctly."

Zain nodded. "Plywood's not hard to get through." He rubbed his thumb over the pads of his fingers. It'd be better if they separated. "If I can get to Dana first, then you can secure the assassin. That'd give us the best option of getting Dana out in one piece."

"All right." He dug into his pocket and pulled out earbuds. "Do you know how to use this?"

He plucked one of the tiny pieces of equipment from Taschen's palm and tucked it into his ear. "Yeah, I used one on occasion with the CIA. Loop around back and drop me off down the alley. I don't want any neighbors spotting me with a fucking assault rifle."

"Copy that." He shifted into gear and rounded the corner, turning down the alleyway. He drove past a few houses before Zain ordered him to stop.

"Let me know if you spot her," Taschen said. "Then I'll go through the front with Micha." A scowl creased his forehead. "We got the bastard."

"I'll believe that when your sister's safe." He grabbed his weapon from the back and got out. Gravel crunched beneath his boots as he made his way toward the rear of the house. Stopping at the fence, he rose up on his toes to glance over the wooden boards.

Dead grass covered the backyard, and a broken birdbath was tipped over in the middle of the lawn. Flower beds riddled with weeds and debris surrounded the sun-bleached back porch. The blinds on the windows were tightly drawn, and he couldn't spot any movement inside.

He slung his gun over his shoulder, grabbed the top of the fence, and hauled himself up. After landing on the earth with a thud, he got to his feet. Holding his weapon, ready to blow the cocksucker holding Dana to pieces, he skirted toward the side of the house.

Dead weeds collapsed beneath his steps as he scanned the perimeter of the foundation. One lone window sat near the ground. He got to his knees and inspected the glass.

The screen was open, and broken glass lay in front of a rectangular chunk of plywood. If he broke the rest of the glass to move it, he'd make too much noise.

He lowered his ear to the wood. "Dana," he

called softly.

Nothing.

"Dana."

Again, no response. Sweat trickled down the back of his neck. If she was here and the asshole was with her, he might end up with a bullet in the face. If she was hurt and unresponsive, he needed to get to her.

Holding his finger on the trigger and the gun aimed at the window, he kicked the plywood. The piece flipped to the floor with a sharp crack, revealing an empty room.

The door was wide open. On the gray concrete floor was a wet dark stain. A bucket sat behind the door and a tattered brown blanket. No sounds came from inside the house.

Unease fisted his stomach.

She was here.

Urgency shot him to his feet. He brought his finger to his ear and pressed on the bud, no longer giving a damn about being quiet. "Taschen. She's gone."

"What the hell do you mean?"

"The room's empty. But she was here."

Taschen cursed a blue streak, echoing the sheer panic rushing through Zain's head.

"I'm going through the back door now," Zain said. "Check the garage."

"On it."

He bounded up the steps and ran at the back

door. His shoulder slammed against the old wood, and the hinges gave way. The door bounced open, and Zain steered his gun around the mudroom. He stalked into the kitchen, moving swiftly, every footstep trained.

Come on, you bastard. Show yourself.

He swept through the living room, three bedrooms, and a bathroom. All fucking empty. He retraced his steps to the kitchen and grabbed the door that led to the basement.

A padlock had been freshly drilled into the white wood frame. It was unlocked. The sweat coating his skin turned to ice. He ripped open the door and banged down the steps. "Dana!"

He raced through the small space. Storage room, utility area, and one bedroom—the one where she'd been held captive.

He dropped to his knee, and agony ripped through him. On the floor next to his jeans was a puddle of blood no bigger than his palm. He touched it with his fingers—cold but wet. Tears clouded his vision, and regret ravaged his soul.

Taking in the rest of the room brought his temper to a breaking point. Vomit splayed the concrete, and there were ropes in a heap. She'd been bound and sick. What the hell had he done to her?

Was the blood from a head wound? Jesus, he'd—

"Zain!" Taschen's bellow came from upstairs.

He forced himself to his feet and wiped his hand down his face. He had to fucking keep it together. Blood didn't necessarily mean death.

But it did mean they were running out of time. He charged for the stairs and met Taschen in the kitchen.

Micha stood still, the hair on her back spikey and her eyes sharp.

"What'd you find?" Taschen demanded.

He ground his back teeth. "A bit of blood in the basement. Was there a vehicle in the garage?"

Taschen glanced toward the open front door. "Nope. Empty."

Zain's phone chirped. He dug it out of his pocket and glanced at the number—Brick. "Hello?"

"Ghost ran the plates again and found them en route. Looks like they're heading out of town."

The meeting point. Fuck.

So much for making it to the house before they moved Dana. Now the question was, were they taking her to the location Maxine had given them?

Or were they killing her and getting rid of her body?

The memory of the puddle of blood hit Zain like a baseball bat to the stomach. She could already be dead. His body temperature climbed, making his heart work harder.

Taschen's eyebrows jumped. "What the hell are we gonna do?"

He turned his attention back to his phone. "Did Rami and August make it there yet?"

"Not sure," Brick said. "But they left minutes after receiving your text, so they should be there by now."

"Good." He jerked his head at Taschen, and they strode out the front door and down the steps. "We just cleared the house. They must have taken her with them."

"Shit."

Taschen jogged to the driver's seat and Zain hopped in the passenger seat. "Let me know if Ghost is able to track anything else. We're going to the location now."

"Roger that."

"I can't believe we just missed them," Taschen murmured. His hands shook as he opened the map on his phone. "Send me the pin."

Seconds later, there was a little red dot on Taschen's screen. "Forty minutes."

"Christ. You'll have to make it in half that if we're gonna get there in time."

Taschen gunned away from the curb. "We'll fucking get there in time."

Zain bounced his knee as his friend whipped them around corners. He might have fallen into this team, but right now he couldn't ask for a better man to help him find Dana.

Both of them cared about her. Both of them would protect her with their lives. Both of them would take a bullet for her.

Both of them loved her.

His heart constricted. Holy shit. He was in love with Dana.

CHAPTER 27

D ANA'S BODY JOSTLED gently, rousing her from sleep. Her head pounded as though someone were operating on her brain without an anesthetic. She squinted against the light filtering in through her eyelids, willing the darkness to take hold of her again. It didn't.

Had she been tased again? She fought to grab hold of memories, but they slipped through as if her mind were made of Swiss cheese. She inhaled a slow breath, burning her nasal passage. A rush of recollection hit her—just like the floor had earlier.

Shit, the bastard had given her a bloody nose and likely a concussion. Both of which would surely be the least of her worries after they arrived wherever he was taking her. She swallowed and focused on slowing her breath so she could assess her surroundings.

The low humming told her she was in a car, and the musty fabric beneath her cheek felt a lot like the one she'd been on after being taken from

Zain's mom's. Her hands were behind her back. She moved her wrists to confirm they were still wrapped with tape.

Hysteria took hold of her psyche. The need to jump up and attack the driver was almost too great. But she'd have a really hard time doing much without the use of her hands. She had to think and figure a way out of this mess.

Maybe they were returning her to Zain. Maybe all of this was some stupid scheme to get what they wanted from him and they had no real intention of killing either of them. Maybe—

She bit back a scoff.

Nope, these people meant business. They'd kill her the second the vehicle stopped.

She cracked open her eyes. Brilliant sun beamed through her lashes. She let her eyes acclimate before opening them the rest of the way.

Pain exploded across her forehead. Everything above her shoulders was in agony. A groan hovered at the back of her throat. She lay on the back seat of a car, her head directly behind the front passenger seat.

As she shifted her gaze to the driver, hate infused every fiber of her being. The brooding bastard stared out the windshield, two hands loosely on the wheel. A gun sat on his lap, the black metal handle just visible. His body was slumped, and the ashen shade of his profile made a little flurry of happiness strike her.

At least she'd done a shitload of damage. Dude needed a doctor ASAP, and if she had anything to do with it, she'd make sure he never saw one.

A call came over the speaker. He swiveled his head back to glance at her, and she quickly closed her eyes. Fear swirled inside her chest. She fought to keep her breathing even and her face relaxed. When she peeked at him again, he was facing the road.

He punched the button on the steering wheel. "Yeah."

She relaxed her muscles a fraction. He probably wouldn't answer the call on Bluetooth if he suspected she was conscious.

"Where are you?" The chilly female voice sliced through the interior of the vehicle.

"Ten minutes or so from Weeks Falls." He spoke laboriously and unevenly.

A sense of foreboding crept over her skin. The water in that area was unpredictable. A great place for a lone hiker to "slip" and die. Alarm fell over her shoulders with the weight of wet fleece.

"What's wrong with you?" the woman snapped. "You sound sick."

"Not sick," he groaned. "She fucking stabbed me. Lost a lot of blood."

Seconds stretched. "Well, it's a good thing I sent you backup. Keep the woman hidden until my team takes care of Zain. My guys are trained to make this look like an accident."

"I could've fucking finished this myself. I'm a professional."

"Maybe," she said dryly. "But Zain's a Green Beret, for god's sake. I need to make sure this is done impeccably. Neither of them can survive."

"Is this going to affect my paycheck?"

"Of course not. Look at them as reinforcements. They'll be there in twenty minutes."

He sighed, long and arduous. "I'll pull over and wait a few until they get there." He slowed the vehicle, and it bumped over a gravel road down a sharp decline.

"Good. And Drake? No one better live."

"Got it, got it." He punched the button, hanging up. "Bitch."

Dana's chest pumped erratically. The need to get up and run was so overpowering she couldn't keep her hands from trying the binding at her back.

"I knew you were awake," said Drake, her soon-to-be killer, his tone ominous.

She wet her lips but didn't respond. He adjusted the rearview and locked his eyes on hers. A breath caught in her throat.

Droplets of sweat dotted his skin. The whites of his eyes were dull and almost as gray as his skin. Despite his rapidly declining health, a spark flashed across his face, lighting his eyes for an instant.

He might be weak, but he had a personal stake

in her demise. The vehicle slowed further, rocking over uneven terrain. "We're gonna sit tight a few minutes until some friends come."

"Whoopie," she sang with disdain.

He grunted. "I gotta piss." He got out and slammed the door. The car shook with the force, rattling Dana even more.

Okay, think. She had a couple of minutes tops before he came back. Using her shoulder to keep her balance, she swung her feet forward so they lay flat on the floor. Grunting and straining, she dragged herself into a sitting position.

Glancing out the window to her left, she caught her creepy friend walking through the grass toward a set of bushes. Rather than reach for his pants, he lifted his shirt, likely to inspect the wound.

Now was her chance.

She inched to her right and reached the door. Panic beat a steady, wild drum against her breastbone. Straining her hands toward the door, she fumbled her fingers along the smooth plastic until she caught the door handle. He'd hear her open the door. She'd have twenty seconds max before he made it back.

Question was, how fast could she run with her hands behind her back? Likely about as fast as she could fight in the same position.

Sucking air through her nostrils, she held her breath and pulled on the lever. The door hinges moaned as she stumbled from the car. Her knees buckled beneath her weight, but she threw herself forward, breaking into a run.

"Fuck!"

Drake's frustrated cry set fire to her heels. A shot rang out.

Dana cried out as the bullet smacked into bark. She ducked, but splinters showered her face. She darted into the woods. Branch after branch swiped her face, neck, and arms. She dodged and swayed, missing the largest ones. Her assailant's maddened footsteps crunched over gravel.

Dana wove between trees and bushes, ducking low to conceal herself. Her legs burned and wobbled, her muscles struggling to counteract the imbalance her tied arms created.

Her breath was frantic, barely audible. Her feet and shoulders screamed, her calves were on fire—but she didn't slow down.

Throwing a glance over her shoulder, she spotted his hunched form, but he was far behind. He might not catch up, but he could damn well blow her head off.

Her toe caught a tree root, and she went down. Her knees connected with the hard, knotty veins clawing up from the earth. A grunt barked from her chest upon impact. Pain exploded through her core as she struggled not to fall on her face. The last thing she needed was to lose consciousness again.

Branches cracked in the distance behind her.

Not close, but not as far as she'd like either. Staying on her knees, she shuffled behind the tree that'd taken her down. With her back pressed against the solid strength of its trunk, she closed her eyes and listened.

Slowing her breath, she focused on the noises around her. Birds fluttered and cawed in the treetops overhead. Water rushed somewhere close by—likely the waterfall. A car whizzed on the highway in the distance.

Another snap of a twig and the unnaturally fast rustling of leaves.

Tears stung her throat, and she clamped her lips tightly together to stop any noises that might escape. Opening her eyes again, she assessed her surroundings. There were trees as far as she could see, but about ten feet away, they dipped toward a ravine.

She had to keep moving before he found her. Drake would lose stamina soon. All she had to do was outlast him and pray Zain found her.

This outcome wasn't impossible. Not when Zain was involved. If—

A ringtone broke through the calm air. Dana jumped and dug her spine deeper against the trunk. Bark dug into her sore scalp.

"Yeah?"

Dana focused on his voice, trying desperately to gauge his location.

"Good. Scratch the meeting point. I need you

in the woods near Weeks Falls. Bitch is on foot."

No!

Zain, where are you?

★　★　★

ZAIN'S EXPECTATIONS FOR Taschen's driving fell short. "My mom drives faster than you."

"Man," Taschen grumbled, "I want to get there more than you do, but I also don't want to get pulled over and have this take even longer. I'm already doing twenty over the speed limit."

All right, he had a point about the cops. But moving at the speed of light probably wouldn't be fast enough for Zain. He also wanted to point out that there was no way in hell Taschen wanted to get there more than he did, but the argument would be a waste of energy.

Instead, he pulled out his phone.

His brother answered after two rings. "Hey, Brick told me you're on your way."

"Yeah, about fifteen minutes out. I take it they're still not there?"

Rami grunted. "Nope. I'm beginning to think this was a setup."

"Well it wasn't. Ghost spotted them en route on I-90. They can't be far."

"Should've been here by now, though."

A vise clamped around Zain's stomach. He didn't want to acknowledge the possibility they'd been given the wrong location. Didn't want to believe they could have already killed Dana before sending men to take care of him. "Keep me posted."

He hung up and pinched his bottom lip between his thumb and forefinger. Dana couldn't be far. The fact that she was so close and he couldn't see or touch her was next-level torture.

As he flicked his gaze out the window, something in the side mirror caught his attention. A large black SUV sent sizzles of awareness through him.

Anyone could drive a fancy SUV. But in the middle of a workday, and heading in the same direction . . .

"You see that?" he asked Taschen softly, almost afraid the people in the SUV would hear him.

"What? They're not tailgating."

"No, but check out the vehicle."

Taschen drummed his thumb on the steering wheel. "I'll let them pass. See if you can get a look." The car slowed a fraction.

A couple of minutes later, the SUV changed lanes and accelerated. Zain looked as it passed. The vehicle had fully tinted windows, so he could see only the outlines of two male figures in the front. "Hard to say if they've got anything to do with Maxine."

"I agree. It's possible but anyone could— They're turning off."

Zain cocked an eyebrow as he watched the

SUV slow and take a dirt road off the highway. Following the gravel path, it snaked into the trees. "Well that's fucking fishy."

"No shit."

Zain sat forward in his seat. "Follow 'em."

"Obviously." He took the same road but paused at the top of a hill. The thicket of forest that sandwiched the road concealed them from whoever was at the bottom.

"What're you doing?" Zain said, failing to keep the annoyance out of his voice.

"Not getting us killed. You can thank me later." He unbuckled his seatbelt. "I say we park here and go for a stroll. We can skirt through the brush and check things out unnoticed."

Good idea. Not that he'd admit it. Micha, sensing they were about to get out, danced in the trunk. "Is she going to give us away?"

"Nah, man. That dog's badass. Only time she's gonna bark is when we want her to." Taschen slid from the vehicle, and Zain followed suit.

While Taschen opened the liftgate, Zain retrieved his AR-15 from the back seat. Strapping it over his chest, he inhaled a stabilizing breath. If these guys worked for Maxine, he'd not only find answers, he'd also find Dana—and he wouldn't stop until he did.

The vehicle beeped as the back door closed. Taschen rounded the SUV with Micha in the lead. The dog snuffled along the ground, her tail straight and in work mode.

Zain patted her back. "Good girl."

"Cut through this way." Taschen nodded toward the trees.

Zain stepped over fallen branches and ducked inside the forest. Pushing away low-lying foliage, he moved in a steady decline along the road the SUV had driven down. Less than three minutes later, they were at the bottom, where a small gravel lot sat. Zain halted in the cover of the trees, and Taschen stopped next to him.

The SUV was parked next to a black sedan. The same fucking car that'd taken Dana. Energy buzzed through Zain's body. He aimed his weapon and stepped forward.

Taschen's hand on his shoulder held him back. "Hang on a second. We need to figure out which way they went."

Zain took a steadying breath and shook off Taschen's hold. He couldn't stand the sensation of anything weighing him down or holding him back. Dana could be anywhere, and if he didn't stop these bastards, they'd kill her any second. But Taschen's level thinking made sense.

A lead weight sat in Zain's stomach as he scanned the area. The sunlight shone on a large sign indicating directions for sightseeing. "There." He nodded at the sign. Taschen and Micha kept pace as he jogged across the gravel, his gaze swiveling side to side, anticipating an ambush.

It didn't come.

He studied the sign. "The waterfall's to the left. I've got a feeling that's a convenient place to throw a body, don't you think?"

Taschen grimaced. "Yeah, I bet that's their plan. Got your earpiece?"

"It's in."

"Let's hope we're heading in the right direction. We'll split up. You go west toward the falls, and I'll head northwest to cover more ground."

"If you spot one of the bastards, just shoot."

Taschen snorted. "No shit." He dragged his hand over Micha's ears. "Let's find Dana, girl, okay?"

Micha panted.

"Let me know if you find anything."

"Roger that." Taschen headed into the trees, making a straight line through the branches.

Zain followed. Satisfaction amplified his heart rate, making his eardrums jump. The cool, comforting weight of the rifle in his hand let him finally release an unrestrained breath as he entered the forest.

He paused, inspecting the scene before he took another step. Taschen's back disappeared ten yards out. No movement to Zain's right or left. He clamped his hands tighter on his weapon and kept his gaze sharp, on the lookout for Maxine's guys.

Part of him wanted to scream to Dana. To let her know he was here, that she wasn't fucking alone and she didn't have to worry. Thinking about the amount of fear she must be experiencing right now almost brought him to the ground.

But if they were on the hunt for her, she was still alive. Still capable. And as long as his heart still beat in his chest, he'd fucking find her . . . because dear god, his heart beat for her.

Crack, crack!

The sharp blast of gunfire ripped through the sky. Birds squawked and critters abandoned their nests.

Every cell in his body turned to stone.

CHAPTER 28

ADRENALINE SCREECHED THROUGH Dana's system. He was getting closer. If she didn't make a run for it, he'd find her. Fire shot from her pinky as her bound hands pressed against the rough tree bark. Forcing the pain away with an uneven breath, she inched her face toward the edge of the tree and locked her gaze on Drake.

He moved like Lurch, every step painfully slow and his hand flat against the wound beneath his arm. His fingers clung to the gun hanging at his side. He wasn't far, maybe forty feet. If she could make it to the ravine before he noticed her, she'd be out of sight before he could get off a shot.

The last thing she wanted to do was give up the security of the tree at her back, but there was no helping it. It was run or be found.

She swallowed, but no saliva went down. Only the sandy texture of fear clung to the insides of her throat. Locking her focus on the ravine, she rose to shaking feet, bent forward to keep her head low, and ran.

The ravine came into view, and she squeezed through bushes. Twigs snapped beneath her feet, screaming with traitorous voices.

Crack, crack!

The deafening blast of gunfire screeched past her ears. Heat singed her arm like a hot poker scraping against her flesh. She cried out and fell on her ass. She slid down the ravine and landed on her back at the bottom.

The sky spun, and her senses fizzled in and out of clarity. Her skin throbbed, and the nerves in her arm spit fire.

Get up, get up!

The insistent voice rushed forth from her sub-conscious, driving her to a sitting position. She gasped and sputtered as pain licked her flesh from the inside out. Blood trickled down her arm, but she didn't try to inspect the wound for fear she'd pass out.

She teetered down the ravine. She couldn't climb the other side of the slope. With her arms behind her it'd be an impossible feat. All she could do was find cover and pray someone found her.

A whistle sounded overhead.

Dana froze. Ice spread from the base of her spine to her neck. She lifted her gaze to the top of the ravine. Two men, guys she'd never seen before, stood above her.

Relief made her choke out a sob. "Help! Please.

There's a shooter!"

One of the men smiled and said, "Sure, honey. We'll give ya a hand. Ain't nothin' to worry 'bout now." He skidded down the hill.

The first guy snickered and followed his friend.

Trepidation seized Dana. Something was wrong.

They weren't concerned about a possible shooter. Didn't seem surprised about finding her either. All the moisture left her mouth, and she retreated a step, then two.

Her gaze fell to the men's hands. They had guns.

Dana turned and ran, panic nipping at her heels. Their laughter boomed through the forest. Her feet squelched in the damp earth, every footstep sucking her down as she sprinted. The acrid taste of fear eroded her tongue.

The men hooted and called as she fled. Bastards knew she had nowhere to go, knew she couldn't climb, knew they'd outrun her. Still, she didn't stop. She'd fight until a bullet entered her head.

Tears ran down her cheeks, mixing with debris and strands of hair. Their footsteps grew louder and louder behind her.

Her toe caught a rock and she flew forward, her stomach landing hard on the ground. The wind coughed from her lungs, and pain exploded across her chest and back. The men cackled, their laughter rolling off the hill.

Combat boots appeared in her vision, and one of the men squatted and moved her hair from her face. If his fingers had been closer, she'd have bitten them off.

She stared into his hard, cold face. He smirked, the smile barely reaching his chalky brown eyes. "Too bad they wanna get rid of such a pretty thing."

"Fuck you," she spat.

His friend guffawed.

The guy's smile fell. "Shut up, Smith." He got to his feet and caught her around the biceps, hauling her upright. The world tilted, and Dana's footing faltered. Too many falls and blows to the head had her equilibrium slipping.

"Come on. We're goin' for a little walk." He turned her toward the incline of the ravine, and her legs turned to mush.

She sank to the ground. Even if she had more stamina, she wouldn't willingly walk to her execution. She'd make every minute of her murder grueling for them—and spread as much of her DNA as possible.

Smith mumbled something derisive. The other guy yanked her up again, this time with less care, and tossed her over his shoulder. His hard muscle dug into her stomach, but with her arms still behind her, she had no way to lessen the weight on her diaphragm.

He climbed the hill. The sharp incline made her

tip farther toward the ground, but he didn't fall. When they reached the top, he dropped her to her feet. "Walk," he ordered.

"Maybe you shouldn't have shot me," she retorted. The pain in her arm had faded to a bone-crushing throb. She suspected shock had something to do with the lessening of the pain, as the hot liquid trickling down to her fingers told her she was bleeding a lot.

He jammed his fingers into her spine, and she staggered forward. "It wasn't a kill shot. Looks like you tore off a chunk of skin from a branch."

She fought the dizziness closing in around her. "Any decent medical examiner will know that's from a bullet."

He chuckled. "You think the people who hired me haven't greased the pockets of your future examiner? Come on now."

Her skin turned clammy. He'd all but admitted the government was behind this. Just peachy. The odds of her surviving a government assassin— make that three—were zero.

"Falls are up ahead, Sharp," Smith said.

Dana swallowed a cry. The taste of fear in her mouth was foul. Her brain started to shut down, her movements on autopilot and her muscles weak. Tears leaked from the corners of her eyes. "You don't have to do this." She spoke the pleading, desperate words knowing they wouldn't do a damn thing.

But she had to try.

The men said nothing, as if her voice were no louder than a mosquito's wings.

"You can just let me go here. I'll find my way. No one has to know." The tears flowed freely now, and her words appeared to be weaving a fairy tale. The rush of the waterfall grew louder, almost deafening.

Sharp grunted. "Lady, this ain't personal. It's a job. We'll make it quick if you just shut up."

Fury spread heat to her cheeks. She stopped in her tracks and pivoted.

Smith jerked back so he didn't bang into her, and Sharp glared with annoyance.

"No. I won't shut up. You can't do this! You won't get away with it."

Smith snorted, and Sharp gave her a sympathetic grin. "Already have." He caught her elbow and steered her around. "Lead the way," he called to Smith.

Smith moved in front and stalked down the sloped trail. Dana sent a gaze toward the woods, willing someone, anyone, to appear. "What happened to Drake?" If she got away, she needed to know who to look out for.

"He, uh, hurt himself on the trail. Real unfortunate."

Smith let out a trill of laughter.

Dana ran her tongue over her chapped lips. Drake was a monster and deserved his fate. But the fact that they'd killed one of their own didn't bode well for her. With no moisture left in her body, she almost ripped off a layer of skin. Drake was gone, which meant she had only these two jerks to escape.

They didn't want to shoot her. That'd make things too difficult to cover up. She darted her gaze to the left then to the right. There was a steep drop-off on her left. She couldn't even see where it ended. But the ground on her right sloped gently into a thicket of bushes. That was her best shot.

As they got closer to the bottom of the path, it pitched at a sharper angle. Dana allowed her pace to pick up and stomped on Smith's heel. He careened forward several steps, caught himself on a tree, and turned to lunge at her. "You—"

She slammed her shoulder into his. He wheeled his free arm backward as he teetered on the edge of the drop-off.

Sharp lunged for him.

Excitement electrified her limbs. She broke free of her captor's hold and ran off the trail to the right, breaking through the bushes.

"Goddammit!" one of the men hollered.

Ragged cries tore from her throat as her feet grew wings. She ran through the bushes at top speed, thorns and branches attacking her arms and face, cutting any exposed skin they could find.

She pushed harder.

Sprinting down the hill, Dana let out a scream

from the depths of her soul.

★ ★ ★

ZAIN RACED WITH everything in him. He ignored the sweat pouring off his face, relished the burn of his muscles. Leaping over fallen logs and tree roots, he ran toward the sound of the gunshot as if his life fucking depended on it—because it did.

It'd been about five minutes since he heard the gun go off. Jesus, he'd better be running in the right direction.

Taschen's voice crackled in his ear.

"What was that?" Zain huffed, the words broken with exertion. "I'm close. They can't be far."

"I found a body. Looks like our guy Drake. He's dead. His skull was bashed in with a rock."

One asshole down. But right now, all that mattered was getting to the bastard who'd fired the—

A scream shook the forest. The bloodcurdling cry made Zain's hair stand on end. He skidded to a stop, chest pumping, as he tried to decipher the direction the cry had come from.

"Holy shit, that was Dana!" Taschen shouted in his ear. "Did you hear that?"

"Yeah," he gasped.

Hope set his shoulders in a determined line as he veered a little more north. She was alive. Had they missed her with the first gunshot? He'd never prayed for anything so hard in his life. *Come on, babe, scream again for me.*

"I don't think I'm far either. Micha's freaking out. I'm going to let her loose."

"Do it." Zain came to a sharp ravine and stopped at the top. His pulse beat fiercely in his ears, conspiring against him. He scanned down to the center of the ravine, and footsteps in the mud caught his eye. He slid down the slope, rushing to the shoe tracks. "I've got prints," he said. He followed them, and eventually, one of the three sets of tracks disappeared.

"Have you reached the ravine?" he asked Taschen, when he got to the top.

"Yup, just went around it."

"Good."

He strained his ears as he followed the muddy footprints, which were becoming harder and harder to decipher on the trail. The path sloped down, and the gushing of the waterfall told him it'd be near the bottom. Only the prints stopped. All of them.

He scanned the ground, but other than skid marks moving toward a tree to his left, there was nothing. Had she fallen?

His heart galloped in his chest as he leaned over the ledge that dropped a good fifty feet. Branches and sharp rocks jutted out, but there was nobody to be seen.

Summoning a deep breath, he cupped his hands over his mouth. "Dana!" He didn't give a damn if a whole army came after him. Let them come.

If Dana was alive, she needed to know he was here.

Silence.

"Dana!" he bellowed again, at the top of his lungs.

"Real subtle, dude," Taschen said dryly in his ear.

"If you've got a better—"

"Zain!" Dana's desperate voice reverberated through the trees. He broke into a run, heading toward a thicket of bushes and charging right through. Twigs clawed at him, but he barreled down the slope at a breakneck pace.

He needed another scream. *One more, baby. Come on.*

★ ★ ★

THUD!

Dana's assailant slammed into her back. She went flying forward, landing on her chest. Stars blipped in front of her vision. Weakness crept over her, muffling the angry sounds disturbing the air.

But she'd heard her name. Right before the jerk had taken her to the ground, she'd heard a man scream.

Zain.

She had to be delirious. There was no way he'd found her. No way she was on the cusp of rescue. But her heart's knowledge was stronger than her doubt.

Zain, I'm here. I'm alive! I knew you'd come for me.

Rough hands seized her shoulders and rolled her onto her back.

Her head lolled, and her consciousness slipped from her fingers like dust in a windstorm. A menacing face glared down at her. Sharp. The flash of a gun caught her eye, and her saliva turned to acid.

She opened her mouth to scream, but his palm slammed over her lips.

"This won't look like an accident," Smith cautioned his colleague.

Dana kicked—his shins, his thighs, his groin. Her captor didn't even flinch. He shoved his knee into her stomach, anchoring her in place as he said something unintelligible to Smith. The gun hovered inches from her temple.

This was her only shot.

She chomped down. Her teeth sunk into the meaty tissue of his palm. She locked her jaw as he howled. He jerked his hand away, and the metallic taste of blood coated her tongue. She threw back her head.

"Zain!" she bellowed, using the power of her diaphragm. Her vocal chords shook.

Using all her strength, she pulled her knee to her chest and jammed her foot between his legs. Her shoe connected with the man's junk, and he careened back. Dana kicked free, but with her arms behind her back she couldn't get up. Smith grabbed her.

He held her down on her knees, his fingers biting into her biceps. "Fucking shoot the bitch already!" he yelled.

Sharp brought the gun to her head. Dana stared down the barrel of the weapon. Her surroundings faded away. Tunnel vision allowed only the sight of the tiny hole that'd take her life any minute.

This was it. There was nothing she could do. A sob escaped her. Her mouth filled with the salty taste of her tears, and anguish twisted her heart. She closed her eyes. Zain's name was like a prayer on her lips.

Crack!

The blast of the gun jolted her body. Dana screamed, the sound shaking her core. Her lips trembled as the wail of terror pulled itself from her chest.

But she wasn't dead.

She opened her eyes to see Sharp fall to the ground. Blood trickled from the left side of his head, where a huge chunk of his skull was missing. Vacant eyes stared at Dana as he landed in the dirt.

"Fuck." Smith yanked her to her feet. He held one arm across her chest, covering his front with her back.

Dana's head swam, and her legs wobbled beneath her. If it weren't for Smith using her as a shield, she'd crumple to the ground. He withdrew a gun and pressed it against her head. The cool, hard steel ground against her sensitive skin.

Movement on the hill made her lift her gaze. Zain came down swiftly, a gun held confidently in his muscled hands, his shoulders so wide and rigid her mouth went dry. She blinked, but he didn't disappear. Didn't fade into her imagination. "Zain!" she choked, needing to say his name, to make his presence stronger.

His golden eyes landed on her, and a red tint crept across his cheekbones. "Let her go!" he bellowed.

Smith retreated. Each step dragged her further and further from Zain. "Put your gun down and I won't shoot her."

Zain didn't move and didn't lower his weapon. "I said let her go," he commanded, his tone deadly.

Smith's arm holding the gun shook. "Back up or—"

A vicious snarl sounded. Something slammed into Smith, and the weapon dropped away from Dana. She fell to the ground and immediately scooted away. A dog—Micha!—was tearing at Smith's arm.

Smith screamed, and a gun went off.

Dana clapped her hands over her ears. Micha whined and skirted to Dana's side. Blood pooled on Smith's chest.

Warm, strong hands scooped her up. Zain's

scent, warm and masculine, pine and spice, filled her nostrils.

She buried her face in the security of his neck, closing her fingers around the material of his shirt. Tears ran down her cheeks, but these ones were different. Their taste didn't fill her with horror. Their sting was filled with gratitude instead of violent fear. "Oh my god. How?" was all she could muster.

His hand, so large and firm, cradled the back of her head. "It's okay. I'm here. It's over." His voice trembled as if he spoke the words more to convince himself than her. "Goddammit, your hands." He cursed again and unsheathed his knife. She watched as the blade disappeared behind her back.

A second later, the rope fell away and her fingers tingled as though millions of little nails were stabbing her skin. She rolled her shoulders. Zain held her against his chest and massaged her wrists and forearms until the burning sensation eased.

He pulled back a few inches, and his eyes probed her face. His hands traced her body. "You're bleeding."

She couldn't respond. A sob tore from her throat, and her lips trembled. Concern flashed across his face. Taschen was there, hovering close.

Zain quickly seized her arm. "She's bleeding a lot," he said to Taschen.

In seconds, her brother had cut off a large strip of his shirt and wrapped it tightly around the wound. She hissed as he knotted the material, but the pressure took away the sting.

"We should call a helicopter." Zain's grave, worry-lined statement made her immediately shake her head.

"No. I'm o-okay."

"It'll probably be faster if we get on the move now," Taschen said. "I'll get ahold of Rami and call for an ambulance."

Zain's arms enveloped her. "I'm going to check you for more injuries. I think you're in shock." The strong, gritty rumble of his words soothed the constriction around her heart, but nothing he could say would be better than him holding her.

His fingers moved along her spine then her neck and around her head. The examination was similar to the one he'd conducted on the plane.

Taschen's voice sounded in the background. Authority coated his words as he spoke to whoever was on the phone.

Zain pulled back and ran his thumb over her cheekbone. "They hit you?"

She nodded. "Yeah. A few times. And I f-fell. I'm fine. Just, my head is pounding."

He touched her lip, and she winced. "Hit you there too." His mouth slashed into an angry line. "Motherfucker."

She caught his wrist. "I'll live. And you already took care of them."

He turned over her hand and touched her pinkie. Somehow the make-shift bandage was still intact. As soon as her attention fell on the appendage, it throbbed. "He—" She wet her lips. "My fingernail."

Zain cursed a blue streak and reached to undo the material she'd wrapped around it.

"Don't. It's okay. It's just a nail."

"They fucking hurt you," he spat. Despair contorted his face. "I'm so fucking sorry, Dana." Moisture collected at the corners of his eyes, and the sight of his pain undid her.

She threw herself at his chest. "You saved me. You're everything to me, Zain," she whispered. "Knowing you'd come for me . . . that's what made me fight."

He caught her chin, tilting her head a fraction, and his eyes ensnared hers. "No, you're alive because you're you. Because you're smart and courageous . . . And god, I love you."

She pressed her palm against his cheek, and appreciation soared inside her. He'd done everything for her. Had fought for her when she was a prisoner, had risked his career and reputation to keep her safe.

The emotions inside her were like water in an overflowing glass. She couldn't contain them but also couldn't verbalize exactly what was in her heart. It was too big for words. Too big to hold down. "I love you too."

Zain gently swiped his thumb beneath her eye.

His lips pressed against her forehead. "Let's get you home."

A minute later, her brother's hand touched her back. "Sis." The simple nickname transported her through time. To a place where Taschen had scared off boys and beat up bullies. Her first protector. She threw her arms around his neck, and he tucked his face into her hair.

"Thank god you're okay," he wheezed.

Locking her gaze on Zain over her brother's shoulder, she smiled. "I am now."

And she would be.

CHAPTER 29

Z AIN'S PULSE PLUMMETED as he watched Dana's teeth chatter and her muscles spasm. Shock was evident, and he didn't like it one fucking bit. After removing his gun from the waistband of his pants, he pulled off his shirt and fit it over her head. The light T-shirt wouldn't do much, but at least it'd give her an extra layer.

She sat on a rock with her back to the dead bodies. They needed to get her to the hospital fast, but he also had to make sure she was well enough to make the trek or they'd need to get a helicopter in despite her protests.

Micha rested her head on Dana's lap. The dog hadn't left her side from the moment they'd killed the assassins.

Taschen hung up the phone and stalked back to them. "Rami and Brick are in the parking lot waiting for us. Can you stand?"

Her throat bobbed on a swallow. "Yes."

"The hell she's walking," Zain snapped. He

passed Taschen his rifle then bent and slipped one arm beneath her knees and his other around her back.

"You can't carry me the whole way," she exclaimed, as he lifted her against his chest.

"Sure I can. You weigh nothing."

"Head north and you can go around the ravine," Taschen said. "It'll be easier and a bit quicker." He whistled to Micha, and she sprang to her feet.

Zain weaved through the branches. Dana curled her body against him, and he held her tighter. She was finally in his arms. The hours she'd been taken had subtracted years from his life. The adrenaline still pushed through his vessels too quickly, still told him he was in fight mode.

And for her he'd never stop fighting.

He'd fight to carry her through this forest to safety. He'd fight to bring justice to the ones who'd hurt her. He'd fight to prove to her how much she meant to him.

Just as long as she was okay. That was all that mattered.

After a few minutes, Taschen and Micha took the lead. Realizing Dana's head hadn't moved from his shoulder, panic rooted inside him. "Dana?" he barked, his tone far sharper than he'd intended.

"What's wrong?" She glanced around.

He relaxed. "You weren't moving. Scared me."

"Oh. Sorry. I think I fell asleep." She squinted

with confusion. Warning struck his heart, and he picked up the pace. Had she lost consciousness? Soon shock would wear off, and not only would she feel more pain, but also any injuries would surface hard and fast.

Her eyes met his. "You're going to be sore tomorrow. I can walk."

"I don't want you to." What he wanted was to get her to a hospital.

She traced her fingers over his jaw. "Zain, you can relax."

He swallowed the knot in his throat. He'd never understand how she could see him so easily. He'd spent years—maybe even a lifetime—building a thick armor to conceal the parts he didn't want seen. He'd gone to war, fought, killed, mourned, and survived.

Yet none of that compared to the crippling fear that'd torn him down when Dana went missing. And she saw it.

He stepped over a fallen tree and tipped his head away from branches, all the while wishing he could form the right words to explain to her that he couldn't just calm down. He couldn't articulate himself.

He cleared the gravel from his throat. "I don't know how to relax, Dana." He dragged his teeth over his top lip. "I don't know how to relax, because I've never been in this situation."

Her thumb traced his chin. The only thing that

kept him remotely sane was her gentle strokes. "It's over now. We're together. I'm so grateful. I—"

He shook his head. "It's not over. I have a list of people to fucking kill. I have evidence I need to take to the FBI. I have to find some way to tell my racing brain that they can't hurt you again." The last part constricted his heart. He stopped and stared down at her. "They *won't* hurt you again. I promise you. I won't allow it."

Tears filled her eyes, and the bright sapphires that'd become his beacon sparkled with adoration and . . . trust. "I don't care about any of that. I just want you. Every day. Can you just promise me that?"

He brushed his lips over her furrowed brow, then he kissed her lips. "I promise you that and all the rest, babe."

She smiled, and tears leaked out of her eyes. "That's more than enough for me. But there's one big question."

"What's that?"

"Will you move in with me? To my apartment."

Relief rippled over him. In the back of his mind, he'd been worried about how they'd figure things out between them—where they'd go from here. Because the last thing he wanted to do was take her home and walk away. But he hadn't realized how truly afraid he'd been that she wouldn't want him around after she was free. That she'd hate him for all he'd brought to her door.

With one simple question, she'd wiped out that uncertainty. He chuckled. "Hell yes, I'll move in with you."

She let out a light laugh, the sound so full of love and ease that his smile spread. Only Dana could make the hardest shit simple.

Despite the ache in his muscles, his heart rate finally found a normal level—one that fell in sync with that of the woman he loved.

★ ★ ★

DANA HOVERED IN the doorway of her bedroom wrapped in her thick baby-blue terry-cloth robe. There was something about being in her own space, her own clothes, her own everything that just erased strain. Some of it anyway. Over-the-counter meds had done the rest.

She'd been worried about how it would feel to be back home after the attack. But Zain's presence removed all the anxious feelings. Allowed her to make new memories to wipe out the bad.

In the living room, Zain spoke on the phone, his voice low as if concerned he might disturb her. She should be resting. But after the longest, hottest bath she could tolerate, she felt almost human.

Although she'd gotten back from the hospital a few hours ago, it was only dinnertime, and the morning's horrors seemed light-years away.

Her body still ached from all the abuse it'd

taken—a mild concussion, bullet graze, contusions, not to mention her battered pinkie and the knife wound on her forearm. She hadn't hesitated to take the ibuprofen the doctor recommended, and she sure as hell was glad she had.

"That's right. I'll send you all the information I have. Thank you." He hung up and lifted his head. His eyes creased with worry when he spotted her in the doorway. "Babe, you should be in bed."

He got to his feet, but she crossed the living room and sat on the couch before he could whisk her back to her room. "I think I'll sleep better once I know what the FBI said."

Zain had returned her phone to her, and she'd found that Suzanne, her old colleague, had responded to her email from earlier that morning. Which turned out to be a great thing—she was putting Zain in contact with the right people; the people with whom to share everything Maxine, Roger, and the CIA had done.

He blew out a breath and lifted her legs onto his lap. "It'll be under investigation. I don't think they'll disclose more than that, but by the sounds of it, they're taking the accusations very seriously."

A little thrill of satisfaction sparked inside her. "I hope Maxine's squirming."

"She must know by now her plan didn't go as expected. I just wish I had a way of knowing how things will go down with Jabar."

She made a sympathetic face. "I get that. You

put so much of yourself into that mission—your life on the line."

He grunted.

She squeezed his shoulder. "You just have to trust everything will work out the way it should. For now, we're all safe."

"You're right," he sighed. His hands wrapped around her foot and massaged.

She melted. "Ohmigod. Please never stop doing that."

His mouth slid into a grin. Although he appeared calm now, the creases around his eyes told her he'd been under intense pressure all day. "You should rest too," she said. "How's your mom?"

"Good. She stayed with Toth and Savannah while we found you. She's going to live with Rami and Ivy for a while until her house is renovated."

"I'm sure that will be stressful for her."

He scrunched his face. "Nah, she's tough as nails. Said she was happy to get a new porch out of the deal. Besides, she'll enjoy Micha's company."

"I'm sure Micha's getting all the treats and snuggles."

He chuckled. "You know it." The planes of his face hardened, and seriousness entered his eyes. "We learned something else."

Her stomach bunched. "What's that?"

He moved his ministrations to her calves. "August spoke to his contact at the police department and they found the DNA of a missing person in the house you were in. It's very likely Drake murdered someone there."

She rounded her eyes and brought her fingertips to her lips. "I found blood on a piece of plastic. It was hidden in the closet beneath wet towels. I totally forgot until now. It'd looked like the floor had been recently mopped." She shook her head. "I'm almost mad he's dead and won't face any prison time."

A muscle in Zain's jaw jumped. She moved closer and let her cheek rest on his sternum. The gentle *thump*, *thump*, *thump* of his heart echoed in her ear, calming the fear that oscillated inside her. One of his large, strong hands held the back of her head and the other moved up and down her leg.

So many things could have gone differently. There were a lot of scenarios that would've resulted in her being another body to search for. Her knees shuddered, but she forced away the intrusive thoughts.

"It really drives home how close I was to losing you," he finally said, his words carrying the weight of an anvil.

She wrapped her arms around his waist. "It's all over now, though."

He lowered his head and brushed his lips over her hair. "Damn right it is."

He pinched her chin between his thumb and forefinger. "I know I said this earlier, but you really need to understand something."

She blinked but didn't move her gaze away from his unwavering golden hues.

"I love you, Dana. I went insane when they took you. I've never been so damn helpless and . . . gutted. I realize I don't have a clear picture of my future right now, but I know for damn sure I want you in it. Will you do that? Be with me."

Tears clouded her vision. She didn't need a play-by-play of their plans, didn't need to know what career he'd find. None of that mattered right now. All she wanted was him. Forever. "Yes," she choked out. "That's all I want."

He brought his lips to hers, and his tongue gently licked into her mouth. The warm scent that was all Zain filled her with promise.

She swept her fingers through his hair, gently tugging the stands.

"Mmm." He pulled his mouth away and kissed her cheek, then her lips again, and then her forehead. "We need to stop before I get carried away. No sex until your concussion's all clear."

She pouted, but in truth, she was much too weak to do anything more than kiss.

A soft, pensive look took hold of his eyes as his fingers traced her chin. "You smell so damn good."

She wrinkled her nose. "Considering I threw up twice today and was covered in sweat and blood, that's quite the compliment." But the gentle look on his face piqued her curiosity. "What do I smell like?"

He touched her cheek with his thumb and was silent for a fraction of a second. "Home."

A warm tingling sensation surrounded her. Before she could respond, he gave her body a gentle shake. "While you were in the bath, Gigi brought over food. You hungry?"

Her salivary glands tingled. "Starving."

"Good. You need to get your strength back."

She grinned. "I sense an ulterior motive."

He laughed, and the sound was so free, so un-restrained, that she grinned ear to ear. He caught her hand and helped her to the kitchen table.

The future might be as dark and scary as the cave in Afghanistan. But with Zain, she'd always have light by her side.

EPILOGUE

D<small>ANA LIFTED THE</small> lid of the slow cooker. The scents of tomato sauce and ginger wafted to her nose and she groaned. Gigi's recipes might be the death of her. She removed the marinating chicken breast, pulled it into strips, then placed the strips in the slow cooker with one cup of coconut milk, just as the cookbook called for.

Zain would be home any minute, and she couldn't wait to sit down and have dinner with him. It'd been almost two weeks since she was kidnapped, and the normalcy she and Zain had fallen into made it seem so much longer. Today was the first time Zain had left the house without her.

Gigi, Ivy, and Savannah had all brought meals over, and she and Zain had holed up in her apartment while she rested and healed. They'd showered, watched movies, lain in bed—and she'd received more foot and back massages than she'd ever had in her life. A few days ago, they'd started taking morning and evening walks.

Life with Zain was an effortless rhythm.

Although nighttime brought the horrors of what she'd survived, her mind replaying the hours of her kidnapping like a broken record, Zain's arms around her, and his sweet kisses and gentle touches, reassured her day after day, nightmare after nightmare, that they'd come out the other side.

Last night was the first time they'd made love since her rescue, and he'd been so careful and loving. Today, she felt like a brand-new woman. Better yet, she also felt like herself.

Keys sounded, and Zain entered. "Hey, babe." He grinned. "Damn that smells amazing."

She chuckled and replaced the lid. "I wish I could take the credit, but it's Gigi's recipe."

His arms came around her waist, and he nuzzled her neck. "Gigi's recipes have nothing on you."

Grinning, she turned in his arms and kissed him, dragging her hand over his stubble like she'd already done a billion times and would never tire of. "What'd you do at the office?"

His mouth slanted in a relaxed, lazy grin. This past week hadn't just been healing for her—it'd been transformative for Zain too. Dana had helped get the evidence Ghost collected to the FBI, and three days ago, Maxine and Roger were arrested.

They'd caused irreparable damage, but knowing they'd rot behind bars gave both Zain and her an ounce of peace. The hellish tsunami's coming to a complete stop was almost jarring. And it was liberating.

Zain leaned back on the counter while she turned off the rice. "Well," he said, "Rami offered me a job. Backcountry's doing really well, and they need another man on salary."

"Oh?" She could have jumped up and down but refrained, struggling to hold in her excitement. Zain hadn't said anything about what he wanted to do now that he was done with the CIA, and she didn't want to sway his decision. "What do you think about that?"

His mouth tipped up at the corner. "I can't think of anything worse than my big brother signing my paychecks." He picked up a piece of chopped green pepper and popped it into his mouth. "But I also love the idea of working with the hottest woman around."

She laughed. "You'd better watch yourself or I'll tell Pearl."

He threw back his head, and the carefree laugh that boomed out warmed her heart.

"So are you going to take it?" she pressed.

His bright white teeth flashed at her. "I start Monday."

She squealed and hugged his waist. "Ohmigod, congratulations. You deserve it Zain, you really do."

He grunted and his hands went to her hair, gently combing back the strands. "I'm thinking in a few months we'll be able to house shop. What do you think about that?"

Warmth and excitement battled in her heart. "I can't think of anything better."

"Yeah? I can." He moved away from the counter and held her hands in both of his then slowly lowered to one knee.

"Dana, you've done more for me than I ever could have done for myself."

Tears rushed to her eyes, and her heart lodged in her throat.

"You came looking for me even though I was a stranger to you. You brought me home and made me remember what it's like to love, to have family, and to enjoy friendships again. You helped me find happiness, and all I want is to make you smile every day." He reached into his pocket and pulled out a small black box.

Revealing a large princess-cut diamond set in a platinum ring and then slipping it on her finger, he said, "Dana McAvery, will you marry me?"

Love gushed from deep inside her. She stared at the glittering stone but could barely see through the salty water filling her eyes. "Yes!" she cried. He could've presented a bread tie and she'd have exploded with just as much happiness.

He let out a hoot, picked her up off the ground, and held her tightly against his chest. "I can't wait to start a life with you, my love."

She grinned and pulled back so she could kiss his mouth. "We already have."

He lowered her to her feet, then nodded at the food cooking. "How about we eat? All I want to do tonight is celebrate by sharing good food and loving you."

"You mean the same thing we do every night?"

He swept his knuckles over her cheek, reminding her of the lingering discoloration still there. "It's a routine I'm happy to repeat for eternity."

She leaned onto her tiptoes and kissed his lips. "Well, I can promise you will."

He laughed, and the passion shining from his eyes filled her with contentment. Some might think her crazy for traveling across the world to find a missing man she'd never met.

But the idea of not having Zain in her life was crazier.

Keep reading for an excerpt
from Taschen . . .

Excerpt from Taschen

DISBELIEF SHROUDED SEPHIE'S mind. Her pulse rapped against the sides of her veins as she pillaged the article with her gaze over and over.

Pippa was dead.

Tears wept from the corners of her eyes as she sat curled on her couch. The Oregon sun sank low on the horizon through her open patio doors. The warm, evening breeze stirred the drapes, making them dance.

Suicide.

The simple word painted a gruesome image. Sephie choked out a sob and dropped her phone to the couch cushion, covering her mouth.

Pippa, no.

It'd been weeks since she'd spoken with her best friend and old co-star. Sephie had been eighteen when she'd left the show and walked away from the entertainment industry. Pippa, however, had went on to star in lead roles left and right. They'd stayed close over the years, but the last time she'd seen Pippa her good friend seemed to turn deeper within herself. No longer the happy-go-lucky kid she'd been ten years ago when Sephie had left the hit teen sitcom.

Pippa's bright brown eyes and freckled face flashed in her brain, causing another gut-wrenching twist. Sephie got to her feet and paced her living room. Kevin lifted his head from the floor by the balcony, his cutely cropped French bulldog ears quirking with interest as if he anticipated another evening walk.

A slideshow of memories played through her mind at lightning speed. Growing up on the set of TV shows and movies, she was no stranger to the dark side of show business. Her skin crawled, sending goosebumps up and down her arms as the reason—among many—she'd left that world came crashing back.

She'd tried to forget. She'd gone to therapy. Pushed it all away. Refused to focus her attention on an industry that'd never change but would always haunt her.

Now, a beautiful young woman was dead. What had gone on in Pippa's life that'd caused her to inflict such harm to herself?

Sephie pressed her knuckles to her lips and sat on the couch again. She closed her eyes against the tremors of guilt that took over her.

You know exactly what went wrong . . .

She and Pippa had been in many uncomfortable situations. Ones a child should never experience. They'd only spoken about their encounters a handful of times over the years, both of them too terrified to give life to the horrific implications.

She should have done something sooner. Never should have tried to sweep things under the rug. She'd escaped, but Pippa hadn't. The tears burning her eyes turned to fire in her core. She hadn't spoken up then. But she could speak up now.

Grabbing her cellphone from the couch, she went to the second bedroom of her house that served as an office space. She needed to do this now and quickly before people created lies and assumptions about Pippa.

Rolling out her desk chair, she sat and switched on her computer. As soon as the desktop screen powered to life, notifications came through. Her relationship with Pippa was well known and everyone expected a reaction from her.

Well, they'd sure as hell get one.

She opened her public social media account and sucked in a deep breath. 1.2 million followers were about to get a story of their life. Wiping her tears from her cheeks, she didn't bother to check her makeup. Didn't give a damn about her appearance. But she had to regain composure if she wanted to get through this without falling apart.

Dragging in one more long, slow breath of oxygenated courage, she hit the LIVE button. A red circle popped up, confirming the broadcast.

"Hello, everyone. I'm coming to you this evening with my deepest regret after hearing the news regarding Pippa Ventura's—" her voice broke. She swallowed the lump pressing on her vocal cords. "—passing."

She paused, sniffing. And her gaze fell to the number of views... over three hundred thousand and the shares climbing by the second.

"I don't know what's true or not. All I know is

Pippa was a beautiful person. Her spirit could light the darkest room. Our time together on Sera and Me was some of the best days of my childhood." She lowered her gaze as her eyes filled with tears again. "But that's not all I want to share with you tonight. As many of you know, I left the show when I turned 18. I've never spoken about this publicly, but here I am."

She turned down the volume of her computer as the dinging of notifications interfered with her concentration. The part of her she'd kept silenced for so long wanted to break free and scream. But the rational part of her mind, the part that held the lock and key, wanted to shut herself up.

A picture sat on her desk of her and Pippa, laughing and smiling when they'd wrapped up season five of the show. She had to do this for Pippa. She had to squash any rumors, had to shine the light on the evil that had permeated her and Pippa's childhood. Because at the very least, what she suspected had contributed to Pippa's downward spiral.

Those involved needed to be held accountable.

More Books by Samantha Wilde

Chosen Few series
Rami
August
Zain
Taschen

Blood Brothers series
Bound
Traced
Unchained
Extracted
Marked
Unbroken

Pretty Thieves series
The Last Heist
Fully Loaded
Straight Shooter

Whistlemore series
Dead of Winter
Dead of Spring
Dead of Summer

Dangerous Distractions series
Abducted
Bait
Exposed

About the Author

Samantha Wilde resides in Saskatchewan, Canada, with her husband, two daughters and son. Ragnar, their mixed terrier, completes her family. Samantha writes steamy, fast-paced romantic suspense novels in the rare moments she has uninterrupted—even interrupted, she manages to apply words to paper. Aside from her love of writing, her other interests include cooking, fantasizing about working out, and eating far too much chocolate.

Want to hear more from Samantha?
Website: samanthakeith.co
Newsletter: eepurl.com/dPyJI5
Facebook: facebook.com/authorsamanthakeith
Goodreads:
goodreads.com/author/show/17716819.Samantha_
Keith
Twitter: twitter.com/authorsamantha
Instagram: instagram.com/authorsamanthakeith
BookBub: bookbub.com/profile/samantha-keith
facebook.com/groups/375343326689529

Acknowledgements

Thank you to my husband, Jesse. I appreciate everything you do for me and our children, and for always prioritizing my dreams. You're a true alpha hero and feed my male characters more lines than I care to admit, haha.

An extra thank you to my two daughters and my son. The three of you motivate me to do better in all areas of my life and work. You might be too young to realize how much apart of this journey you've been, but I couldn't do it without you.

For my mom, who's always been a constant support in my life. I'm so fortunate to have you and am thankful you're such an amazing grandma.

Fellow author, critique partner, and best friend, Danielle M. Haas, you helped bring this book to life. I love and appreciate you and our friendship so much! I feel incredibly lucky to share this passion and purpose with you.

Rachel Small, you've been with me from that very first (and very rough) draft of Abducted. Thank you for your keen eye, close attention to detail, and encouragement—you're the best of the best!

I also owe much gratitude to my arc team and beta readers! You guys rock.

Last but not least, thank you to you, my readers. Many of you have been around from the very beginning of my career and I'm so incredibly grateful I can offer you this fun escape—in the form of a spicy, up-to-no-good heroine and no holds barred hero.

I hope you love Zain and Dana.

All my best,
Samantha Wilde